Tongues of Conscience

by

Robert Hichens

Double 9
BOOKS

Tongues of Conscience
by Robert Hichens

ISBN: 978-93-65788-83-9

Published by

DOUBLE 9 BOOKS
2/13-B, Ansari Road
Daryaganj, New Delhi – 110002
info@double9books.com
www.double9books.com
Tel. 011-40042856

ABOUT THE AUTHOR

Robert Hichens (1864–1950) was a versatile British author and journalist, best known for his work in the Gothic and supernatural fiction genres. Born in Speldhurst, Kent, Hichens initially studied music before turning to writing, a field where he would leave a lasting mark. He gained early fame with his novel "The Green Carnation" (1894), a satire that drew attention for its thinly veiled portrayal of prominent figures in British society. Hichens's literary career spanned several decades, during which he explored a variety of themes, but he is particularly remembered for his contributions to supernatural and horror fiction. His works often delve into psychological drama, blending the eerie and the mysterious with profound character studies. "The Return of the Soul," one of his notable works, exemplifies his skill in creating atmospheric and suspenseful narratives that engage readers on multiple levels. Aside from his fiction, Hichens was also a successful journalist, traveling extensively and drawing upon his experiences in his writing. His ability to capture the uncanny and the supernatural, while also providing deep psychological insight, has secured his place as a significant figure in British literature, particularly within the Gothic and horror traditions.

CONTENTS

SEA CHANGE

PART I

THE RAINBOW 7

PART II

THE GRAVE 35

"WILLIAM FOSTER" 68

THE CRY OF THE CHILD

PART I

THE DEAD CHILD 109

PART II

THE LIVING CHILD...130

HOW LOVE CAME TO PROFESSOR GUILDEA...................................153

THE LADY AND THE BEGGAR 196

SEA CHANGE

PART I
THE RAINBOW

"Nothing of him that doth fade,
But doth suffer a sea change,
Into something rich and strange."

Shakespeare.

In London nightfall is a delirium of bustle, in the country the coming of a dream. The town scatters a dust of city men over its long and lighted streets, powders its crying thoroughfares with gaily dressed creatures who are hidden, like bats, during the hours of day, opens a thousand defiant yellow eyes that have been sealed in sleep, throws off its wrapper and shows its elaborate toilet. The country grows demure and brown, most modest in the shadows. Labourers go home along the damp and silent lanes with heavy weariness. The parish clergyman flits like a blackbird through the twinkling village. Dogs bark from solitary farms. A beautiful and soft depression fills all the air like incense or like evening bells. But whether night reveals or hides the activities of men it changes them most curiously. The difference between man in day, man in night, is acute.

The arrival of darkness always meant something to the Rev. Peter Uniacke, whose cure of souls now held him far from the swarming alleys and the docks in which his early work had been done. He seldom failed to give this visitor, so strange and soft-footed, some slight greeting. Sometimes his welcome was a sigh, sometimes a prayer, sometimes a clenching of the hands, a smile, a pause in his onward walk. Looking backward along his past he could see his tall figure in many different places, aware of the first footfalls of the night, now alone and thinking of night's allegory of man's end, now in company, when the talk insensibly changed its character, flowing into deeper, more mysterious or confidential channels. Peter Uniacke had listened to informal confessions, too, as the night fell, confessions of sin that at first surprised him, that at last could no longer surprise him. And he had confessed himself, before the altar of the twilight, and had wondered why it is that sometimes Nature seems to have the power of absolution, even as God has it.

Now, at the age of thirty-two, he heard the footsteps of night on a windy evening of November. They drew near to the wall of the churchyard in which stood the sturdy and rugged building where now he ministered, on a little isle set lonely in a harsh and dangerous northern sea. He listened to them, leaning his arms along this wall, by which the grey and sleepless waves sang loudly. In the churchyard, growing gradually dim and ethereal, were laid many bodies from which the white vampires of the main had sucked out the souls. Here mouldered fisher lads, who had whistled over the nets, and dreamed rough dreams of winning island girls and breeding hardy children. Here reposed old limbs of salty mariners, who had for so long defied the ocean that when they knew themselves taken at the last, they turned their rugged faces down to their enemy with a stony and an ironic wonder. And here, too, among these cast-up bodies of the drowned, lay many women who had loved the prey of the sea, and kissed the cheeks turned acrid by its winds and waters. Some of them had died from heart-sickness, cursing the sea. Some had faded, withering like the pale sand roses beside the sea. Some had lived to old age by empty hearths, in the sound of the sea.

Inscriptions faded upon the stones that lay above them. Texts of comfort in which the fine, salt films crept, faint verses of sweet hymns defiled by the perching sea-birds, old rhymes like homely ejaculations of very simple hearts, sank into the gathering darkness on every hand. The graves seemed murmuring to the night: "Look on me, I hold a lover;" "And I—I keep fast a maiden;" "And within my arms crumbles a little child caught by the sea;" "And I fold a mother, whose son is in the hideous water foliage of the depths of the sea;" "And I embrace an old captain whom the sea loved even in his hollow age." The last inscription that stood clear to Peter Uniacke's eyes in the dying light ran thus:

> "Here lies the body of Jack Pringle, cast up by the sea
> on December 4th, 1896. He was boy on the schooner
> 'Flying Fish.' His age seventeen. 'Lead kindly Light.'"

Uniacke watched this history go into the maw of the darkness, and when it was gone he found himself environed by the cool sea noises which seemed to grow louder in the night, wondering whether the "Kindly Light" was indeed leading on Jack Pringle, no longer boy on the schooner "Flying Fish," but—what? The soul of a fisher lad, who had kissed his girl, and drunk his glass, and told many a brave and unfitting tale, and sworn many a lusty oath, following some torch along the radiant ways of Heaven! Was that it? Uniacke had, possibly, preached now and then that so indeed it was. Or, perhaps, was the light-hearted and careless living lad caught fast, like sunk wreckage, in the under sea of Hell, where pain is like a living fire in the moving dimness? "His age seventeen." Could that be true and God merciful? With such thoughts, Uniacke greeted the falling of night. In the broad daylight, full of the songs and of the moving figures of his brawny fisher folk, he had felt less poetically uncertain. He had said like men at sea, "All's well!" More, he had been able to feel it. But now he leaned on the churchyard wall and it was cold to his arms. And the song of the sea was cold in his ears. And the night lay cold upon his heart. And his mind — in the grim, and apparently unmeaning way of minds set to sad music in a sad atmosphere — crept round and round about the gravestone of this boy; bereft of boyhood so early, of manhood ere he won to it, and carried so swiftly into mystery beyond the learning of all philosophy. Ignorance, in jersey and dripping sea-boots, set face to face with all knowledge, and that called a tragedy!

Yet now to Peter Uniacke it was tragedy, and his own situation, left in the safety of ignorance preaching to the ignorant, tragedy too, because of the night, and the winds and the sea noises, and the bareness of this Isle.

Beyond the church a light shone out, and a bearded shadow towered and dwindled upon a white blind. Uniacke, a bachelor, and now almost of necessity a recluse, entertained for the present a visitor. Remembering the substance of the shadow he opened the churchyard gate, threaded his way among the gravestones, and was quickly at the Vicarage door. As he passed within, a yellow glow of lamplight and of firelight streamed into the narrow passage from a chamber on the left hand, and he heard his piano, surprised to learn that it could be taught to deliver passionately long winding melodies from *Tristan and Isolde*. Uniacke laid down his hat and stick and entered his sitting-room, still companioned by the shadowy thought-form of the boy of the schooner "Flying Fish," who seemed to tramp at his side noiselessly, in long sea-boots that streamed with the salt water.

The man at the piano turned round, showing a handsome and melancholy face, and eyes that looked as if they were tired, having seen too many men and deeds and cities.

"I make myself at home, you see," he said, "as I hope you will some day in my studio, when you visit me at Kensington."

Uniacke smiled, and laid his hand on a bell which tinkled shrewishly.

"It is a great treat for me to hear music and a voice not my own in this room," he answered. "Are you ready for tea?"

"Thank you, I painted till it was dark. I was able to paint."

"I'm glad of that."

"When it was too dim to see, and too cold to feel the brush between my fingers, I came back in the twilight to my new roof tree. I am thankful to be out of the inn, yet I've stayed in worse places in Italy and Greece. But they were gilded by the climate."

He sat down by the fire and stretched his limbs. Uniacke looked at him rather curiously. To the lonely clergyman it was a novel experience to play host to a man of distinction, to a stranger who had filled the world with his fame years ago. Three days before, in one of his island walks, Uniacke had come upon a handsome bearded man in a lane full of mud, between bleak walls of stone. The man stopped him courteously, asked if he were not the clergyman of the Isle, and, receiving an affirmative reply, began to make some enquiries as to lodging accommodation.

"My name is Sir Graham Hamilton," he said presently.

Uniacke started with surprise and looked at the stranger curiously. He had read much of the great sea painter, of his lonely wanderings, of his melancholy, of his extraordinary house in Kensington, and, just recently, of his wretched condition of health, which, it was said, had driven him suddenly from London, the papers knew not whither.

"I thought you were ill," he blurted out.

"I am not very well," the painter said simply, "and the inn here is exceedingly uncomfortable. But I want to stay. This is the very home of the sea. Here I find not merely the body of the sea but also its soul."

"There are no good lodgings, I am afraid," said the clergyman. "Nobody ever wants to lodge here, it seems."

"I do. Well, then, I must keep on at the inn."

"Come to stay with me, will you?" Uniacke suddenly said. "I have a spare room. It is scarcely ever occupied. My friends find this island a far cry, except in the height of summer. I shall be glad of your company and glad to make you as comfortable as I can."

"You are very kind," said the painter, hesitating. "But I scarcely—"

"Come as my guest," said the clergyman, reddening slightly.

"Thank you, I will. And some day you must come to me in London."

Now the painter was installed at the Vicarage, and blessed, each hour, his happy escape from the inn, whose walls seemed expanded by the forcible and athletic smell of stale fish.

Uniacke's servant girl brought in the tea. The two men had it by the fire. Presently Hamilton said:

"Nightfall is very interesting and curious here."

"I find it so almost everywhere," Uniacke said.

"Yes. It can never be dull. But here, in winter at least, it is extraordinarily—" he paused for the exactly right word, in a calm way that was peculiar to him and that seemed to emphasise his fine self-possession—"pathetic, and suggestive of calamity."

"I have noticed that, indeed," Uniacke answered, "and never, I think, more than to-night."

Hamilton looked across at him in the firelight.

"Where did you see it fall?" he asked.

"I was by the wall of the churchyard."

"It was you, then, whom I saw from the window. It seemed to be a mourner looking at the graves."

"I was looking at them. But nobody I care for deeply is buried there. The night, however, in such an island as this, makes every grave seem like the grave of a person one has known. It is the sea, I daresay."

"So close on every hand. Why, this house of yours might be a ship afloat a hundred miles from land, judging by the sounds of the waves."

He sighed heavily.

"I hope the air will do you good," Uniacke remarked, with a sudden relapse into conversational lameness.

"Thank you. But sea air is no novelty to me. Half of my life, at least, has been spent in it. I have devoted all the best of my life, my powers, my very soul to the service of the sea. And now, when I am growing old, I sometimes think that I shall hate it before I go."

"Hate it!"

"Yes."

"Well—but it has brought you fame."

"H'm. And wealth and a thousand acquaintances. Yes, that's quite true. Sometimes, nevertheless, we learn in the end to hate those who have brought us most. Perhaps, because they have educated us in the understanding of disappointment. You love the sea?"

"Yes."

"You wouldn't be here otherwise."

"I did not come here exactly because of that," Uniacke said slowly.

"No," said the painter.

"Rather to forget something."

"I doubt if this is a place which could teach one to forget. I find it quite otherwise."

The two men looked at each other, the elderly painter on his height of fame, the young clergyman in his depth of obscurity, and each felt that there was a likeness between them.

"I came here to forget a woman," Uniacke said at last, moved by a strange impulse to speak out.

"Yes, I see. It is the old idea of sorrowful men, a hermitage. I have often wondered in London, in Rome, in Athens, whether a hermitage is of any avail. Men went out into the desert in old days. Legend has it that holiness alone guided them there. All their disciples believed that. Reading about them I have often doubted it."

He smiled rather coldly and cynically.

"You don't know what a hermitage can mean. You have only been here three days. Besides, you come in search of—"

"Search!" Hamilton interrupted, with an unusual quickness.

"Of work and health."

"Oh, yes. Do you care, since we are on intimate topics, to tell me any more about yourself and—and—"

"That woman?"

"Yes."

"I loved her. She disappeared out of my life. I don't know at all where she is, with whom, how she lives, anything at all about her. I don't suppose I ever shall. She may be dead."

"You don't think you would know it if she were?"

"How could I? Who would tell me?"

"Not something within you? Not yourself?"

Uniacke was surprised by this remark. It did not fit in precisely with his conception of his guest's mind, so far as he had formed one.

"Such an idea never occurred to me," he said. "Do you believe that such an absolute certainty could be put into a man's mind then, without a reason, a scrap of evidence, a hint to eye, or ear?"

"I don't know. I—I want to know."

"That someone's dead?"

"That someone is not dead. How loud the sea is getting!"

"It always sounds much like that at night in winter."

"Does the winter not seem very long to you up here quite alone?"

"Oh, yes."

"And monotonous?"

"Often. But we have times of keen excitement, of violent, even of exhausting activity. I have had to rush from the pulpit up to my shoulders in the sea."

"A wreck?"

"Yes, there have been many. There was the schooner 'Flying Fish.' She broke up when I was holding service one December morning. Only the skipper was saved alive. And he—"

"What of him?"

"He went what the people here call 'silly' from the shock—not directly. It came on him gradually. He would not leave the island. He would never trust the sea again."

"So he's here still?"

"Yes."

Just then the two plaintive bells of the church began to ring on the wind.

"There he is!" Uniacke said.

"Where?"

"He's our bell-ringer. It's the only thing he takes any pleasure in, ringing the bells for church and at nightfall. I let him do it, poor fellow. He's got a queer idea into his brain that his drowned mates will hear the bells some night and make the land, guided by the sound. When the darkness falls he always rings for a full hour."

"How strange! How terrible!"

They sat by the fire listening to the pathetic chime of the two bells, whose voices were almost hidden in the loud sea voices that enveloped the little island with their cries. Presently the painter shifted in his armchair.

"There is something—I—there is something very eerie to me in the sound of those two bells now I know why they are ringing, and who is ringing them," he said, with a slight irritation. "Don't you find they affect your nerves at all?"

"No. I like to hear them. They tell me that one poor creature is happy. The Skipper—all we Island folk call him so—believes he will bring his mates safe to shore some day. And each time he sets those bells going he thinks the happy hour is perhaps close at hand."

"Poor fellow! And he is summoning the drowned to come up out of their world."

They sat silent again for three or four minutes. Then Sir Graham said:

"Uniacke, you have finished your tea?"

"Yes, Sir Graham."

"Has your day's work tired you very much?"

"No."

"Then I wish you would do me a favour. I want to see your skipper. Can I get into the church?"

"Yes. He always leaves the door wide open while he rings the bells—so that his mates can come in from the sea to him."

"Poor fellow! Poor fellow!"

He got up.

"I shall go across to the church now," he said.

"I'll take you there. Wrap yourself up. It's cold to-night."

"It is very cold."

The painter pulled a great cloak over his shoulders and a cap down over his glittering and melancholy eyes, that had watched for many years all the subtle changes of the colour and the movement of the sea. Uniacke opened the Vicarage door and they stood in the wind. The night was not dark, but one of those wan and light grey nights that seemed painted with the very hues of wind and of cloud. It was like a fluid round about them, and surely flowed hither and thither, now swaying quietly, now spreading away, shredded out as water that is split by hard substances. It was full of noise as is a whirlpool, in which melancholy cries resound forever. Above this noise the notes of the two bells alternated like the voices of stars in a stormy sky.

"Even living men at sea to-night would not hear those bells," said the painter. "And the drowned—how can they hear?"

"Who knows?" said the clergyman. "Perhaps they are allowed to hear them and to offer up prayers for their faithful comrade. I think faithfulness is heaven in a human heart."

They moved across the churchyard, and all the graves of the drowned flickered round their feet in the gusty greyness. They passed Jack Pringle's grave, where the "Kindly Light" lay in the stone. When they gained the church Sir Graham saw that the door was set wide open to the night. He stood still.

"And so those dead mariners are to pass in here," he said, "under this porch. Uniacke, cannot you imagine the scene if they came? Those dead men, with their white, sea-washed faces, their dripping bodies, their wild eyes that had looked on the depths of the sea, their hanging hands round which the fishes had nibbled with their oval lips! The procession of the drowned to their faithful captain. If I stood here long enough alone my imagination would hear them, would hear their ghostly boat grate its keel upon the Island beach, and the tramp of their sodden sea-boots. How many were there?"

"I never heard. Only one body was cast up, and that is buried by the churchyard wall. Shall we go in?"

"Yes."

They entered through the black doorway. The church was very dim and smelt musty and venerable, rather as the cover of an old and worn Bible smells. And now that they were within it, the bells sounded different, less magical, more full of human music; their office—the summoning of men to pray, the benediction of the marriage tie, the speeding of the departed on the eternal road—became apparent and evoked accustomed thoughts.

"Where is the belfry?" said Sir Graham in a whisper.

"This way. We have to pass the vestry and go up a stone staircase."

Uniacke moved forward along the uncarpeted pavement, on which his feet, in their big nailed boots, rang harshly. The painter followed him through a low and narrow door which gave on to a tiny stairway, each step of which was dented and crumbled at the uneven edge. They ascended in the dark, not without frequent stumbling, and heard always the bells which seemed sinking down to them from the sky. Presently a turn brought them to a pale ray of light which lay like a thread upon the stone. At the same moment the bells ceased to sound. Both Uniacke and Sir Graham paused simultaneously, the vision of the light and the cessation of the chimes holding them still for an instant almost without their knowledge. There was a silence that was nearly complete, for the tower walls were thick, and kept the sea voices and the blowing winds at bay. And while they waited, involuntarily holding their breath, a hoarse and uneven voice cried out, anxiously and hopefully from above:

"Are ye comin', mates? Are ye comin'? Heave along, boys! D'ye hear me! I'm your skipper. Heave along!"

Uniacke half turned to the painter, whose face was very white.

"What are ye waitin' for?" continued the voice. "I heard ye comin'. I heard ye at the door. Come up, I say, and welcome to ye! Welcome to ye all, mates. Ye've been a damned long time comin'."

"He thinks—he thinks—" whispered Uniacke to his companion.

"I know. It's cruel. What shall we—"

"Ye've made the land just in time, mates," continued the voice. "For there's a great gale comin' up to-night. The 'Flying Fish' couldn't live in her under bare poles, I reckon. I'm glad ye've got ashore. Where are ye, I say? Where are ye?"

The sound of the voice approached the two men on the stairs. The thread of light broadened and danced on the stone. High up there appeared the great figure of a man in a seaman's jersey with a peaked cap on his head. In his broad rough hands he held a candle, which he shaded with his fingers while he peered anxiously and expectantly down the dark and narrow funnel of the stairway.

"Hulloh!" he cried. "Hulloh, there!"

The hail rang down in the night. Sir Graham was trembling.

"I see ye," cried the Skipper. "It's Jack, eh? Isn't it little Jack, boys? Young monkey! Up to his damned larks that I've reckoned up these many nights while I've stood ringin' here! I'll strike the life out of ye, Jack, I will. Wait till I come down, lads, wait till I come down!"

And he sprang forward, his huge limbs shaking with glad excitement. His feet missed a stair in his hurry of approach, and throwing abroad his hands to the stone walls of the belfry in an effort to save himself, he let fall the candlestick. It dropped on the stones with a dull clatter as the darkness closed in. The Skipper, who had recovered his footing, swore a round oath.

Sir Graham and Uniacke heard his heavy tread descending until his breath was warm on their faces.

"Where are ye, lads?" he cried out. "Where are ye? Can't ye throw a word of welcome to a mate?"

He laid his hands heavily on Uniacke's shoulders in the dark, and felt him over with an uncertain touch.

"Is it Jack?" he said. "Why, what 'a ye got on, lad? Is it Jack, I say?"

"Skipper," Uniacke said, in a low voice, "it's not Jack." As he spoke he struck a match. The tiny light flared up unevenly right in the Skipper's eyes. They were sea-blue and blazing with eagerness and with the pitiful glare of madness. Over the clergyman's shoulder the pale painter with his keen eyes swept the bearded face of the Skipper with a rapid and greedy glance. By the time the match dwindled and the blackness closed in again the face was a possession of his memory. He saw it even though it was actually invisible; the rugged features dignified by madness, the clear, blue eyes full of a saddening fire, and—ere the match faded—of a horror of disappointment, the curling brown beard that flowed down on the blue jersey. But he had no time to dwell on it now, for a dreary noise rose up in that confined space. It was the great seaman whimpering pitifully in the dark.

"It isn't Jack," he blubbered, and they could hear his huge limbs shaking. "Ye haven't come back, mates, ye haven't come back. And the great gale comin' up, the great gale comin'."

As the words died away, a gust of wind caught the belfry and tore at its rough-hewn and weather-worn stones.

"Let us go down," said Sir Graham, turning to feel his way into the church.

"Come, Skipper," said Uniacke, "come with us."

He laid hold of the seaman's mighty arm and led him down the stairs. He said nothing. On a sudden all the life and hope had died out of him. When they gained the grey churchyard and could see his face again in the pale and stormy light, it looked shrunken, peaked and childish, and the curious elevation of madness was replaced by the uncertainty and weakness of idiocy. He shifted on his feet and would not meet the pitiful glances of the two men. Uniacke touched him on the shoulder.

"Come to the Vicarage, Skipper," he said kindly. "Come in and warm yourself by the fire and have some food. It's so cold to-night."

But the seaman suddenly broke away and stumbled off among the gravestones, whimpering foolishly like a dog that cannot fight grief with thought.

"The sea—ah, the hatefulness of the sea!" said the painter, "will it ever have to answer for its crimes before God?"

Uniacke and his guest sat at supper that night, and all the windows of the Vicarage rattled in the storm. The great guns of the wind roared in the sky. The great guns of the surf roared on the island beaches. And the two men were very silent at first. Sir Graham ate little. He had no appetite, for he seemed to hear continually in the noises of the elements the shrill whimpering of a dog. Surely it came from the graves outside, from those stone breasts of the dead.

"I can't eat to-night," he said presently. "Do you think that man is lingering about the church still?"

They got up from the table and went over to the fire. The painter lit a pipe.

"I hope not," Uniacke said, "but it is useless attempting to govern him. He is harmless, but he must be left alone. He cannot endure being watched or followed."

"I wish we hadn't gone to the church. I can't get over our cruelty."

"It was inadvertent."

"Cruelty so often is, Uniacke. But we ought to look forward and foresee consequences. I feel that most especially to-night. Remorse is the wage of inadvertence."

As he spoke, he looked gloomily into the fire. The young clergyman felt oddly certain that the great man had more to say, and did not interrupt his pause, but filled it in for himself by priestly considerations on the useless illumination worldly success seems generally to afford to the searchers after happiness. His reverie was broken by the painter's voice saying:

"I myself, Uniacke, am curiously persecuted by remorse. It is that, or partly that, which has affected my health so gravely, and led me away from my home, my usual habits of life, at this season of the year."

"Yes?" the clergyman said, with sympathy, without curiosity.

"And yet, I suppose it would seem a little matter to most people. The odd thing is that it assumes such paramount importance in my life; for I'm not what is called specially conscientious, except as regards my art, of course, and the ordinary honourable dealings one decent man naturally has with his fellows."

"Your conscience, in fact, limits its operations a good deal, I know."

"Precisely. But if it will not bore you, I will tell you something of all this."

"Thank you, Sir Graham."

"How the wind shakes those curtains!"

"Nothing will keep it out of these island houses. You aren't cold?"

"Not in body, not a bit. Well, Uniacke, do you ever go to see pictures?"

"Whenever I can. That's not often now. But when my work lay in cities I had chances which are denied me at present."

"Did you ever see a picture of mine called 'A sea urchin'?"

"Yes, indeed—that boy looking at the waves rolling in!—who could forget him? The soul of the sea was in his eyes. He was a human being, and yet he seemed made of all sea things."

"He had never set eyes upon the sea."

"What?" cried Uniacke, in sheer astonishment, "the boy who sat for that picture? Impossible! When I saw it I felt that you had by some happy chance lit on the one human being who contained the very soul of an element. No merman could so belong of right to the sea as that boy."

"Who was a London model, and had never heard the roar of waves or seen the surf break in the wind."

"Genius!" the clergyman exclaimed.

"Uniacke," continued the painter, "I got £1,000 for that picture. And I call the money now blood-money to myself."

"Blood-money! But why?"

"I had made studies of the sea for that picture. I had indicated the wind by the shapes of the flying foam journeying inland to sink on the fields. I wanted my figure, I could not find him. Yet I was in a sea village among sea folk. The children's legs there were browned with the salt water. They had clear blue eyes, sea eyes; that curious light hair which one associates with the sea and with spun glass sometimes. But they wouldn't do for my purpose. They were unimaginative. As a fact, Uniacke, they knew the sea too well. That was it. They were familiar with it, as the little London clerk is familiar with Fleet Street or Chancery Lane. The twin brother of a prophet thinks prophecy boring table-talk—not revelation. These children chucked the sea under the chin. That didn't do for me, and for what I wanted."

"I understand."

"After a great deal of search and worry I came to this conclusion: that my purpose required of me this—the discovery of an exceptionally imaginative child, who was unfamiliar with the sea, but into whose heart and brain I could pour its narrated wonders, whose soul I could fill to the brim with its awe, its majesty, its murmuring sweetness, its wild romance and its inexhaustible cruelty. I must make this child see and know, but through the medium of words alone, of mental vision. If I took it to the sea the imagination would be stricken down—well, by such banalities as paddling and catching shrimps."

Uniacke smiled.

"But on the contrary, in London, far from the sea, I could give to the child only those impressions of the sea that would wake in it the sort of sea-soul I desired to print. I should have it in my power. And a child's soul cannot be governed by a mere painter, when a conflict arises between him and sand-castles and crabs and prawns and the various magicians of the kind that obsess the child so easily and so entirely."

"Yes, children are conquered by trifles."

"And that, too, is part of their beauty. Under this strong impression, I packed up my traps and came back to London with the studies for my picture. I placed them on an easel in my studio and began my search for the child. At first I sought this child among my cultivated friends; married artists, musicians, highly-strung people, whose lives were passed in an atmosphere vibrating with quick impressions. But I went unrewarded. The children of such people are apt to be peevishly receptive, but their moods are often cloudy, and I wished for a pellucid nature. After a time I went lower down, and I began to look about the streets for my wonder-child."

"What a curious quest!" said Uniacke, leaning forward till the firelight danced on his thin face and was reflected in his thoughtful hazel eyes.

"Yes, it was," rejoined the painter, who was gradually sinking into his own narrative, dropping down in the soft realm of old thoughts revived. "It was curious, and to me, highly romantic. I sometimes thought it was like seeking for a hidden sea far inland, watching for the white face of a little wave in the hard and iron city thoroughfares. Sometimes I stopped near Victoria Station, put my foot upon a block, and had a boot half ruined while I watched the bootblack. Sometimes I bought a variety of evening papers from a ragged gnome who might be a wonder-child, and made mistakes over the payment to prolong the interview. I leaned against gaunt houses and saw the dancing waifs yield their poor lives to ugly, hag-ridden music. I endured the wailing hymns of voiceless women on winter days in order that I might observe the wretched ragamuffins squalling round their knees the praise of a Creator who had denied them everything. Ah! forgive me!"

"For some purpose that we shall all know at last," said Uniacke gently.

"Possibly. In all these prospectings I was unlucky. By chance at length I found the wonder-child when I was not seeking him."

"How was that?"

"One day the weather, which had been cold, changed and became warm, springlike, and alive with showers. When it was not raining, you felt the rain was watching you from hidden places. You smelt it in the air. The atmosphere was very sweet and depressing, and London was full of faint undercurrents of romance, and of soft and rapidly changing effects of light. I went out in the afternoon and spent an hour in the National Gallery. When I came out my mind was so full of painted canvas that I never looked at the unpainted sky, or at the vaporous Square through which streamed the World, opening and shutting umbrellas. I believe I was thinking over some new work of my own, arranged for the future. Now the rain ceased, I went down the steps and walked across the road into the stone garden of the lions. Round their feet played pigmy children. I heard their cries mingling with the splash of the fountains, but I took no notice of them. Sitting down on a bench, I went on planning a picture—the legendary masterpiece, no doubt. I was certainly very deep in thought and lost to my surroundings, for when a hand suddenly grasped my knee I was startled. I looked up. In front of me stood a very dirty and atrociously-dressed boy, whose head was decorated with a tall, muddy paper cap, funnel-shaped and bending feebly in the breeze. This boy was clutching my knee tightly with one filthy hand, while with the other he pointed to the sky on which his eyes were intently fixed.

"'Look at that there rainbow!' he said. 'Look at that there rainbow!'

"I glanced up and saw that the clouds had partially broken and that London lay under a huge and perfect coloured arch.

"'I never did!' continued the boy.

"He stared at me for an instant with the solemn expression of one who reveals to the ignorant a miracle. Then he took his hand from my knee, hurried to an adjoining seat, woke up a sleeping and partially intoxicated tramp, requested him to observe closely the superb proceedings of Nature, took no heed of his flooding oaths, and passed on in the waving paper cap from seat to seat, rousing from their dreams, and sorrows, and newspapers, the astounded habitués of the Square, that they might share his awe and happiness. Before he had finished teaching a heavy policeman the lessons of the sky, I knew that I had found my wonder-child."

"You followed him?"

"I captured him in the midst of a group of emaciated little girls in the shadow of Lord Nelson. All the childish crowd was looking upward, and every eye was completely round over each widely-opened mouth, while paper-cap repeated his formula. Poor children, looking at the sky! Ah, Uniacke, what do you think of that for a sermon?"

The young clergyman cleared his throat. The red curtains by the narrow window blew outward towards the fire, and sank in again, alternately forcible and weak. The painter looked towards the window and a sadness deepened in his eyes.

"Where is my wonder-child now?" he said.

"You have lost sight of him?"

"Yes—though the blood-money lies at my bank and the paper-cap is in my studio."

"Is he not in London?"

"No, no; I learnt his history, the history of a gamin of fifteen or thereabouts. It was much the same as a history of a London pavement, with this exception, that the gamin had a mother to whom he presented me without undue formality. The impression made upon me by that lady at first was unfavourable, since she was slatternly, drank, and was apparently given to cuffing and kicking the boy—her only child. I considered her an abandoned and unfeeling female. She dwelt in Drury Lane and sold something that most of us have never heard of."

"I can see her."

"I wish to heaven I could not," the painter said, with a sudden outburst of fire.

He was silent a moment and then continued: "I had no difficulty in persuading her to let me paint the boy. I don't think she rightly understood what I meant, except that for some foolish reason I was prepared to give her money, apparently in return for nothing, that I meant to have little Jack decently dressed—"

"Jack—was that his name?"

"Yes, and that he was to spend certain hours—snatched from Trafalgar Square—in my house in Kensington."

"I see."

"The boy turned up in the jersey and cap and boots I had bought him. And then his education began. On first entering my studio he was numb with surprise, a moving and speechless stare—more overcome than by rainbows."

"Poor little chap!"

"I let him stray about examining everything. He did so completely oblivious of my presence, and of the fact that all the things in the place were mine. By his demeanour one might have supposed him engaged in an examination of works of God never before brought to his notice. While I smoked and pretended to read, he crept about like a little animal, penetrating into corners where statues stood, smelling—so it seemed—the angles of painted walls, touching the petals of flowers, smoothing rugs the wrong—but soon the right—way. I can hear his new boots creaking still. He was a very muscular little chap, but small. When he was able to speak I questioned him. He had never seen the sea. He had never been out of London for a day or slept away from Drury Lane for a night. The flask was empty; now to pour the wine into it. I told him to sit down by the open hearth. He obeyed, staring hard at me before he sat, hard at the chair when he was sitting. I interested him much less than old brocade and lighted wax candles, which inspired him with a solemnity that widened his eyes and narrowed his features. He looked on a new, and never-before-imagined, life. And he was grave to excess, though, later, I found plenty of the London child's impish nature in him."

"That impish quality hides in nearly all street-bred children," said Uniacke. "I have seen larkiness dawn in them for an instant at some recollection, even when they were dying."

"I daresay. I can believe it. But Jack was solemn at first, his brow thunderous with thought, as he examined his chair and the rug under his new boots. Then in the firelight I began my task. I wrought to bring about in this Trafalgar Square soul a sea change. For a time I did not attempt to paint. I merely let the boy come to me day by day, get accustomed to the studio, and listen to my talk—which was often of the sea. I very soon found that my intention had led me to the right mind for my purpose; for the starved gaze that had been fixed on the rainbow could turn itself, with equal wonder, similar rapture, on other things. And the mind also could be brought to see what was not visible to the eye. My studio—you must see it some day—is full of recollections of sea days and nights. Jack explored them. I eliminated from the studio important objects of art which might lead him to think of towns, of villages inland, of wonderful foreign interiors. I fixed all his nature upon this marvellous element which had never murmured round his life before. I played to him music in which the sea could be heard. I described to him the onward gallop of the white horses, racing over impenetrable depths. I painted for him in words the varying colours of waves in different seas, the black purple of tropical waters, the bottle-green turmoil of a Cornish sea on a choppy day, the brown channel waves near shore, the jewelled smoothness of the Mediterranean in early morning sunshine, its silver in moonrise, melting into white and black. I told him of the crowd of voices that cry in the sea, expressing all the emotions which are uttered on land by the voices of men; of the childish voices that may be heard on August evenings in fiords, of the solemn sobbing that fills an autumn night on the Northumbrian coast, of the passionate roaring in mid Atlantic, of the peculiar and frigid whisper of waters struggling to break from the tightening embrace of ice in extreme northern latitudes, of the level moan of the lagoons. I explained to him how this element is so much alive that it is never for a moment absolutely still, even when it seems so to the eyes, as it sleeps within the charmed embrace of a coral reef, extended, like an arm, by some Pacific island far away. I drew for him the thoughts of the sea, its intentions, its desires, its regrets, its griefs, its savage and its quiet joys. I narrated the lives in it, of fishes, of monsters; its wonders of half human lives, too, the mermaids who lie on the rocks at night to see the twinkling lights on land, the mermen who swim round them, wondering what those lights may mean. I made him walk with me on the land under the sea, where go the divers through the wrecks, and ascend the rocky mountains and penetrate the weedy valleys, and glide across the slippery, oozy plains. In fine, Uniacke, I drowned little Jack—I drowned him in the sea, I drowned him in the sea."

The painter spoke the last words in a voice of profound, even of morbid, melancholy, as if he were indeed confessing a secret crime, driven by some wayward and irresistible impulse. Uniacke looked at him in growing surprise.

"And why not?" Uniacke asked.

But the painter did not reply. He continued:

"I made him see the rainbows of the sea and he looked no more at the rainbows of the sky. For at length I had his imagination fast in my net as a salmon that fishermen entice within the stakes. His town mind seemed to fade under my fostering, and, Uniacke, 'nothing of him that did fade but did suffer a sea change into something rich and strange.'"

The painter got up from his chair and walked over to the blowing wind that crept in at the window fastenings. The red curtains flew out towards him. He pushed them back with his hands.

"Into something rich and strange," he repeated, as if to himself. "And strange."

"Ah, but that was said, surely, of one who was actually drowned in the sea," said the clergyman. "It might be suitably placed on many of the memorial slabs in the church yonder," he continued, waving his hand towards the casement that looked on the churchyard. "But your sea-urchin—"

"Oh, I speak only of the fading of the town nature into the sea nature," rejoined the painter quickly, "only of that. The soil of the childish mind was enriched; his eyes shone as if touched with a glow from the sun, swaying in the blue sea. The Trafalgar Square gamin disappeared, and at last my sea-urchin stood before me. As the little Raleigh may have looked he looked at me, and I saw in the face then rather the wonder of the sea itself than the crude dancing desire of the little adventurer who would sail it. And it was the wonder of the sea embodied in a child that I desired to paint, not the wakening of a human spirit of gay seamanship and love of peril. That's for a Christmas number—but that came at last."

He stopped abruptly and faced the clergyman.

"Why does the second best succeed so often and so closely the best, I wonder," he said. "It is very often so in the art life of a man, even of a great man. And it is so sometimes—perhaps you know this better than I—in the soul life of a nature. Must we always sink again after we have soared? Must we do that? Is it an immutable law?"

"Perhaps for a time. Surely, surely, not forever," said Uniacke.

His guest's conversation and personality began to stir him more and more powerfully. It seemed so new and vital an experience to be helped to think, to have suggestion poured into him now, after his many lonely island evenings.

"Ah, well, who can say?" said the painter. "I had the best for a time—long enough for my immediate purpose; for now I painted, and I felt that I was enabled by little Jack to do fine work. It seems he told his drinking mother in Drury Lane, in his lingo, of the wonders of the sea. This I learnt later. And, in his occasional, and now somewhat fleeting visits to Trafalgar Square, he explained to the emaciated little girls, in the shadow of Nelson, the fact that there was to be found, and seen, somewhere, water of a very different kind from that splashing and churning in the dingy basins guarded by the lions. Meanwhile I painted little Jack, all the time keeping alive in his nature the sea change, which was, in the end, to bring into my pocket £1,000 in hard cash."

Sir Graham said this with an indescribable cold irony and bitterness.

"I can hear that money jingling in the wind, upon my soul, Uniacke," he added, frowning heavily.

The young clergyman was touched by a passing thought of the painter's notorious ill-health.

"Before the picture was finished—quite completed—the impish child began to waken in the wonder-child, and I had to comply with the demands of this new-born youngster. Our conversation—little Jack's and mine—drifted from the sea itself to the men and ships that travel it, to the deeds of men that are done upon it; raidings of Moorish pirates, expeditions to the Spanish Main in old days, to the whaling grounds in new, and so forth. When we got to this sort of thing my work was nearly done and could not be spoiled. So I let myself go, and talked several boys' books in those afternoons. I was satisfied, damnably satisfied—your pardon, Uniacke—with my work, and I was heedless of all else. That is the cursed, selfish instinct of the artist; that is the inadvertence of which we spoke formerly. You remember?"

Uniacke nodded.

"My picture was before me and a child's budding soul, and I thought of nothing at all but my picture. That's sin, if you like. Little Jack, in his jersey and squeaky boots, with his pale face and great eyes, was my prey on canvas and my £1,000. I hugged myself and told him wild stories of bold men on the sea. Uniacke, do you believe in a personal devil?"

"I do," replied the young clergyman, simply.

"Well, if there is one, depend upon it he sometimes requires an introduction before he can make a soul's acquaintance. I effected the introduction between him and my wonder-child when I sat in the twilight and told Jack those tales of the sea. The devil came to the boy in my studio, and I opened the door and bowed him in. And once he knew the boy, he stayed with him, Uniacke, and whispered in his ear—'Desert your duty. Life calls you. The sea calls you. Go to it. Desert your duty!' Even a dirty little London boy can have a duty and be aware of it, I suppose. Eh?"

"Yes. I think that. But—"

"Wait a moment. I've nearly finished my tale, though I'm living the sequel to it at this moment. One day I completed my picture; the last touch was given. I stood back, I looked at my canvas. I felt I had done well; my sea urchin was actually what I had imagined. I had succeeded in that curious effort—to accomplish which many of us give our lives—in the effort to project perfectly my thought, to give the exactly right form to my imagination. I exulted. Yes, I had one grand overwhelming moment of exultation. Then I turned from my completed picture. 'Jack,' I cried out, 'little Jack, I've made you famous. D'you know what that means?'

"I took the little chap by the shoulders and placed him before the picture. 'See yourself,' I added. The boy stared at the sea urchin, at those painted eyes full of the sea wonder, at those parted lips, that mouth whispering to the sea. His nose twisted slightly.

"'That ain't me,' he said. 'That ain't me.'

"I looked down at him, and knew that he spoke the truth; for already the wonder-child was fading, even had faded. And a little adventurer, a true boy, stood before me, a boy to pull ropes, lend a hand at an oar, whistle in the rigging, gaze with keen dancing eyes through a cold dawn to catch the first sight of a distant land. I looked, understood, didn't care; although the poetry of wonder had faded into the prose of mere desire.

"'It isn't you, Jack?' I answered. 'Well, perhaps not. But it is what you were, what you may be again some day.'

"He shook his head.

"'No, it ain't me. Go on tellin' about them pirits.'

"And, full of gladness, a glory I had never known before, I went on till it was dark. I said good-by to little Jack on the doorstep. When he had gone, I stood for a moment listening to the sound of his footsteps dying away down the road. I did not know that I should never hear them again. For, although I did not want Jack any more as a model, I was resolved not to lose sight of him. To him I owed much. I would pay my debt by making the child's future very different from his past. I had vague thoughts of educating him carefully for some reasonable life. I believe, Uniacke, yes, on my soul, I believe that I had bland visions of the sea-urchin being happy and prosperous on a high stool in an office, at home with ledgers, a contented little clerk, whose horizon was bounded by an A B C shop, and whose summer pastime was fly-killing. My big work finished, a sort of eager idiocy seized me. I was as a man drugged. My faculties must have been besotted, I was in a dream. Three days afterwards I woke from it and learnt that there may be grandeur, yes, grandeur, dramatic in its force, tragic in its height and depth, in a tipsy old woman of Drury Lane."

"Jack's mother?"

The painter nodded. All the time he had been talking the wind had steadily increased, and the uproar of the embracing sea had been growing louder. The windows rattled like musketry, the red curtains shook as if in fear. Now there came a knock at the door.

"Come in," said the clergyman.

The maid appeared.

"Do you want anything more to-night, sir?"

"No, thank you, Kate. Good-night."

"Good-night, sir."

The door shut.

"Is it late?" said the painter.

"Nearly eleven. That is all."

"Are you tired, Uniacke? perhaps you are accustomed to go to bed early?"

"Not very. Besides to-night the gale would keep me awake; and I want to hear the end of your story."

"Then—Drury Lane invaded me one evening, smelling of gin, with black bonnet cocked over one eye, an impossible umbrella, broken boots, straying hair, a mouth full of objurgation, and oaths, and crying between times, 'Where's Jack? Where's my boy? What 'a yer done with my boy,—yer!' I received Drury Lane with astonishment but, I hope, with courtesy, and explained that my picture was finished, that Jack had left me to go home, that I meant to take care of his future.

"My remarks were received with oaths, and the repeated demand to know where Jack was. 'Isn't he at home?' I asked. 'No, nor he ain't been 'ome.' After a while I gathered that Jack had disappeared in darkness from my house on the night when I put the last touch to my picture, and had not been seen by his mother since. She now began to soften and to cry, and I observed that maternity was in her as well as cheap gin. I endeavoured to comfort her and promised that little Jack should be found.

"'If he ain't found,' she sobbed, 'I'm done for, I am; 'e's my hall.'

"There was something horribly genuine in the sound of this cry. I began to see beyond the gin in which this poor woman was soaked; I began to see her half-drowned soul that yet had life, had breath.

"'We'll find him,' I said.

"'Never, never,' she wailed, rocking her thin body to and fro, 'I know 'e's gone to sea, 'e 'as. Jack's run away fur a sailor.'

"At these words I turned cold, for I felt as if they were true. I saw in a flash the result of my experiment. I had shown the boy the way that led to the great sea. Perhaps that night, even as he left my door, he had seen in fancy the white waves playing before him in the distance, the ships go sailing by. He had heard siren voices calling his youth and he had heeded them. His old mother kept on cursing me at intervals. Instinct, rather than actual knowledge, led her to attribute this disappearance to my initiative. I did not attempt to reason her out of the belief, for alas! I began to hold it myself, Uniacke."

"You thought Jack had run away to sea, prompted by all that you had told him of the sea?"

"Yes. And I think it still."

"Think—then you don't—"

"I don't know it, you'd say? Do I not? Uniacke, a little while ago, when you told me of that—that woman for whom you cared much, you remember my saying to you, was there not something within you that would tell you if she were dead?"

"Yes, I remember."

"That something which makes a man know a thing without what is generally called knowledge of it. Well, that something within me makes me know that little Jack did run away to sea. I searched for him, I strove, as far as one can do such a thing, to sift all the innumerable grains of London through my fingers to find that one little grain I wanted. I spared no pains in my search. Conceive, even, that I escorted Drury Lane in the black bonnet to the Docks, to ships lying in the Thames, to a thousand places! It was all in vain; the wonder-child was swallowed up. I had indeed drowned little Jack in the sea. I have never set eyes on him since he left me on the evening of the day when I completed my picture. Shall I ever set eyes on him again? Shall I, Uniacke? Shall I?"

Sir Graham put this strange question with a sort of morose fierceness, getting up from his chair as he spoke. The young clergyman could think of no reply.

"Why not?" he said at last. "He may be well, happy, active in a life that he loves, that he glories in."

"No, Uniacke, no, for he's far away from his duty. That hideous old woman, in her degradation, in her cruelty, in her drunkenness, loved that boy, loves him still, with an intensity, a passion, a hunger, a feverish anxiety that are noble, that are great. Her hatred of me proves it. I honour her for her hatred. I respect her for it! She shows the beauty of her soul in her curses. She almost teaches me that there is indeed immortality—at least for women—by her sleepless horror of me. Her hatred, I say, is glorious, because her love shines through it. I feed her. She doesn't know it. She'd starve rather than eat my bread. She would kill me, I believe, if she didn't fancy in her vague mind, obscured by drink, that the man who had sent her boy from her might bring him back to her. For weeks she came every day—walking all the way from Drury Lane, mind you—to ask if the boy had returned. Then she endured the nightmare of my company, as I told you, while we searched in likely places for the vanished sea urchin. Jack did nothing for the support of his mother. It was she who kept him. She beat him. She cursed him. She fed him. She loved him; like an animal, perhaps, like a mother, certainly. That says all, Uniacke. It was I who sent that boy away. I must give him back to that old woman. Till I do so I can never find peace. This thing preys upon my life, eats into my heart. It's the little worm gnawing, always gnawing at me. The doctors tell me I am morbid because I am in bad health, that my bad health makes the malady in my mind. On the contrary, it is my mind that makes the malady in my body. Ah! you are wondering! You are wondering, too, whether it's not the other way! I see you are!"

"I cannot deny it," Uniacke said gently.

"You are wrong. You are wrong, I assure you. And surely you, a clergyman, ought to be the very man to understand me, to know how what seems a slight thing, a small selfishness, well, the inadvertence we spoke of lately, may punish the soul, may have a long and evil train of consequences. I was careless of that child, careful only of my ambition. I ground the child in the mortar of my ambition; is it not natural that I should suffer now? Does not your religion tell you that it is right? Answer me that?"

Uniacke hesitated. A conviction had been growing up in him all the evening that his guest was suffering severely under some nervous affliction; one of those obscure diseases which change the whole colour of life to the sufferer, which distort all actions however simple and ordinary, which render diminutive trials monstrous, and small evils immense and ineffably tragic. It seemed to Uniacke to be his duty to combat Sir Graham's increasing melancholy, which actually bordered upon despair. At the same time, the young clergyman could not hide from his mind—a mind flooded with conscience—that the painter was slightly to blame for the action which had been followed by so strange a result.

"I see you hesitate, Uniacke," said Sir Graham. "Ah, you agree with me!"

"No; I think you may have been careless. But you magnify a slight error into a grievous sin; and I do indeed believe that it must be your present bad state of health which acts as the magnifying glass. That is my honest opinion."

"No, no," said the painter, almost with anger, "my illness is all from the mind. If I could find that boy, if I could give him back to his mother, I should recover my peace, I should recover my health—I should no longer be haunted, driven as I am now. But, Uniacke, do you know what it is that I fear most of all, what it is that dogs me, night and day; though I strive to put it from me, to tell myself that it is a chimera?"

"What?"

"The belief that little Jack is dead; that he has been drowned at sea, perhaps lately, perhaps long ago."

"Why should you think that? You do not even know for certain that he ran away to sea."

"I am sure of it. If he is dead! If he is dead!"

The painter, as if in an access of grief, turned abruptly from the fire, walked over to the window, pulled one of the blowing curtains aside and approached his face to the glass.

"In spite of the storm it is still so light that I can see those graves," he said in a low voice.

"Don't look at them, Sir Graham. Let us talk of other things."

"And—and—yes, Uniacke, that poor, mad Skipper is still out there, lingering among them. He is by the churchyard wall, where you were standing this evening in the twilight: one would say he was watching."

The clergyman had also risen from his seat. He moved a step or two across the little room, then stood still, looking at Sir Graham, who was half concealed by the fluttering curtains.

"He is just where I stood?" Uniacke asked.

"Yes."

"Then he is watching."

"By a grave?"

"Yes. Only one of his crew ever gained the land. He gained it—a corpse. He is buried by that wall. I was reading the inscription upon his tombstone, and wondering—"

"Wondering? Yes?"

"Where he is, how he is now, far away from the voice of the sea which took his life, the wind which roared his requiem."

"Poor man! You were here when he was washed up on the beach?"

"Yes. I buried him. The Skipper—sane then, though in terrible grief—was able to identify him, to follow the drowned body as chief mourner, to choose the inscription for the stone."

"What was it?" asked Sir Graham, without curiosity, idly, almost absently.

"'Lead, kindly light.' He would have that put. I think he had heard the boy sing it, or whistle the tune of it, at sea one day."

"The boy? It was a boy then?"

"Yes."

The clergyman spoke with a certain hesitation, a sudden diffidence. He looked at the painter, and an abrupt awkwardness, almost a shamefacedness, crept into his manner, even showed itself in his attitude. The painter did not seem to be aware of it. He was still engrossed in his own sorrow, his own morbid reflections. He looked out again in the night.

"Poor faithful watch-dog," he murmured.

Then he turned away from the window.

"The Skipper does not wait for that boy," he said. "He knows at least that he can never come to him from the sea."

"Strangely—no. Indeed, he always looks for the boy first."

"First, do you say? Was it so to-night?"

Again Uniacke hesitated. He was on the verge of telling a lie, but conscience intervened.

"Yes," he said.

"Didn't he speak of little Jack?" said Sir Graham slowly, and with a sudden nervous spasm of the face.

"Yes, Sir Graham."

"That's curious."

"Why?"

"The same name—my wonder-child's name."

"And the name of a thousand children."

"Of course, of course. And—and, Uniacke, the other name, the other name upon that tomb?"

"What other name?"

"Why—why the surname. What is that?"

The painter was standing close to the clergyman and staring straight into his eyes. For a moment Uniacke made no reply. Then he answered slowly:

"There is no other name."

"Why not?"

"Why—the—the Skipper would only have Jack put, that was all. Jack— he was the boy on the schooner 'Flying Fish'—'Lead, kindly light.'"

"Ah!"

The exclamation came in a sigh, that might have been a murmur of relief or of disappointment. Then there was a silence. The painter went over again to the fire. Uniacke stood still where he was and looked on the ground. He had told a deliberate lie. It seemed to grow as he thought of it. And why had he told it? A sudden impulse, a sudden fear, had led him into sin. A strange fancy had whispered to him, "What if that boy buried by the wall yonder should be the wonder-child, the ragamuffin who looked at the rainbow, the sea urchin, the spectre haunting your guest?" How unlikely that was! And yet ships go far, and the human fate is often mysteriously sad. It might be that the wonder-child was born to be wrecked, to be cast up, streaming with sea-water on the strand of this lonely isle. It might be that the eyes which worshipped the rainbow were sightless beneath that stone yonder; that the hands which pointed to it were folded in the eternal sleep. And, if so, was not the lie justified? If so, could Peter Uniacke regret it? He saw this man who had come into his lonely life treading along the verge of a world that made him tremble in horror. Dared he lead him across the verge into the darkness? And yet his lie troubled him, and he saw a stain spreading slowly out upon the whiteness of his ardent soul. The painter turned from the fire. His face was haggard and weary.

"I will go to bed," he said. "I must try to get some sleep even in the storm."

He held out his thin hand. Uniacke took it.

"Good-night," he said.

"Good-night. I am sorry I have troubled you with my foolish history."

"It interested me deeply. By the way—what did you say your wonder-child's name was, his full name?"

"Jack—Jack Pringle. What is it?"

"Nothing. That gust of wind startled me. Good-night."

The painter looked at Uniacke narrowly, then left the room.

The clergyman went over to the fire, leaned his arms on the mantelpiece, and rested his head on them.

Presently he lifted his head, went softly to the door, opened it and listened. He heard the tread of his guest above stairs, moving to and fro about the spare room. He waited. After a while there was silence in the house. Only the wind and the sea roared outside. Then Uniacke went into the kitchen, pulled out a drawer in a dresser that stood by the window, and took from it a chisel and a hammer. He carried them into the passage, furtively put on his coat and hat, and, with all the precaution of a thief, unlocked the front door and stole out into the storm.

PART II
THE GRAVE

In the morning the storm was still fierce. Clouds streamed across a sky that bent lower and lower towards the aspiring sea blanched with foam. There was little light, and the Rectory parlour looked grim and wintry when Sir Graham and Uniacke met there at breakfast time. The clergyman was pale and seemed strangely discomforted and at first unable to be natural. He greeted his guest with a forcible, and yet flickering, note of cheerfulness, abrupt and unsympathetic, as he sat down behind the steaming coffee-pot. The painter scarcely responded. He was still attentive to the storm. He ate very little.

"You slept?" asked Uniacke presently.

"Only for a short time towards dawn. I sat at my window most of the night."

"At your window?" Uniacke said uneasily.

"Yes. Somebody—a man—I suppose it must have been the Skipper—came out from the shadow of this house soon after I went to my bedroom, and stole to that grave by the churchyard wall."

"Really," said Uniacke. "Did he stay there?"

"For some time, bending down. It seemed to me as if he were at some work, some task—or perhaps he was only praying in his mad way, poor fellow!"

"Praying—yes, yes, very likely. A little more coffee?"

"No, thank you. The odd thing was that after a while he ceased and returned to this house. One might have thought it was his home."

"You could not see if it was the Skipper?"

"No, the figure was too vague in the faint stormy light. But it must have been he. Who else would be out at such a time in such a night?"

"He never heeds the weather," said Uniacke.

His pale face had suddenly flushed scarlet, and he felt a pricking as of needles in his body. It seemed to him that he was transparent like a thing of glass, and that his guest must be able to see not merely the trouble of his soul, but the fact that was its cause. And the painter did now begin to observe his host's unusual agitation.

"And you—your night?" he asked.

"I did not sleep at all," said Uniacke quickly, telling the truth with a childish sense of relief, "I was excited."

"Excited!" said Sir Graham.

"The unwonted exercise of conversation. You forget that I am generally a lonely man," said the clergyman, once more drawn into the sin of subterfuge, and scorching in it almost like a soul in hell.

He got up from the breakfast-table, feeling strangely unhappy and weighed down with guilt. Yet, as he looked at the painter's worn face and hollow eyes, his heart murmured, perhaps deceitfully, "You are justified."

"I must go out. I must go into the village," he said.

"In this weather?"

"We islanders think nothing of it. We pursue our business though the heavens crack and the sea touches the clouds."

He went out hurriedly and with the air of a man painfully abashed. Once beyond the churchyard, in the plough-land of the island road, he continued his tormented reverie of the night. Never before had he done evil that good might come. He had never supposed that good could come out of evil, but had deemed the supposition a monstrous and a deadly fallacy, to be combated, to be struck down to the dust. Even now he was chiefly conscious of a mental weakness in himself which had caused him to act as he had acted. He saw himself as one of those puny creatures whose so-called kind hearts lead them into follies, into crimes. Like many young men of virtuous life and ascetic habit, Uniacke was disposed to worship that which was uncompromising in human nature, the slight hardness which sometimes lurks, like a kernel, in the saint. But he was emotional. He was full of pity. He desired to bandage the wounded world, to hush its cries of pain, to rock it to rest, even though he believed that suffering was its desert. And to the individual, more especially, he was very tender. Like a foolish woman, perhaps, he told himself to-day as he walked on heavily in the wild wind, debating his deed of the night and its consequences.

He had erased the name of Pringle from the stone that covered little Jack, the wonder-child. And he felt like a criminal. Yet he dreaded the sequel of a discovery by the painter, that his fears were well founded, that his sea urchin had indeed been claimed by the hunger of the sea. Uniacke had worked in cities and had seen much of sad men. He had learnt to read them truly for the most part, and to foresee clearly in many instances the end of their journeys. And his ministrations had taught him to comprehend the tragedies that arise from the terrible intimacy which exists between the body and its occupant the soul. He could not tell, as a doctor might have been able to tell, whether the morbid condition into which Sir Graham had come was primarily due to ill-health of the mind acting upon the body or the reverse. But he felt nearly sure that if the painter's fears were proved suddenly to him to be well founded, he might not improbably fall into a condition of permanent melancholia, or even of active despair. Despite his apparent hopelessness, he was at present sustained by ignorance of the fate of little Jack. He did not actually know him dead. The knowledge would knock a prop from under him. He would fall into some dreadful abyss. The young clergyman's deceit alone held him back. But it might be discovered at any moment. One of the islanders might chance to observe the defacement of the tomb. A gossiping woman might mention to Sir Graham the name that had vanished. Yet these chances were remote. A drowned stranger boy is naught to such folk as these, bred up in familiarity with violent death. Long ago they had ceased to talk of the schooner "Flying Fish," despite the presence of the mad Skipper, despite the sound of church bells in the night. Fresh joys, or tragedies, absorbed them. For even the island world has its record. Time plants his footsteps upon the loneliest land. And the dwellers note his onward tour.

Uniacke reckoned the chances for and against the discovery of his furtive act of mercy and its revelation to his guest. The latter outnumbered the former. Yet Uniacke walked nervously as one on the verge of disaster. In the Island cottages that morning he bore himself uneasily in the presence of his simple-minded parishioners. Sitting beside an invalid, whose transparent mind was dimly, but with ardent faith, set on Heaven, he felt hideously unfitted to point the way to that place into which no liar shall ever come. He was troubled, and prayed at random for the dying—thinking of the dead. At the same time he felt himself the chief of sinners and knew that there was a devil in him capable of repeating his nocturnal act. Never before had he gathered so vital a knowledge of the complexity of man. He saw the threads of him all ravelled up. When he finished his prayers at the bedside, the invalid watched him with the critical amazement of illness.

He went out trembling and conscience-stricken. When he reached the churchyard on his way homewards, he saw Sir Graham moving among the graves. He had apparently just come out from the Rectory and was making his way to the low stone wall, over which shreds of foam were being blown by the wind. Uniacke hastened his steps, and hailed Sir Graham in a loud and harsh voice. He paused, and shading his eyes with his arched hands, gazed towards the road.

Uniacke hurried through the narrow gate and joined his guest, who looked like a man startled out of some heavy reverie.

"Oh, it is you," he said. "Well, I—"

"You were going to watch the sea, I know. It is worth watching to-day. Come with me. I'll take you to the point—to the nigger."

"The nigger?"

"The fishermen call the great black rock at the north end of the Island by that name. The sea must be breaking magnificently."

Uniacke took Sir Graham's arm and led him away, compelling him almost as if he were a child. They left the churchyard behind them, and were soon in solitary country alone with the roar of wind and sea. Branching presently from the road they came into a narrow, scarcely perceptible, track, winding downward over short grass drenched with moisture. The dull sheep scattered slowly from them on either side of the way. Presently the grass ceased at the edge of an immense blunt rock, like a disfigured head, that contemplated fixedly the white turmoil of the sea.

"A place for shipwreck," said Sir Graham. "A place of death."

Uniacke nodded. The painter swept an arm towards the sea.

"What a graveyard! One would say the time had come for it to give up its dead and it was passionately fighting against the immutable decree. Is Jack somewhere out there?"

He turned and fixed his eyes upon Uniacke's face. Uniacke's eyes fell.

"Is he?" repeated Sir Graham.

"How can I tell?" exclaimed Uniacke, almost with a sudden anger. "Let us go back."

Towards evening the storm suddenly abated. A pale yellow light broke along the horizon, almost as the primroses break out along the horizon of winter. The thin black spars of a hurrying vessel pointed to the illumination and vanished, leaving the memory of a tortured gesture from some sea-thing. And as the yellow deepened to gold, the Skipper set the church bells ringing. Sir Graham opened the parlour window wide and listened, leaning out towards the graves. Uniacke was behind him in the room. Vapour streamed up from the buffeted earth, which seemed panting for a repose it had no strength to gain. Ding dong! Ding dong! The wild and far-away light grew to flame and faded to darkness. In the darkness the bells seemed clearer, for light deafens the imagination. Uniacke felt a strange irritability coming upon him. He moved uneasily in his chair, watching the motionless, stretched figure of his guest. Presently he said:

"Sir Graham!"

There was no reply.

"Sir Graham!"

He got up, crossed the little room and touched the shoulder of the dreamer. Sir Graham started sharply and turned a frowning face.

"What is it?"

"The atmosphere is very cold and damp after the storm."

"You wish me to shut the window? I beg your pardon."

He drew in and shut it, then moved to the door.

"You are going out?" said Uniacke uneasily.

"Yes."

"I—I would not speak to the Skipper, if I were you. He is happier when he is let quite alone."

"I want to see him. I want him to sit for me."

"To sit!" Uniacke repeated, with an accent almost of horror.

"Yes," said Sir Graham doggedly. "I have a great picture in my mind."

"But—"

"The Skipper's meeting with his drowned comrades, in that belfry tower. He will stand with the ropes dropping from his hands, triumph in his eyes. They will be seen coming up out of the darkness, grey men and dripping from the sea, with dead eyes and hanging lips. And first among them will be my wonder-child, on whom will fall a ray of light from a wild moon, half seen through the narrow slit of the deep-set window."

"No, no!"

"What do you say?"

"Your wonder-child must not be there. Why should he? He is alive."

"You think so?"

Uniacke made no reply.

"I say, do you think so?"

"How can I know? It is impossible. But—yes, I think so."

The clergyman turned away. A sickness of the conscience overtook him like physical pain. Sir Graham was by the door with his hand upon it.

"And yet," he said, "you do not believe in intuitions. Nothing tells you whether that woman you loved is dead or living. You said that."

"Nothing."

"Then what should tell you whether Jack is dead or living?"

He turned and went out. Presently Uniacke saw his dark figure pass, like a shadow, across the square of the window. The night grew more quiet by slow degrees. The hush after the storm increased. And to the young clergyman's unquiet nerves it seemed like a crescendo in music instead of like a diminuendo, as sometimes seems the falling to sleep of a man to a man who cannot sleep. The noise of the storm had been softer than the sound of this increasing silence in which the church bells presently died away. Uniacke was consumed by an apprehension that was almost like the keen tooth of jealousy. For he knew that the Skipper had ceased from his patient task and Sir Graham did not return. He imagined a colloquy. But the Skipper's madness would preserve the secret which he no longer knew, and, therefore, could not reveal. He made the bells call Jack Pringle. He would never point to the defaced grave and say, "Jack Pringle lies beneath this stone." And yet sanity might, perhaps, return, a rush of knowledge of the past and recognition of its tragedy.

Uniacke took his hat and went to the door. He stood out on the step. Sea-birds were crying. The sound of the sea withdrew moment by moment, as if it were stealing furtively away. Behind, in the rectory passage, the servant clattered as she brought in the supper.

"Sir Graham!" Uniacke called suddenly. "Sir Graham!"

"Yes."

The voice came from somewhere in the shadow of the church.

"Will you not come in? Supper is ready."

In a moment the painter came out of the gloom.

"That churchyard draws me," he said, mounting the step.

"You saw the Skipper?"

"Yes, leaving."

"Did he speak to you?"

"Not a word."

The clergyman breathed a sigh of relief.

In the evening Uniacke turned his pipe two or three times in his fingers and said, looking down:

"That picture of yours—"

"Yes. What of it?"

"You will paint it in London, I suppose?"

"How can I do that? The imagination of it came to me here, is sustained and quickened by these surroundings."

"You mean to paint it here?" the clergyman faltered.

Sir Graham was evidently struck by his host's air of painful discomfiture.

"I beg your pardon," he said hastily. "Of course I do not mean to inflict myself upon your kind hospitality while I am working. I shall return to the inn."

Uniacke flushed red at being so misunderstood.

"I cannot let you do that. No, no! Honestly, my question was only prompted by—by—a thought—"

"Yes?"

"Do not think me impertinent. But, really, a regard for you has grown up in me since you have allowed me to know you—a great regard indeed."

"Thank you, thank you, Uniacke," said the painter, obviously moved.

"And it has struck me that in your present condition of health, and seeing that your mind is pursued by these—these melancholy sea thoughts and imaginings, it might be safer, better for you to be in a place less desolate, less preyed upon by the sea. That is all. Believe me, that is all."

He spoke the last words with the peculiar insistence and almost declamatory fervour of the liar. But he was now embarked upon deceit and must crowd all sail. And with the utterance of his lie he took an abrupt resolution.

"Let us go away together somewhere," he exclaimed, with a brightening face. "I need a holiday. I will get a brother clergyman to come over from the mainland and take my services. You asked me some day to return your visit. I accept your invitation here and now. Let me come with you to London."

Sir Graham shook his head.

"You put me in the position of an inhospitable man," he said. "In the future you must come to me. I look forward to that. I depend upon it. But I cannot go to London at present. My house, my studio are become loathsome to me. The very street in which I live echoes with childish footsteps. I cannot be there."

"Sir Graham, you must learn to look upon your past act in a different light. If you do not, your power of usefulness in the world will be crushed."

The clergyman spoke with an intense earnestness. His sense of his own increasing unworthiness, the fighting sense of the necessity laid upon him to be unworthy for this sick man's sake, tormented him, set his heart in a sea of trouble. He strove to escape out of it by mental exertion. His eyes shone with unnatural fervour as he went on:

"When you first told me your story, I thought this thing weighed upon you unnecessarily. Now I see more and more clearly that your unnatural misery over a very natural act springs from ill-health. It is your body which you confuse with your conscience. Your remorse is a disease removable by medicine, by a particular kind of air or scene, by waters even it may be, or by hard exercise, or by a voyage."

"A voyage!" cried Sir Graham bitterly.

"Well, well—by such means, I would say, as come to a doctor's mind. You labour under the yoke of the body."

"Do you think that whenever your conscience says, 'You have done wrong'? Tell me!"

Uniacke, who had got up in his excitement, recoiled at these words which struck him hard.

"I—I!" he almost stammered. "What have I got to do with it?"

"I ask you to judge yourself, to put yourself in my place. That is all. Do you tell me that all workings of conscience are due to obscure bodily causes?"

"How could I? No, but yours—"

"Are not. They hurt my body. They do not come from my body's hurt. And they increase upon me in this place, yes, they increase upon me."

"I knew it," cried Uniacke.

"Why is that?" said Sir Graham, with a melancholy accent. "I feel, I begin to feel that there must be some powerful reason—yes, in this island."

"There cannot be. Leave it! Leave it!"

"I am held here."

"By what?"

"Something intangible, invisible—"

"Nothing, then."

"All-powerful. I cannot go. If I would go, I cannot. Perhaps—perhaps Jack is coming here."

The painter's eyes were blazing. Uniacke felt himself turn cold.

"Jack coming here!" he said harshly. "Nonsense, Sir Graham. Nobody ever comes here."

"Dead bodies come on the breast of the sea."

The painter looked towards the window, putting himself into an attitude of horrible expectation.

"Is it not so?" he asked, in a voice that quivered slightly as if with an agitation he was trying to suppress.

Uniacke made no reply. He was seized with a horror he had not known before. He recognised that the island influence mysteriously held his guest. After an interval he said abruptly:

"What is your doctor's name, did you say?"

"Did I ever say whom I had consulted?" said Sir Graham, almost with an invalid's ready suspicion, and peering at the clergyman under his thick eyebrows.

"Surely. But I forget things so easily," said Uniacke calmly.

"Braybrooke is the man—Cavendish Square. An interesting fellow. You may have heard of his book on the use of colour as a sort of physic in certain forms of illness."

"I have. What sort of man is he?"

"Very small, very grey, very indecisive in manner."

"Indecisive?"

"In manner. In reality a man of infinite conviction."

"May I ask if you told him your story?"

"The story of my body—naturally. One goes to a doctor to do that."

"And did that narrative satisfy him?"

"Not at all. Not a bit."

"Well—and so?"

"I did not tell him my mental story. I explained to him that I suffered greatly from melancholy. That was all. I called it unreasoning melancholy.

Why not? I knew he could do no more than put my body a little straight. He did his best."

"I see," said Uniacke, slowly.

That night, after Sir Graham had gone to bed, Uniacke came to a resolution. He decided to write to Doctor Braybrooke, betray, for his guest's sake, his guest's confidence, and ask the great man's advice in the matter, revealing to him the strange fact that fate had led the painter of the sea urchin to the very edge of the grave in which he slept so quietly. No longer did Uniacke hesitate, or pause to ask himself why he permitted the sorrow of a stranger thus to control, to upset, his life. And, indeed, is the man who tells us his sorrow a stranger to us? Uniacke's creed taught him to be unselfish, taught him to concern himself in the afflictions of others. Already he had sinned, he had lied for this stricken man. He, a clergyman, had gone out in the night and had defaced a grave. All this lay heavy on his heart. His conscience smote him. And yet, when he saw before him in the night the vision of this tortured man, he knew that he would repeat his sin if necessary.

The next day was Sunday. He sat down and tried to think of the two sermons he had to preach. The sea lay very still on the Sabbath morning, still under a smooth and pathetic grey sky. The atmosphere seemed that of a winter fairyland. All the sea-birds were in hiding. Small waves licked the land like furtive tongues seeking some dainty food with sly desire. Across the short sea-grass the island children wound from school to church, and the island lads gathered in knots to say nothing. The whistling of a naughty fisherman attending to his nets unsabbatically pierced the still and magically cruel air with a painful sharpness. People walked in silence without knowing why they did not care to speak. And even the girls, discreet in ribbons and shining boots, thought less of kisses than they generally did on Sunday. The older people, sober by temperament, became sombre under the influence of sad, breathless sky, and breathless waters. The coldness that lay in the bosom of nature soon found its way to the responsive bosom of humanity. It chilled Uniacke in the pulpit, Sir Graham in the pew below. The one preached without heart. The other listened without emotion. All this was in the morning. But at evening nature stirred in her repose and turned, with the abruptness of a born coquette, to pageantry. A light wind got up. The waves were curved and threw up thin showers of ivory spray playfully along the rocks. The sense of fairyland, wrapped in ethereal silences, quivered and broke like disturbed water. And the grey womb of the sky swelled in the west to give up a sunset that became tragic in its crescendo of glory. Bursting forth in flame—a narrow line of fire along the sea—it pushed its way slowly up the sky. Against the tattered clouds a hidden host thrust forth their spears of gold. And a wild-rose colour descended upon the gentle sea and floated to the island, bathing the rocks, the grim and weather-beaten houses, the stones of the churchyard, with a radiance so delicate, and yet so elfish, that enchantment walked there till the night came down, and in the darkness the islanders moved on their way to church. The pageant was over. But it had stirred two imaginations. It blazed yet in two hearts. The shock of its coming, after long hours of storm, had stirred Uniacke and his guest strangely. And the former, leaving in the rectory parlour the sermon he had composed, preached extempore on the text, "In the evening there shall be light."

He began radiantly and with fervour. But some spirit of contradiction entered his soul as he spoke, impelling him to a more sombre mood that was yet never cold, but rather impassioned full of imaginative despair. He was driven on to discourse of the men who will not see light, of the men who draw thick blinds to shut out light. And then he was led, by the egoism that so subtly guides even the best among men, to speak of those fools who, by fostering darkness, think to compel sunshine, as a man may mix dangerous chemicals in a laboratory, seeking to advance some cause of science and die in the poisonous fumes of his own devilish brew. Can good, impulsive and radiant, come out of deliberate evil? Must not a man care first for his own soul if he would heal the soul of even one other? Uniacke spoke with a strange and powerful despair on this subject. He ended in a profound sadness and with the words of one scourged by doubts.

There was a pause, the shuffle of moving feet. Then the voice of the clerk announced the closing hymn. It was "Lead, Kindly Light," chosen by the harmonium player and submitted to Uniacke, who, however, had failed to notice that it was included in the list of hymns for the day. The clerk's voice struck on him like a blow. He stared down from the pulpit and met the upward gaze of his guest. Then he laid his cold hands on the wooden ledge of the pulpit and turned away his eyes. For he felt as if Sir Graham must understand the secret that lay in them. The islanders sang the hymn lustily, bending their heads over their books beneath the dull oil lamps that filled the church with a dingy yellow twilight. Alone, at the back of the building, the mad Skipper stood up by the belfry door and stared straight before him as if he watched. And Uniacke's trouble increased, seeming to walk in the familiar music which had been whistled by Jack Pringle as he swarmed to the mast-head, or turned into his bunk at night far out at sea. Sir Graham had spoken of intuitions. Surely, the clergyman thought, to-night he will feel the truth and my lie. To-night he will understand that it is useless to wait, that the wonder-child can never come to this island, for he came on the breast of the sea long ago. And if he does know, now, at this moment, while the islanders are singing,

"And with the morn those angel faces smile—"

how will he regard me, who have lied to him and who have preached to him, coward and hypocrite? For still the egoism was in Uniacke's heart. There is no greater egoist than the good man who has sinned against his nature. He sits down eternally to contemplate his own soul. When the hymn was over Uniacke mechanically gave the blessing and knelt down. But he did not pray. His mind stood quite still all the time he was on his knees. He got up wearily, and as he made his way into the little vestry, he fancied that he heard behind him a sound as of some one tramping in sea-boots upon the rough church pavement. He looked round and saw the bland face of the clerk, who wore perpetually a little smile, like that of a successful public entertainer. That evening he wrote to Doctor Braybrooke.

On the morrow Sir Graham began the first sketch for his picture, "*The Procession of the Drowned to their faithful Captain.*"

Three mornings later, when Uniacke came to the breakfast-table, Sir Graham, who was down before him, handed to him a letter, the envelope of which was half torn open.

"It was put among mine," he said in apology, "and as the handwriting was perfectly familiar to me, I began to open it."

"Familiar?" said Uniacke, taking the letter.

"Yes. It bears an exact resemblance to Doctor Braybrooke's writing."

"Oh!" said Uniacke, laying the letter aside rather hastily.

They sat down on either side of the table.

"You don't read your letter," Sir Graham said, after two or three minutes had passed.

"After breakfast. I don't suppose it is anything important," said the clergyman hastily.

Sir Graham said nothing more, but drank his coffee and soon afterwards went off to his work. Then Uniacke opened the letter.

"Cavendish Square,

London, Dec.—

"Dear Sir:

"I read your letter about my former patient, Sir Graham Hamilton, with great interest. When he consulted me I was fully aware that he was concealing from me some mental trouble, which reacted upon his bodily condition and tended to retard his complete recovery of health. However, a doctor cannot force the confidence of a patient even in that patient's own interest, and I was, therefore, compelled to work in the dark, and to work without satisfaction to myself and lasting benefit to Sir Graham. You now let in a strange light upon the case, and I have little doubt what course would be the best to pursue in regard to the future. Sir Graham's nervous system has broken down so completely that, as often happens in nervous cases, his very nature seems to have changed. The energy, the remarkable self-confidence, the hopefulness and power of looking forward, and of working for the future, which have placed him where he is—these have vanished. He is possessed by a fixed idea, and imagines that it is this fixed idea which has preyed upon him and broken him down. But my knowledge of nerve-complaints teaches me that the fixed idea follows on the weakening of the nervous system, and seldom or never precedes it. I find it is an effect and not a cause. But it is a fact that the fixed idea which possesses a man under such circumstances is often connected, and closely, with the actual cause of his illness. Sir Graham Hamilton is suffering from long and habitual overwork in connection with the sea; overwork of the imagination, of the perceptive faculty, and in the mere mechanical labour of putting on canvas what he imagines and what he perceives. In consequence of this overstrain and subsequent breakdown, he has become possessed by a fixed sea-idea, and traces all his wretchedness to this episode of the boy and the picture. You will say I did not succeed in curing him because I did not discover what this fixed idea was. How can that be, if the idea comes from the illness and not the illness from the idea. In reply I must inform you that a tragic idea, once it is fixed in the mind of a man, can, and often does, become in itself at last a more remote, but effective, cause of the prolonged continuance of the ill-health already started by some other agent. It keeps the wound, which it has not made, open. It is most important, therefore, that it should, if possible, be banished, in the case of Sir Graham as in other cases. Your amiable deception has quite possibly averted a tragedy. *Continue in it, I counsel you.* The knowledge that his fears are well founded, that the boy—for whose fate he morbidly considers himself entirely responsible—has in very truth been lost at sea, and lies buried in the ground beneath his feet, might, in his present condition of invalidism, be attended by most evil results. Some day it is quite possible that he may be able to learn all the facts with equanimity. But this can only be later when long rest and change have accomplished their beneficent work. It cannot certainly be now. Endeavour, therefore, to dissuade him from any sort of creative labour. Endeavour to persuade him to leave the island. Above all things, do not let him know the truth. It is a sad thing that a strong man of genius should be brought so low that he has to be treated with precautions almost suitable to a child. But to a doctor there are many more children in the world than a statistician might be able to number. I wish I could take a holiday and come to your assistance. Unfortunately, my duties tie me closely to town at the present. And, in any case, my presence might merely irritate and alarm our friend.

"Believe me,

Faithfully yours,

John Braybrooke."

Uniacke read this letter, and laid it down with a strange mingled feeling of relief and apprehension. The relief was a salve that touched his wounded conscience gently. If he had sinned, at least this physician's letter told him that by his sin he had accomplished something beneficent. And for the moment self-condemnation ceased to scourge him. The apprehension that quickly beset him rose from the knowledge that Sir Graham was in danger so long as he was in the Island. But how could he be persuaded to leave it? That was the problem.

Uniacke's reverie over the letter was interrupted by the appearance of the painter. As he came into the room, the clergyman rather awkwardly thrust the doctor's letter into his pocket and turned to his guest.

"In already, Sir Graham?" he said, with a strained attempt at ease of manner. "Ah! work tires you. Indeed you should take a long holiday."

He spoke, thinking of the doctor's words.

"I have not started work," the painter said. "I've—I've been looking at that grave by the church wall—the boy's grave."

"Oh!" said Uniacke, with sudden coldness.

"Do you know, Uniacke, it seems—it seems to me that the gravestone has been defaced."

"Defaced! Why, what could make such an idea come to you?" exclaimed the clergyman. "Defaced! But—"

"There is a gap in the inscription after the word 'Jack,'" the painter said slowly, fixing a piercing and morose glance on his companion. "And it seems to me that some blunt instrument has been at work there."

"Oh, there was always a gap there," said Uniacke hastily, touching the letter that lay in his pocket, and feeling, strangely, as if the contact fortified that staggering pilgrim on the path of lies—his conscience. "There was always a gap. It was a whim of the Skipper's—a mad whim."

"But I understood he was sane when his shipmate was buried? You said so."

"Sane? Yes, in comparison with what he is now. But one could not argue with him. He was distraught with grief."

Sir Graham looked at Uniacke with the heavy suspicion of a sick man, but he said nothing more on the subject. He turned as if to go out. Uniacke stopped him.

"You are going to paint?"

"Yes."

Again Uniacke thought of the doctor's advice.

"Sir Graham," he said, speaking with obvious hesitation, "I—I would not work."

"Why?"

"You are not fit to bear any fatigue at present. Creation will inevitably retard your recovery."

"I am not ill in body, and work is the only panacea for a burdened mind. If it cannot bring me happiness, at least—"

"Happiness!" Uniacke interrupted. "And what may not bring that! Why, Sir Graham, even death—should that be regarded as a curse? May not death bring the greatest happiness of all?"

The painter's forehead contracted, but the clergyman continued with gathering eagerness and fervour:

"Often when I pray beside a little dead child, or—or a young lad, and hear the mother weeping, I feel more keenly than at any other time the fact that blessings descend upon the earth. The child is taken in innocence. The lad is bereft of the power to sin. And their souls are surely at peace."

"At peace," said the painter heavily. "Yes, that is something. But the mother—the mother weeps, you say."

"Human love, the most beautiful thing in the world must still be earth-bound, must still be selfish."

"But—"

"Sir Graham, I'll confess to you even this, that on Sunday evening, when, after the service, we sang that hymn, 'Lead, Kindly Light,' I thought would it not be a very beautiful thing if the body mouldering beneath that stone in the churchyard yonder were indeed the body of—of your wonder-child."

"Uniacke!"

"Yes, yes. Don't you remember how he looked up from his sordid misery to the rainbow?"

"How can I ever forget it?"

"Does that teach you nothing?"

There was a silence. Then the painter said:

"Death may be beautiful, but only after life has been beautiful. For it is beautiful to live as Jack would have lived."

"Is living—somewhere," interposed Uniacke quickly.

"Perhaps. I can't tell. But I hear the mother weeping. I hear the mother weeping."

That night Uniacke lay long awake. He heard the sea faintly. Was it not weeping too? It seemed to him in that dark hour as if one power alone was common to all people and to all things—the power to mourn.

Next day, despite Uniacke's renewed protests, Sir Graham began to paint steadily. The clergyman dared not object too strongly. He had no right. And brain-sick men are bad to deal with. He could only watch over Sir Graham craftily and be with him as much as possible, always hoping that the painting frenzy would desert him, and that he would find out for himself that his health was too poor to endure any strain of labour.

The moon was now past its second quarter, and the weather continued cold and clear. Sir Graham and Uniacke went out several times by night to the belfry of the church, and the painter observed the light effects through the narrow window. In the daytime he made various studies from memory of these effects. And presently Uniacke began to grow more reconciled to this labour of which—prompted by the doctor's letter—he had at first been so much afraid. For it really seemed that toil could be a tonic to this man as to many other men. Sir Graham spoke less of little Jack. He was devoured by the fever of creation. In the evenings he mused on his picture, puffing at his pipe. He no longer continually displayed his morbid sorrow, or sought to discuss at length the powers of despair. Uniacke was beginning to feel happier about him, even to doubt the doctor's wisdom in denouncing work as a danger, when something happened which filled him with a vague apprehension.

The mad Skipper, whom nothing attracted, wandering vacantly, according to his sad custom, about the graveyard and in the church, one day ascended to the belfry, in which Sir Graham sat at work on a study for the background of his picture. Uniacke was with his friend at the time, and heard the Skipper's heavy and stumbling footsteps ascending the narrow stone stairs.

"Who's that coming?" the painter asked.

"The Skipper," Uniacke answered, almost under his breath.

In another minute the huge seaman appeared, clad as usual in jersey and peaked cap, his large blue eyes full of an animal expression of vacant plaintiveness and staring lack of thought. He showed no astonishment at finding intruders established in his domain, and for a moment Uniacke thought he would quietly turn about and make his way down again. For, after a short pause, he half swung round, still keeping his eyes vaguely fixed on the artist, who continued to paint as if quite alone. But apparently some chord of curiosity had been struck in this poor and benumbed mind. For the big man wavered, then stole rather furtively forward, and fixed his sea-blue eyes on the canvas, upon which appeared the rough wall of the belfry, the narrow window, with a section of wild sky in which a weary moon gleamed faintly, and the dark arch of the stairway up which the drowned mariners would come to their faithful captain. The Skipper stared at all this inexpressively, turned to move away, paused, waited. Sir Graham went on painting; and the Skipper stayed. He made no sound. Uniacke could scarcely hear him breathing. He seemed wrapped in dull and wide-eyed contemplation. Only when at last Sir Graham paused, did he move away slowly down the stairs with his loose-limbed, shuffling gait, which expressed so plainly the illness of his mind.

In the rectory parlour, a few minutes later, Uniacke and Sir Graham discussed this apparently trifling incident. A feeling of unreasonable alarm besieged Uniacke's soul, but he strove to fight against and to expel it.

"How quietly he stood," said the painter. "He seemed strangely interested."

"Yes, strangely. And yet his eyes were quite vague and dull. I noticed that."

"For all that, Uniacke, his mind may be waking from its sleep."

"Waking from its sleep!" said Uniacke, with a sudden sharpness. "No—impossible!"

"One would almost think you desired that it should not," rejoined Sir Graham, with obvious surprise.

Uniacke saw that he had been foolishly unguarded.

"Oh, no," he said, more quietly, "I only fear that the poor fellow can never recover."

"Why not? From what feeling, from what root of intelligence does his interest in my work spring? May it not be that he vaguely feels as if my picture were connected with his sorrow?"

Uniacke shook his head.

"I am not sure that it is impossible," continued Sir Graham. "To-morrow I begin to make studies for the figures. If he comes to me again, I shall sketch him in."

Uniacke's uneasiness increased. Something within him revolted from the association of his guest and the Skipper. The hidden link between them was a tragedy, a tragedy that had wrecked the reason of the one, the peace of the other. They did not know of this link, yet there seemed horror in such a companionship as theirs, and the clergyman was seized with fear.

"You are going to draw your figures from models?" he said, slowly, speaking to cover his anxiety, and speaking idly enough.

The painter's reply struck away his uncertainty, and set him face to face with a most definite dread.

"I shall have models," said Sir Graham, "for all the figures except for little Jack. I can draw him from memory. I can reproduce his face. It never leaves me."

"What!" said Uniacke. "You will paint an exactly truthful portrait of him then?"

"I shall; only idealised by death, dignified, weird, washed by the sad sea."

"The Skipper watched you while you were painting. He saw all you were doing."

"Yes. And I think he'll come again."

"But then—he'll—he'll see—"

The clergyman stopped short.

"See—see what?" Sir Graham asked.

"Himself," Uniacke replied, evasively. "When you paint him with the ropes dropping from his hands. May it not agitate, upset him, to see himself as he stands ringing those bells each night? Ah! there they are!"

It was twilight now, cold, and yellow, and grim; twilight of winter. And the pathetic, cheerless appeal of the two bells stole out over the darkening sea.

"Perhaps it may agitate him," Sir Graham said. "What then? To strike a sharp blow on the gates of his mind might be to do him a good service. A shock expelled his reason. Might not a shock recall it?"

"I can't tell," Uniacke said. "Such an experiment might be dangerous, it seems to me, very dangerous."

"Dangerous?"

Uniacke turned away rather abruptly. He could not tell the painter what was in his mind, his fear that the mad Skipper might recognise the painted face of the dead boy, for whom he waited, for whom, even at that moment, the bells were ringing. And if the Skipper did recognise this face that he knew so well—what then? What would be the sequel? Uniacke thought of the doctor's letter. He felt as if a net were closing round him, as if there could be no escape from some tragic finale. And he felt too, painfully, as if a tragic finale were all that he—he, clergyman, liar, trickster,—deserved. His conscience, in presence of a shadow, woke again, and found a voice, and told him that evil could not prevail for good, that a lie could not twist the course of things from paths of sorrow to paths of joy. Did not each lie call aloud to danger, saying, "Approach! approach!" Did not each subterfuge stretch out arms beckoning on some nameless end? He seemed to hear soft footsteps. He was horribly afraid and wished that, in the beginning of his acquaintance with Sir Graham, he had dared consequence and spoken truth. Now he felt like a man feebly fighting that conqueror, the Inevitable, and he went in fear. Yet he struggled still.

"Sir Graham," he said, on the following day, "forgive me, but I feel it my duty to urge you not to let that poor fellow watch you at work. It is not safe. I do not think it is safe. I have a strong feeling that—that the shock of seeing—"

"Himself?"

"Exactly!—might be dangerous."

"To him?"

"Or to you. That is my feeling. Possibly to you. He is not sane, and though he seems harmless enough—"

"I'm fully prepared to take the risk," said Sir Graham abruptly, and with a return of his old suspicious expression. "I'm not afraid of the man."

He got up and went out. The mere thought of danger, in his condition, warmed and excited him. He had resolved before actually starting upon his picture to make some *plein air* studies of the islanders. Therefore he now made his way into the village, engaged a fisher-lad to stand to him, returned to the rectory for his easel and set it up just beyond the churchyard wall. He posed the shamefaced and giggling boy and set to work. Uniacke was writing in the small bow-window, or pretending to write. Often he looked out, watching the painter, waiting, with a keen anxiety, to know whether the interest shown in his work by the Skipper was only the passing whim of insanity, or whether it was something more permanent, more threatening perhaps.

The painter worked. The sailor posed, distending his rough cheeks with self-conscious laughter. Uniacke watched. It seemed that the Skipper was not coming. Uniacke felt a sense of relief. He got up from his writing-table at last, intending to go into the village. As he did so, the tall form of the Skipper came into view in the distance. Dark, bulky, as yet far off, it shambled forward slowly, hesitatingly, over the short grass towards the painter. While Uniacke observed it, he thought it looked definitely animal. It approached, making détours, like a dog, furtive and intent, that desires to draw near to some object without seeming to do so. Slowly it came, tacking this way and that, pausing frequently as if uncertain or alarmed. And

Uniacke, standing in the shadow of the red curtain, watched its movements, fascinated. He did not know why, but he had a sensation that Fate, loose-limbed, big-boned, furtive, was shambling over the grass towards his guest. Sir Graham went on quietly painting. The Skipper made a last détour, got behind the painter, stole up and peered over his shoulder. Once there, he seemed spellbound. For he stood perfectly still and never took his large blue eyes from the canvas. Uniacke went into the little passage, got his hat and hastened out, impelled yet without purpose. As he crossed the churchyard he saw Sir Graham put something into the sailor's hand. The sailor touched his cap awkwardly and rolled off. Uniacke hurried forward.

"You've finished your work?" he said, coming up.

Sir Graham turned and made him a hasty sign to be silent.

"Don't alarm him," he whispered, with a slight gesture towards the Skipper, who stood as if in a vacant reverie, looking at the painted sailor boy.

"But—" Uniacke began.

"Hush!" the painter murmured, almost angrily. "Leave us alone together."

The clergyman moved away with a sinking heart. Indefinable dread seized him. The association between these two men was fraught with unknown peril. He felt that, and so strongly, that he was almost tempted to defy convention and violently interfere to put an end to it. But he restrained himself and returned to the rectory, watching the two motionless figures beyond the churchyard wall from the parlour window as from an ambush, with an intensity of expectation that gave him the bodily sensation of a man clothed in mail.

In the late afternoon Sir Graham showed him an admirable study of the Skipper, standing with upraised arms as if ringing the church bells, his blue eyes fixed as if he scanned a distant horizon, or searched the endless plains of the sea for his lost companions.

"Forgive my abruptness this morning," the painter said. "I was afraid your presence would scare the Skipper."

Uniacke murmured a word in admiration of the painting.

"And to-morrow," he added.

"To-morrow I shall start on the picture," Sir Graham replied.

After supper he drew aside the blind and looked forth.

"The moon is rising," he said. "I shall go out for a little while. I want to observe light effects, and to think over what I am going to do. My mind is full of it, Uniacke; I think it should be a great picture."

His eyes were shining with excitement. He went out. He was away a long time. The clock in the rectory parlour struck eleven, half-past eleven, he did not return. Beginning to feel anxious, Uniacke went to the window and looked out. The night was quiet and clear, bathed in the radiance of the moon, which defined objects sharply. The dark figure of the painter was approaching the house from the church. Uniacke, who did not wish to be thought curious, drew hastily back from the window and dropped the blind. In a moment Sir Graham entered. He was extremely pale and looked scared. He shut the door very hastily, almost as if he wished to prevent some one from entering after him. Then he came up to the fire without a word.

"You are late," Uniacke said, unpleasantly affected, but trying to speak indifferently.

"Late, am I? Why—what time is it?"

"Nearly midnight."

"Indeed. I forgot the hour. I was engrossed. I—" He looked up hastily and looked down again. "A most strange, most unaccountable, thing has happened."

"What?" said Uniacke. "Surely the Skipper hasn't—"

"No, no. It's nothing to do with him. I haven't seen him. No, no—but the most unaccountable—how long have I been out there?"

"You went out at nine. It's a quarter to twelve now."

"Two hours and three-quarters! I should have said ten minutes. But then—how long was I with it?"

"With it?" repeated Uniacke, turning cold.

"Yes, yes—how long? It seemed no time—and yet an eternity, too."

He got up and went to and fro uneasily about the room.

"Horrible!" he muttered, as if to himself. "Horrible!"

He stopped suddenly in front of Uniacke.

"Do you believe," he said, "that when we think very steadily and intensely of a thing we may, perhaps, project—give life, as it were, for the moment to our thought?"

"Why do you ask me?" said Uniacke. "It has never happened to me to do such a thing."

"Why do I ask? Well, I'll—"

He hesitated, keeping his eyes fixed on Uniacke's face.

"Yes, I'll tell you what took place. I went out thinking of my picture, of its composition, of the light effect, of the faces of the drowned men, especially of the face of little Jack. I seemed to see him coming into that belfry tower—yes, to greet the Skipper, all dripping from the sea. But—but—no, Uniacke, I'll swear that, in my mind, I saw his face as it used to be. That was natural, wasn't it? I imagined it white, with wide, staring eyes, the skin wet and roughened with the salt water. But that was all. So it couldn't have been my thought projected, because I had never imagined.—"

He was evidently engrossed by his own reflections. His eyes had an inward expression. His voice died in a murmur, almost like the murmur of one who babbles in sleep.

"Never had imagined what?" said Uniacke, sharply.

"Oh, forgive me. I cannot understand it. As I paced in the churchyard, thinking of my picture, and watching the moon and the shadows cast by the church and by the stones of the tombs, I came to that grave by the wall."

"The grave of the boy I told you about?" said Uniacke with an elaborate indifference.

"Yes, the boy."

"Well?"

"I suppose I stood there for a few minutes, or it may have been longer. I can't tell at all. I don't think I was even aware that I was no longer walking. I was entirely wrapped up in my meditations, I believe. I saw my picture before me, the Skipper, the dripping sailors—Jack first. I saw them quite distinctly with my mental vision. And then, by degrees, somehow those figures in the picture all faded into darkness, softly, gradually, till only one was left—Jack. He was still there in the picture. The moonlight through the narrow belfry window fell on him. It seemed to make the salt drops sparkle, almost like jewels, in his hair, on his clothes. I looked at him,—mentally, still. And, while I looked, the moonlight, I thought, grew stronger. The belfry seemed to fade away. The figure of Jack stood out in the light. It grew larger—larger. It reached the size of life. And then, as I stared upon it, the face altered before my eyes. It became older, less childish, more firm and manly—but oh, Uniacke! a thousand times more horrible."

"How? How?"

"Why, it became puffy, bloated, dropsical. The eyes were glazed and bloodshot. On the lips there was foam. The fingers of the hands were twisted and distorted. The teeth grinned hideously. The romance of death dropped away. The filthy reality of death stood before me, upon the grave of that boy."

"You imagined it," muttered Uniacke.

He spoke without conviction.

"I did not. I saw it. For now I knew that I was no longer thinking of my picture. I looked around me and saw the small clouds and the night, the moon in the pale sky, the black church, this house, the graves like creatures lying side by side asleep. I saw them all. I heard the dull wash of the sea. And then I looked again at that grave, and on it stood Jack, the dead thing I sent to death, bloated and silent, staring upon me. Silent—and yet I seemed to feel that it said, 'This is what I am. Paint me like this. Look at what the sea has done to me! Look—look at what the sea has done!'—Uniacke! Uniacke!"

He sank down into a chair and stared before him with terrible eyes. A shudder ran over the clergyman, but he said, in a voice that he tried to make calm and consolatory,

"Of course it was your fancy, Sir Graham. You had conjured up the figures in your picture. There was nothing unnatural in your seeing one— the one you had known in life—more distinctly than the others."

"I had not known it like that. I had never imagined anything so distorted, so horrible, tragic and yet almost grotesque, a thing for the foolish to—to laugh at, ugh! Besides, it stood there. It was actually there on that grave, as if it had risen out of that grave, Uniacke."

"Your fancy."

Uniacke spoke with no conviction, and his lips were pale.

"I say it is not. The thing—Jack, come to that!—was there. Had you been with me, you must have seen it as I did."

Uniacke shook his head.

"Believe me, Sir Graham," he exclaimed, "you ought to go from here. The everlasting sound of the sea—the presence of the Skipper—your idea for this terrible picture—"

"Terrible! Yes, I see it must be terrible. My conception—how wrong it was! I meant to make death romantic, almost beautiful. And it is like that. To-morrow—to-morrow—ah, Jack! I can paint you now!"

He sprang up and hurried from the room. Uniacke heard him pacing up and down above stairs till far into the night.

The clergyman was deeply and sincerely religious, but he was in nowise a superstitious man. Association with Sir Graham, however, and the circumstances attendant upon that association, had gradually unnerved him. He was now a prey to fear, almost to horror. Was it possible, he thought, as he sat listening to that eternal footfall overhead, that Providence permitted a spirit to rise from the very grave to proclaim his lie, and to show the truth in a most hideous form? He could almost believe so. It seemed that the dead boy resented the defacement of his tomb, resented the deliberate untruth which concealed from the painter his dreary destiny, and came up out of the other world to proclaim the clergyman's deception. It seemed as if God himself fought with a miraculous means the battle of truth and tore aside the veil in which Uniacke had sought to shroud the actuality of death. Uniacke could not bring himself to speak to the painter, to acknowledge the trickery resorted to for a sick man's sake. But this vision of the night paralysed his power to make any further effort in deception. He felt benumbed and impotent. A Power invisible to him fought against him. He could only lay down his weapons,—despicable, unworthy, as they were,—and let things take their course, while he looked on as one in a sad dream, apprehensive of the ending of that dream.

Sir Graham began his picture on the morrow. His first excitement in the conception of it, which had been almost joyous, was now become feverish and terrible. He was seized by the dreary passion of the gifted man who means to use his gifts to add new and vital horrors to the horrors of life. He no longer felt the pathos, the almost exquisite romance, of his subject. He felt only its tragic, its disgusting terror. While he painted feverishly the mad Skipper hovered about him, with eyes still vacant but a manner of increasing unrest. It seemed as if something whispered to him that this work of a stranger had some connection with his life, some deep, though as yet undiscovered, meaning for him. The first figure in the picture was the Skipper himself. When it was painted the likeness was striking. But the poor mad seaman stared upon it with an ignorant vagueness. It was evident that he looked without seeing, that he observed without comprehending.

"Surely he will not know Jack," Uniacke thought, "since he does not know his own face."

And he felt a faint sense of relief. But this passed away, for the unrest of the Skipper seemed continually to grow more marked and seething. Uniacke noticed it with gathering anxiety. Sir Graham did not observe it. He thought of nothing but his work.

"I shall paint Jack last of all," he said grimly, to Uniacke. "I mean to make a crescendo of horror, and in Jack's figure the loathsomeness of death shall reach a climax. Yes, I will paint him last of all. Perhaps he will come again and pose for me upon that grave." And he laughed as he sat before his easel.

"What painter ever before had such a model?" he said to Uniacke.

And that night after supper, he got up from the table saying:

"I must go and see if Jack will give me a sitting to-night."

Uniacke rose also.

"Let me come with you," he said.

Sir Graham stopped with his hand on the door. There was a smile on his lips, but his eyes were full of foreboding.

"Do you want to see Jack, then?" he asked, with a dreadful feigning of jocularity. "But you are not a painter. You require no model, living or dead." He burst again into a laugh.

"Let me come with you," the clergyman repeated doggedly.

Sir Graham made no objection, and they went out together.

The moon was now growing towards the full, but it was yet low in the sky, and the night was but faintly lit, as a room is lit by a heavily shaded lamp. Sir Graham's manner lost its almost piteous bluster as he stood on the doorstep and felt the cold wind that blew from the wintry sea. He set his lips, and his face twitched with nervous agitation as he stole a furtive glance at the clergyman, whose soft hat was pulled down low over his eyes as if to conceal their expression.

The two men walked forward slowly into the churchyard. Uniacke's heart was beating with violence and his mind was full of acute anticipation. Yet he would scarcely acknowledge even to himself the possibility of such an appearance as that affirmed by Sir Graham. They drew near to the grave of little Jack, round which the chill winds of night blew gently and the dull voices of the waves sang hushed and murmurous nocturnes. Uniacke was taken by an almost insurmountable inclination to pause, even to turn back. Their progress to this grave seemed attended by some hidden and ghastly danger. He laid his hand upon the painter's arm, as if to withhold him from further advance.

"What is it?" Sir Graham asked, speaking almost in a whisper.

"Nothing," said Uniacke, dropping his hand.

Sir Graham's eyes were full of sombre questioning as they met his. Moving slowly on, the two men stood at length by Jack's grave. The moon rose languidly, and shed a curious and ethereal twilight upon the stone at its head. The blurred place from which Uniacke had struck the name was plainly visible. Instinctively the clergyman's eyes sought the spot and stared upon it.

"Does it not bear all the appearance of having been defaced?" said Sir Graham in his ear.

Uniacke shook his head.

"The Skipper would have it so," he murmured, full of a heavy sense of useless contest against the determination of something hidden that all should be known to his companion, perhaps even that very night.

They waited, as mourners wait beside a tomb. As the moon rose, the churchyard grew more distinct. The surrounding graves came into view, the crude bulk of the rectory, the outline of the church tower, and the long wall of the churchyard. On the white faces of the two men the light fell pitilessly, revealing the strained and anxious expression of Uniacke, the staring watchfulness of the painter. The minutes ran by. Uniacke shivered slightly in the wind. By degrees he began to lose the expectation of seeing any apparition. Presently he even sneered silently at himself for his folly in having ever entertained it. Nevertheless he was strongly affected by the nearness of the wonder-child's grave, from which seemed to emanate an influence definite and searching, and—so he felt—increasingly hostile, either to himself or to the artist. It came up like a thing that threatened. It crept near like a thing that would destroy. Uniacke wondered whether Sir Graham was conscious of it. But the painter said nothing, and the clergyman dared not ask him. At length, however, his fanciful sense of this dead power, speaking as it were from the ground under his feet, became so intolerable to him that he was resolved to go; and he was about to tell Sir Graham of his intention when the painter suddenly caught his arm in a tight grip.

"There it is," he whispered.

He was staring before him over the grave. Uniacke followed his eyes. He saw the short grass stirring faintly in the night wind. He thought it looked like hair bristling, and his hair moved on his head. He saw the churchyard in a maze of moon-rays. And with the moonlight had come many shadows. But not one of them was deceptive. Not one took the form of any spectre. Nevertheless Uniacke recoiled from this little grave at his feet, for it seemed to him as if the power that had been sleeping there stirred, forsook its recumbent position, rose up warily, intent on coming forth to confront him.

"You see it?" whispered Sir Graham, still keeping hold of his arm.

"No, no I see nothing; there is nothing. It's your fancy, your imagination that plays tricks on you."

"No, it's Jack. Oh, Uniacke, see—see how he poses! He knows that I shall paint him to-morrow. How horrible he is! Do the drowned always look like that?"

"Come away, Sir Graham. This is a hideous hallucination. Come away."

"How he is altered. All his features are coarsened, bloated. My wonder-child! He is tragic now, and he is disgusting. How loathsomely he twists his fingers! Must I paint him like that—with that grinning, ghastly mouth—little Jack? Ah! ah! He poses—he poses always. He would have me paint him now,—here in the moonlight—here—here—standing on this grave!"

"Sir Graham, come with me!" exclaimed Uniacke.

And this time he forcibly drew his companion with him from the grave. The painter seemed inclined to resist for a moment. He turned his head and looked long and eagerly behind him. Then suddenly he acquiesced.

"It has gone," he said. "You have driven it away."

Uniacke hurried forward to the Rectory. That night he implored the painter for the last time to leave the island.

"Can't you feel," he said, almost passionately, "the danger you are running here, the terrible danger to yourself? The sea preys upon your mind. You ought not to be near it. Every murmur of the waves is suggestive to your ears. The voices of those bells recall to your mind the drowning of men. The sigh of that poor maniac depresses you perpetually. Leave the sea. Try to forget it. I tell you, Sir Graham, that your mind is becoming actually diseased from incessant brooding. It begins even to trick your eyes in this abominable way."

"You swear you saw nothing?"

"I do. There was nothing. You have thought of that boy until you actually see him before you."

"As he is?"

"As he is not, as he will never be."

The painter got up from his chair, came over to Uniacke, and looked piercingly into his eyes.

"Then you declare—on your honour as a priest," he said slowly, "that you do not know that my wonder-child is the boy who is buried beneath that stone?"

"I buried that boy, and I declare on my honour as a priest that I do not know it," Uniacke answered, desperately but unflinchingly.

It was his last throw for this man's salvation.

"I believe you," the painter said.

He returned to the fireplace, and leaned his face on his arm against the mantelpiece.

"I believe you," he repeated presently. "I have been mistaken."

"Mistaken—how?"

"Sometimes I have thought that you have lied to me."

Uniacke's heart grew heavier at the words.

In the morning Sir Graham said to him, with a curious calmness:

"I think perhaps you are right, Uniacke. I have been considering your words, your advice."

"And you will take it?" Uniacke said, with a sudden enormous sense of gratefulness.

"I think I shall."

"Think—Sir Graham!"

"I'll decide to-night. I must have the day to consider. But—yes, you are right. That—that horrible appearance. I suppose it must be evoked by the trickery of my own brain."

"Undoubtedly."

"There can be no other reason for it?"

"None—none."

"Then—then, yes, I had better go from here. But you will come with me?"

"To London?"

"Anywhere—it does not matter."

He looked round him wistfully.

"If I am to leave the island," he said sorrowfully, "it does not matter where I go."

"To London then," Uniacke said, almost joyously. "I will make my arrangements."

"To-morrow?"

"To-morrow. Yes. Excuse me for the present. I must run over to the mainland to settle about the Sunday services. I shall be back in a few hours."

He went out, feeling as if a weight had been lifted from brain and heart. So good could come out of evil. Had he not done right to lie? He began to believe that he had. As he crossed to the mainland he wrapped himself in warm and comfortable sophistries. The wickedness of subterfuge vanished now that subterfuge was found to be successful in attaining a desired end. For that which is successful seldom appears wholly evil. To-day Uniacke glowed in the fires of his sinfulness.

He transacted his business on the mainland and set out on his return home, driving through the shallow sea in a high cart. The day, which had opened in sunshine, was now become grey, very still and depressing. An intense and brooding silence reigned, broken by the splashing of the horse's hoofs in the scarcely ruffled water, and by the occasional peevish cackle of a gull hovering, on purposeless wings, between the waters and the mists. The low island lay in the dull distance ahead, wan and deprecatory of aspect, like a thing desiring to be left alone in the morose embrace of solitude. Uniacke, gazing towards it out of the midst of the sea, longed ardently for the morrow when Sir Graham would be caught away from this pale land of terror. He no longer blamed himself for what he had done. Conscience was asleep. He exulted, and had a strange feeling that God smiled on him with approval of his sin.

As he reached the island, the grey pall slightly lifted and light broke through the mist. He came up out of the sea, and, whipping the wet and weary horse, drove along the narrow lanes towards the Rectory. But when he came within hail of the churchyard all his abnormal exultation was suddenly quenched, and the oppressive sense of threatening danger which had for so long a time persecuted him, returned with painful force. He saw ahead of him Sir Graham seated before his easel painting. Behind the artist, bending down, his eyes fixed intently on the canvas, his huge hands gripping one another across his chest, stood the mad Skipper. As the wheels of the cart ground the rough road by the churchyard wall, Sir Graham looked up and smiled.

"I'm doing a last day's work," he called.

Uniacke stopped the cart and jumped out. The Skipper never moved. His eyes never left the canvas. He seemed utterly absorbed.

"You are not working on the picture?" said Uniacke hastily.

"No."

"Thank God."

"Why d'you say that?"

"I—the subject was so horrible."

"This is only a study. I shall leave the picture as I am leaving the Island. Perhaps some day—" He paused. Then he said: "I call this 'Sea Change.' Go indoors. In about half an hour I will come and fetch you to see it. Where will you be?"

"In my little room at the back of the house. I have some letters to write."

"I'll come there. Don't disturb me, till then. I think the picture will be strange—and I hope beautiful."

And again he smiled. Reassured, Uniacke made his way into the Rectory. He sat down at his writing-table, took up his pen and wrote a few words of a letter. But his mind wandered. The pen dropped on the table and he fell into thought. It was strangely still weather, and there was a strange stillness in his heart and conscience, a calm that was sweet to him. He felt the relief of coming to an end after a journey that had not been without dangers. For, during his intercourse with Sir Graham, he had often walked upon the edge of tragedy. Now he no longer looked down from that precipice. He leaned his arm on the table, among the litter of papers connected with parish affairs, and rested his head in his hand. Almost unconsciously, at that moment he began to rejoice at his own boldness in deviating from the strict path of uncompromising rectitude. For he thought of it as boldness, and of his former unyielding adherence to the principles he believed to be right, as timidity. After all, he said to himself, it is easy to be too rigid, too strict. In all human dealings we must consider not only ourselves, but also the individuals with whom we have to do. Have we the right to injure them by our determination to take care of the welfare of our own souls? It seemed to him just then as if virtue was often merely selfishness and implied a lack of sympathy with others. He might have refused to lie and destroyed his friend. Would not that have been selfishness? Would not that have been sheer cowardice? He told himself that it would.

Calm flowed upon him. He was lost in the day-dream of the complacent man whose load of care has fallen away into the abyss from which he has fortunately escaped. The silence of the Island was intense to-day. His conscience slept with the winds. And the sea slept too with all its sorrow. He sat there like a carven figure with his face in his hand. And, by degrees, he ceased to feel, to think actively. Conscious, not asleep, with open eyes he remained in a placid attitude, lulled in the arms of a quiet happiness.

He was distracted at length by some sound at a distance. It broke through his day-dream. At first he could not tell what it was, but presently he became aware that a hoarse voice was ejaculating some word outside, probably in the churchyard. He took his hand from his face, sat up straight by the writing-table and began to listen, at first with some slight irritation. For he had been happy in his day-dream. The voice outside repeated the word. Uniacke thought of the street-cries of London to which he was going, and that this cry was like one of them. He heard it again. Now it was nearer. Short and sharp, it sounded both angry and—something else—what? Dolorous, he fancied, keen with a horror of wonder and of despair. He remembered where he was, and that he had never before heard such a cry on the Island. But he still sat by the table. He was listening intently, trying to hear what was the word the voice kept perpetually calling.

"Jack! Jack!"

Uniacke sprang up, pushing back his chair violently. It caught in a rug that lay on the bare wooden floor and fell with a crash to the ground.

"Jack! Jack!"

The word came to his ears now in a sort of strident howl that was hardly human. He began to tremble. But still he did not recognise the voice.

"Jack!"

It was cried under the window of the parlour, fiercely, frantically. Uniacke knew the voice for the mad Skipper's. He delayed no longer, but hastened to the front room and stared out across the churchyard.

The Skipper, with his huge hands uplifted, his fingers working as if they strove to strangle something invisible in the air, was stumbling among the graves. His face was red and convulsed with excitement.

"Jack!" he shouted hoarsely, "Jack!"

And he went on desperately towards the sea, pursuing—nothing.

Uniacke looked away from him towards the place where Sir Graham had been painting. The easel stood there with the canvas resting upon the wooden pins. On the ground before it was huddled a dark thing.

Uniacke went out from his house. Although he did not know it he walked very slowly as if he dragged a weight. His feet trod upon the graves. As he walked he could hear the hoarse shout of the skipper dying away in the distance towards the sea.

"Jack!"

The voice faded as he gained the churchyard wall.

The dark thing huddled at the foot of the easel was the painter's dead body. On his discoloured throat there were the marks of fingers. Mechanically Uniacke turned his eyes from those purple and red marks to the picture the dead man had been painting. He saw the figure of a boy in a seaman's jersey and long sea-boots dripping with water. The face of the boy was pale and swollen. The mouth hung down hideously. The hair was matted with moisture. Only the eyes were beautiful, for they looked upward with a rapt and childlike expression.

"He sees the rainbow!" murmured the clergyman.

And he fell forward against the churchyard wall with his face buried in his arms. The voice of the grey sea was very loud in his ears. Darkness seemed to close in on him. He had done evil to do good, and the evil he had done had been in vain. His heart beat hard, and seemed to be in his throat choking him. And in the darkness he saw a vision of a dirty child, dressed in rags and a tall paper cap, and pointing upwards.

And he heard a voice, that sounded far off and unearthly, say:

"Look at that there rainbow! Look at that there rainbow!"

He wondered, as a man wonders in a dream, whether the dead painter heard the voice too, but more clearly—and elsewhere.

"WILLIAM FOSTER"

One sad cold day in London, city of sad cold days, a man in a Club had nothing on earth to do. He had glanced through the morning papers and found them full of adjectives and empty of news. He had smoked several cigarettes. He had exchanged a word or two of gossip with two or three acquaintances. And he had stared moodily out of a bow window, and had been rewarded by a vision of wet paving stones, wet beggars and wet sparrows. He felt depressed and inclined to wonder why he existed. Turning from the window to the long room at his back he saw an elderly Colonel yawning, with a sherry and bitters in one hand and a toothpick in the other. He decided not to remain in the Club. So he took his hat and went out into the street. It was raining in the street and he had no umbrella. He hailed a hansom and got in.

"Where to, sir?" asked the cabby through the trap door.

"What?" said the man.

"Where to, sir?"

"Oh! go to—to——"

He tried to think of some place where he might contrive to pass an hour or two agreeably.

"Sir?" said the cabby.

"Go to Madame Tussaud's," said the man.

It was the only place he could think of at the moment. He had lived in London for years but he had never been there. He had never had the smallest desire to go there. Wax and glass eyes did not attract him. Dresses that hung from corpses, which had never been alive, did not appeal to him. Nor did he care for buns. He had never been to Tussaud's. He was only going there now because literally, at the moment, he knew not where to go. He leaned back in the cab and looked at the wet pedestrians, and at the puddles.

When the cab stopped he got out and entered a large building. He paid money at a turnstile and drifted aimlessly into a waxen world. Some fat men in strange costumes, with bulging eyes like black velvet, and varying expressions of heavy lethargy, played Hungarian music on violins. It was evident that they did not thrill themselves. Their aspect was at the same time fierce and dull, they looked like volcanoes that had been drenched with water. The man passed on, the music grew softer and the waxen world pressed more closely round. Kings, cricketers, actresses, and statesmen beset him in vistas. He trod a maze of death that had not lived. There were very few school treats about, for the fashionable school treat season had not yet fully set in. So the man had the wax almost entirely to himself. He spread his wings to it like a bird to the air. By degrees, as he wandered—pursued by the distant music from the drenched volcanoes—a feeling of suffocation overtook him. All these men and women about him stared and smiled, but all were breathless. They wore their gaudy clothes with an air, no doubt. The Kings struck regal attitudes. The cricketers had a set manner of bringing off dreamy, difficult catches. The actresses were properly made up to charm, and the statesmen must surely have brought plenty of empires to ruin, if insipidity has power to cause such wreckage. But they were all decisively breathless. They seemed caught by some ghastly physical spell. And this spell was laid also upon the man who wandered among them. The breath of life withdrew from him to a long, long distance—he fancied. He felt as one who, taken by a trance, is bereft of power though not of knowledge. The staring silence was as the silence of a tomb, whose walls were full of eyes, intent and fatigued. He started when a person in uniform, hitherto apparently waxen, said in a cockney voice,

"See the Chamber of Horrors, sir?" But he recovered in time to acquiesce.

He descended towards a subterranean vault: as if to a lower circle of this inferno full of breathless demons. Here there were no rustic strangers, no clergymen with their choirs, no elderly ladies in command of "Bands of Hope." The silence was great, and the murderers stood together in companies, looking this way and that as if in search of victims. Some sat on chairs or stools. Some crouched in the dock. Some prepared for a mock expiation in their best clothes. One was at work in his house, digging in quicklime a hole the length of a human body. His waxen visage gleamed pale in the dim light, and he appeared to pause in his digging and to listen for sounds above his head. For he was in the cellar of his house.

The man stood still and looked at him. He had a mean face. All the features were squeezed and venomous, and expressive of criminal desires and of extreme cruelty. And so it was with most of his comrades. They varied in height, in age, in social status and in colouring. But upon all their faces was the same frigid expression, a sort of thin hatefulness touched with sarcasm. The man wandered on among them and saw it everywhere, on the lips of a youth in rags, in the eyes of an old woman in a bonnet, lurking in the wrinkles of a labourer, at rest upon the narrow brow of a doctor, alive in the puffed-out wax of an attorney's bloated features. Yes, it was easy to recognise the Devil's hall-mark on them all, he thought. And he wondered a little how it came about that they had been able, in so many cases, to gain the confidence of their unhappy victims. Here, for instance, were the man and woman who had lured servant girls into the depths of a forest and there murdered them for the sake of their boxes. Even the silliest girl, one would have supposed, must have fled in terror from the ape-like cunning of those wicked faces. Here was the housekeeper who had made away with her aged mistress. Surely any one with the smallest power of observation would have refused to sit in the evening, to sleep at night, in company with so horrible a countenance. Here was the man who killed his paramour with a knife. How came he to have a paramour? The desire to kill lurked in his bony cheeks, his small, intent eyes, his narrow slit of a mouth, but no desire to love. God seemed to have set his warning to humanity upon each of these creatures of the Devil. Yet they had deceived mankind to mankind's undoing. They had won confidence, respect, even love.

The man was confused by this knowledge, as he moved among them in the dimness and the silence, brushing the sleeve of one, the skirt of another, looking into the curiously expressive eyes of all. But presently his wondering recognition of the world's fatuous and frantic gullibility ceased. For at the end of an alley of murderers he stood before a woman. She was young, pretty and distinguished in appearance. Her features were small and delicate. Her brow was noble. Her painted mouth was tender and saintly; and, though her eyes were sightless, truth and nobility surely gazed out of them. For a moment the man was seized by a conviction that a mistake had been made by the proprietors of the establishment, and that some being, famous for charitable deeds, or intellect, or heroic accomplishment had been put in penance among these tragic effigies. He glanced at her number, consulted his catalogue, and found that this woman was named Catherine Sirrett, and that she had been convicted of the murder of her husband by poison some few years before. Then he looked at her again and, before this criminal, he felt that she might, nay, must, have deceived any man, the most acute and enlightened observer. No one could have looked into that face and seen blackness in the heart of that woman. Everyone must have trusted her. Many must have loved her. Her appearance inspired more than confidence—reverence; there was something angelic in its purity. There was something religious in its quiet gravity. His heart grew heavy as he looked at her, heavy with a horror far more great than any that had overcome him as he examined the bestial company around. And when he came away, and long afterwards, Catherine Sirrett's face remained in his memory as the most horrible face in all that silent, watchful crowd of beings who had wrought violence upon the earth. For it was dressed in deceit. The other faces were naked. So he thought. He did not know Catherine Sirrett's story, though he remembered that a woman of her name had been hanged in England some years before, when he was in India, and that she had gained many sympathisers by her bearing and roused some newspaper discussion by her fate.

This is her story, the inner story which the world never knew.

Catherine Sirrett's mother was an intensely, even a morbidly, religious woman. Her father was an atheist and an æsthete. Yet her parents were fond of each other at first and made common cause in spoiling their only child. Sometimes the mother would whisper in the little girl's ear that she must pray for poor father who was blind to the true light and deaf to the beautiful voice. Sometimes the father would tell her that if she would worship she must worship genius, the poet, the painter, the musician; that if she would pray she must pray to Nature, the sea, the sunset and the spring-time. But as a rule these two loving antagonists thought it was enough for their baby, their treasure, to develop quietly, steadily, in an atmosphere of adoration, in which arose no mist of theories, no war of words. Till she was ten years old Catherine was untroubled. At that age a parental contest began to rage—at first furtively,—about her. With the years her mother's morbidity waxed, her father's restraint waned. The one became more intensely and frantically devout, the other more frankly pagan. And now, as the child grew, and her mind and heart stood up to meet life and girlhood, each of her parents began to feel towards her the desire of sole possession. She had been brought up a Christian. The father had permitted that. So long as she was an ignorant infant he had felt no anxiety to attach her to his theories. But when he saw the intelligence growing in her eyes, the dawn of her soul deepening, there stirred within him a strong desire that she should face existence as he faced it, free from trammels of superstition. The mother, with the quick intuition of woman, soon understood his unexpressed feeling and thrilled with religious fear. Although—or indeed because—she loved her husband so much she was tortured by his lack of faith. And now she was alarmed at the thought of the effect his influence might have upon Catherine. She was roused to an intense activity of the soul. She said nothing to her husband of her fear and horror. He said nothing to her of his secret determination that his only child should grow up in his own faithless faith. But a silent and determined battle began to rage between them for the possession of Catherine's soul. And, at last, this battle turned the former love of the parents into a sort of uneasy hatred. The child did not fully comprehend what was going on around her, but she dimly felt it. And it influenced her whole nature.

Her mother, who was given over to religious forms, who was ritualistic and sentimental as well as really devout and fervent, at first gained the ascendancy over Catherine. Holy but narrow-minded, she compressed the girl's naturally expansive temperament, and taught her something of the hideous and brooding melancholy of the bigot and the fanatic. Then the father, quick-sighted, and roused to an almost angry activity by his appreciation of Catherine's danger, threw himself into the combat, and endeavoured to imbue the girl with his own comprehension of life's meaning, exaggerating all his theories in the endeavour to make them seem sufficiently vital and impressive. Catherine lived in the centre of this battle, which became continually more fierce, until she was eighteen. Then she fell in love with Mark Sirrett, married him, and left her parents alone with their mutual hostility, now complicated by a sort of paralysis of surprise and sense of mutual failure. They had forgotten that their child's future might hold a lover, a husband. Now they found themselves in the rather absurd position of enemies who have quarrelled over a shadow which suddenly vanishes away. They had lost their love for each other, they had lost Catherine. But her soul, though it was given to Mark Sirrett, had not lost their impress. Both the Puritanism of her mother and the paganism of her father were destined to play their parts in the guidance of her strange and terrible destiny.

Mark Sirrett, when he married Catherine, was twenty-five, dark, handsome, warm-hearted and rich. It seemed that he had an exceptionally sweet and attractive nature. He had been an affectionate son, a kind brother in his home, a generous comrade at school and college. Everybody had a good word for him; his family, his tutors, his friends, his servants. Like most young and ardent men he had had some follies. At least they were never mean or ungenerous. He entered upon married life with an unusually good record. Those who knew him casually, even many who knew him well, considered that he was easily read, that he was transparently frank, that, though highly intelligent, he was not particularly subtle, and that no still waters ran deep in Mark Sirrett. All these people were utterly wrong. Mark had a very curious side to his nature, which remained almost unsuspected until after his marriage with Catherine, but which eventually was to make a name very well known to the world. He was, although apparently so open, in reality full of reserve. He was full of ambition. And he had an exceptionally peculiar, and exceptionally riotous, imagination. And this imagination he was quite determined to express in an art—the art of literature. But his reserve kept him inactive until he had left Oxford, when he went to live in London, where eventually he met Catherine.

His reserve, and his artistic hesitation to work until he felt able to do good work, held Mark's imagination in check as a dam holds water in check. He sometimes wrote, but nobody knew that he wrote except one friend, Frederic Berrand. And Berrand could be a silent man. Even to Catherine, when he fell in love with her and wooed her, Mark did not reveal his desire for fame, or his intention to win it. The girl loved her lover for what he was, but not for all he was. Of the still water that ran deep she as yet knew nothing. She thought her husband, who was rich, who appeared gay, who had lived so far, as it seemed, idly enough, would continue to live with her, as he had apparently lived without her, brightly, honestly, a little thoughtlessly, a little vainly.

She had no sort of suspicion that she had married that very curious phenomenon—a born artist. Had her mother suspected it she would have been shocked. Had her father dreamed it he would have been delighted. And Catherine herself? well, she was still a child at this time.

She and Mark went to Spain for their honeymoon, and lived in a tiny white villa at Granada. It stood on the edge of the hill whose crown is the exquisite and dream-like Alhambra. Its long and narrow garden ran along the hillside, a slope of roses and of orange flowers, of thick, hot grass and of tangled green shrubs. The garden wall was white and uneven, and almost hidden by wild, pink flowers. Beneath was spread the plain in which lies the City, bounded by the mountains over which, each evening, the sun sets. And every day the drowsy air hummed in answer to the huge and drowsy voice of the wonderful Cathedral bell, which struck the hours and filled this lovely world with almost terrible vibrations of romance. In the thick woods that steal to the feet of the ethereal Palace the murmur of the streams was ever heard, and the white snows of the Sierra Nevada stared over the yellow and russet plain, and were touched with a blue blush as the night came on.

Catherine, although she loved her parents and had never fully realised the enmity grown up between them, felt a strange happiness, that was more than the happiness of new-born passion, in her emancipation. She was by nature exquisitely sensitive, and she had often been vaguely troubled by the contest between her parents. Their fighting instincts had sometimes set her face to face with a sort of shadowed valley, in whose blackness she faintly heard the far-off clash of weapons. Now she was caught away from this subtle tumult, and as she looked into her husband's vivacious dark eyes she felt that a little weight which had lain long on her heart was lifted from it. She had thought herself happy before, now she knew herself utterly happy. Life seemed to have no dark background. Even love itself was not spoiled by a too great wonder of seriousness. They loved in sunshine and were gay—like grasshoppers in the grass that the sun has filled with a still rapture of warmth. Not till two days before their departure for England was this chirping, grasshopper mood disturbed or dispelled.

At one end of the long and narrow garden there was a little crude pavilion, open to the air on three sides. The domed roof was supported on painted wooden pillars up which red and white roses audaciously climbed. Rugs covered the floor. A wooden railing ran along the front facing the steep hillside. The furniture was simple and homely, a few low basket chairs and an oval table. In this pavilion the newly married pair took tea nearly every afternoon after their expeditions in the neighbourhood, or their strolls through the sunny Moorish Courts. After tea they sat on and watched the sunset, and fancied they could see the birds that flew away above the City towards the distant mountains drop down to their nests in Seville ere the darkness came. This last evening but one was intensely hot; the town at their feet seemed drowning in a dust of gold. Cries, softened and made utterly musical, rose up to them from this golden world, beyond which the sky reddened as the sun sank lower. Sometimes they heard the jingling bells of mules and horses in the hidden streets; they saw the pigeons circling above the house-tops, and doll-like figures moving whimsically in gardens that seemed as small as pocket-handkerchiefs. Thin laughter of playing children stole to them. And then the huge and veiled voice of the Cathedral bell tolled the hour, like Time become articulate.

A voice may have an immense influence over a sensitive nature. This bell of the Cathedral of Granada has one of the most marvellous voices in the world, deep with a depth of old and vanished ages, heavy with the burden of all the long-dead years, and this evening it seemed suddenly to strike away a veil from Catherine's husband. She was leaning her arms on the painted railing and searching the toy city with her happy eyes. Mark, standing behind her, was solicitously winding a shawl round her to protect her from the chill that falls from the Sierra Nevada with the dropping downward of the sun. As the bell tolled, Catherine felt that Mark's hands slipped from her shoulders. She glanced round and up at him. He was standing rigid. His eyes were widely opened. His lips were parted. All the gaiety that usually danced in his face had disappeared. He looked like an entranced man.

"Mark!" Catherine exclaimed. "Mark! why, how strange you look!"

"Do I?" he said, staring out over the wide plain below.

The voice of the bell died reluctantly on the air, but some huge and vague echo of its heavy romance seemed to sway, like a wave, across the little houses to the sunset and faint towards Seville.

"Yes, you look sad and stern. I have never seen your face like this—till now."

He made no answer.

"Are you sad because we are going so soon?" she asked. "But then why should we go? We are perfectly happy here. There is nothing to call us away."

"Kitty, does not that bell give you the lie?" he answered.

"The bell of the Cathedral?" she asked, wondering.

"Yes. Just now when I listened to it, I seemed to hear it whispering of the mysterious things of life, of the hidden currents in the great river, of the sorrows, of the terrors, of the crimes."

"Mark!" said Catherine in amazement.

"Nothing to call us away from our idle happiness here!" he continued. "Do you say—nothing?"

"Why—no. For we are free; we have no ties. You have no profession, Mark. You have no art even to call you back to England. Dear father—how he worships the arts!"

"And you, Kitty—you?"

Mark spoke with a curious pressure of excitement.

"He has taught me to love them too."

"How much, Kitty? As he loves them, more than anything else on earth?"

She had never heard him speak at all like this. She answered:

"Ah no. For my mother——"

She paused.

"My mother has made me understand that there is something greater than any art, more important, more beautiful."

"What can that be?"

"Oh, Mark—religion!"

He leaned over the railing at her side, and the white and red roses that embraced the pillar shook against his thick dark hair in the infant breeze of evening.

"But there are many religions," he said. "A man's art may be his religion."

A troubled look came into her eyes and made them like her mother's.

"Oh no, Mark."

"Yes, Kitty," he said, with growing earnestness, putting aside his reserve for the first time with her. "Indeed it may."

"You mean when he uses it to do good?"

He shook his head. The roses shivered.

"The true artist never thinks of that. To have a definite moral purpose is destructive."

The City at their feet was sinking into shadow now, and the air grew cold, filled with the snowy breath of the Sierra.

"When we go back to England I will teach you the right way to follow an art, to worship it; the way that will be mine."

"Yours, Mark? But I don't understand."

"No," he said. "You don't understand all of me yet, Kitty. Do you want to?"

"Yes," she said.

There was a sound of fear in her voice. Mark sat down beside her and put his arm round her.

"Kitty," he began. "I'm only on the threshold of my life, of my real life, my life with you and with my work."

"You are going to work?" she exclaimed.

"Yes. That bell just now seemed to strike the hour of commencement— to tell me it was time for me to begin. I should like, some day—far in the future, Kitty,—to hear it strike that other hour, the hour when I must finish, when the little bit of work that I can do in the world is done. I shan't be afraid of that hour any more than I'm afraid of this one. Perhaps, when you and I are old we shall come here again, and listen to that bell once more, the same, when we are changed."

He pointed towards the Cathedral which was still touched by the sun. Catherine leaned against his shoulder. She said nothing, and did not move.

"Everything in life has its appointed recorder," he continued. "They are a big band, the band of the recorders who strive accurately to write down life as it is. Well, Kitty, I am going to be one of that band."

"You are going to be a writer, Mark?"

"Yes."

"Then, you will record the beauty, the joy, the purity, the goodness of life?"

His usually bright face had become sombre and thoughtful. It looked strangely dark and saturnine in the twilight.

"I shall record what I see most clearly."

"And what is that?"

"Not the things on the surface, but the things beneath the surface, of life."

And then he told Catherine more fully of his ambition and gave her a glimpse of the hidden side of his duplex nature.

She gazed up at him in the gathering twilight and it seemed to her that she was looking at a stranger. The climbing roses still shook against Mark in the wind. While he talked his voice grew almost fierce, and his dark eyes shone like the eyes of a fanatic. When he ceased to speak, Catherine's lips were pursed together, like her mother's when she listened to the pagan rhapsodies of Mr. Ardagh.

Two days later the Sirretts left Granada for England.

On their return they paid a short visit to Catherine's parents, who were living in Eaton Square. Mr. and Mrs. Ardagh received them with a sort of dulled and narcotic affection. In truth, for different reasons, the Puritan and the pagan cherished a certain resentment against the man who had stepped in and robbed them of their cause of warfare. Nevertheless they desired his company in their house. For each was anxious to study him and to discover what influence he was likely to have upon Catherine. During her daughter's absence Mrs. Ardagh had found the emptiness of her childless life insupportable, and she had, therefore, engaged a young girl, called Jenny Levita, to come to her every day as companion. Jenny was intelligent and very poor, bookish and earnest, even ardent in nature. Mrs. Ardagh gained a certain amount of interest and pleasure from forming the pliant mind of her protégée, who was with her always from eleven till six in the evening, who read aloud to her, accompanied her on her charitable missions, and took—so far as a stranger might,—the place of Catherine in her life. Catherine met Jenny upon the doorstep of her parents' house on the evening of her arrival, and hastened to ask her mother who the slim girl, with the tall figure, narrow shoulders, fluffy brown hair, and large oriental eyes was.

"My paid daughter," said Mrs. Ardagh, almost bitterly. "But she can't fill the place of my lost Catherine."

Nevertheless, Catherine discovered that her mother was truly attached to Jenny.

"I took her partly because she is easily led," she said, "easily influenced and so very pretty and poor. I want to save her for God, and when I met her there was one who wished to lead her to the devil. She won't see him now. She won't hear his name."

Then she dropped the subject.

Catherine was alternately questioned by her father and by her mother as to the influence of Mark. But something within her prevented her from telling them of the conversation in the Pavilion, when the cries of the toy city died down into the night. Mrs. Ardagh, now sinking in the confusion of a rather dreary middle age, complicated by a natural melancholy, and by incessant confession to a ritualistic clergyman seductive in receptivity, was relieved to think that Mark was harmless.

Art for Art's sake—the motto of her husband—had apparently little meaning for Mark. As Mrs. Ardagh thought it the devil's motto she was glad of this and said so to Catherine. Mr. Ardagh, on the other hand, was vexed to find Mark apparently so frivolous; and he also expressed his feelings to Catherine, who became slightly confused.

"I should like to see your husband doing something," he said. "You have much of me in you, Kit, despite your poor dear mother's extravagant attempts to limit your reading to Frances Ridley Havergal. Why didn't you marry an artist, eh? A painter or an author, somebody who can give us more beauty than we have already, or more truth? You're too good for Frances Ridley Havergal. Leave her to your mother and that girl, Jenny, who is like wax in your mother's hands and the hands of the Rev. Father Grimshaw. Piff!"

Catherine said nothing, but she sought an opportunity of seeing something of Jenny. She found it, just before the day on which she and Mark were to leave London for their country house. Jenny had come as usual one morning, to read aloud to Mrs. Ardagh. They were just then deep in the "Memoirs" of a certain pious divine, whose chief claim upon the attention and gratitude of posterity seemed to be that, during a very long career, he had "confessed" more Anglican notabilities than any of his rivals, and had used up, in his church, an amount of incense that would have put a Roman Catholic priest to shame. On the morning in question the reading was interrupted. Mrs. Ardagh was called away to consult with a lay-worker in the slums upon some scheme for reclaiming the submerged masses, and Catherine, running in to her mother's boudoir after a walk with Mark, found the tall, narrow-shouldered girl with the oriental eyes sitting alone with the apostolic memoirs lying open upon her knees. Catherine was not sorry. She took off her fur coat and sat down.

"What are you and my mother reading, Miss Levita?" she asked.

Jenny told her.

"Is it interesting?"

"I suppose it ought to be," Jenny answered, thoughtlessly.

Then a flush ran over her thin cheeks, on which there were a great many little freckles.

"I mean that it is very interesting," she added. "Your mother will tell you so, Mrs. Sirrett."

"Perhaps. But I was asking your opinion."

It struck Catherine that Jenny had her opinion and was scarcely as compliant as Mr. Ardagh evidently supposed her to be. At Catherine's last remark Jenny glanced up. The two girls looked into each other's eyes, and, in Jenny's, Catherine thought she saw a flickering defiance.

"I was asking your opinion," she repeated.

"Well, Mrs. Sirrett," Jenny said, more hardily, "I don't know why it is. I admire and love goodness, yes, as your mother—who's a saint, I think—does. But I'll tell you frankly that I think it's often very dull to read about. Don't you think so?"

She blushed again, and let the heavy white lids droop over her eyes, which had glittered almost like the eyes of a fever patient while she was speaking.

"Only when dull people write about it, surely," said Catherine.

"I don't know," Jenny said, twisting her black stuff dress with nervous fingers. "I often think that in the books of the cleverest authors there are dull moments, and that those dull moments are nearly always when the good, the really excellent, characters are being written about."

"And in real life, Miss Levita?" asked Catherine. "Do you find the good people duller, less interesting, than the bad ones in real life?"

"I haven't known many very bad ones, Mrs. Sirrett."

"Well—but those you have known!"

Jenny hesitated. She was obviously embarrassed. She even shifted, like an awkward child, in her chair. But there was something of obstinate honesty in her that would have its way.

"If you must know,—I mean, if you care to know, please," she said at length, "the most interesting person I ever met was—yes, I suppose he was a wicked man."

Her curious, sharp-featured, yet attractive, face was hot all over as she finished. Catherine divined at once that she was speaking of the person who, according to Mrs. Ardagh, had wished "to lead her to the devil." At this moment, while the two girls were silent, Mrs. Ardagh returned to the room. As Catherine left it she heard the soft and high voice of Jenny taking up once more the parable of the highly-honoured divine.

Catherine was not altogether sorry when she and her husband left Eaton Square for the house in Surrey which Mark had rented for the summer months.

In this house the young couple were to face for the first time the reality of married life. Hitherto they had only faced its romance.

The house was beautiful in an old-fashioned way. Its rooms were low and rather dark. A wood stood round it. The garden was a wild clearing, fringed with enormous clumps of rhododendron. Wood doves cooed in the trees like invisible lovers unable to cease from gushing. Under the trees ferns grew in masses. Squirrels swarmed, and in the huge rhododendron flowers the bees lost themselves in an ecstasy of sipping sensuality. It was a fine summer, and this house was made to be a summer house. In winter it must have been but a dreary hermitage.

The servants greeted them respectfully. The horses neighed in the stables. The dogs barked, and leaped up in welcome, then, when they were noticed and patted, depressed their backs in joyous humility, and, lifting their flexible lips, grinned amorously, glancing sideways from the hands that they desired. It was an eminently unvulgar, and ought to have been a very sweet, home-coming.

But was it sweet to Catherine?

She asked herself that question, and the fact that she did so proved that it was not wholly sweet. Already the future oppressed her. In this house, which seemed full of the smell of the country, of the very odour of peace, she felt that the stranger, the second Mark—scarcely known to her as yet—was to be born, was to gain strength and grow. She feared him. She watched for him. But, for the first few days, he did not show himself. The grasshoppers chirped and revelled in the grass. Mark and Catherine sat in the wood, wandered on the hills, rode in the valleys, cooed a little even, like the doves hidden in the green shadows of the glades, and making ceaseless music. The lovers—for they were still lovers at this time—made a gay dreamland for themselves. But dreams cannot and ought not to last. If they did they would become painfully enervating. One day, in the wood, Mark resumed the conversation of the Pavilion.

"Because I am rich I must not be idle, Kitty," he said.

And into his dark eyes there crept that look of the stranger man.

"Thank God that I am rich," he added.

"Why, Mark dear?"

"Because I can dare to do what sort of work I choose," he answered. "The pot boils without my labour. So I am independent of the public, whom I will win in my own way. If I have to wait it will not matter."

And then, speaking with growing enthusiasm, he gave Kitty a sketch of a book he had projected. The doves cooed all through the plot, which was a sad and terrible one, very uncommon and very unlike Mark. Catherine listened to it with, alternately, the mind of her father and the mind of her mother. It was the old antagonism of the Puritan and the pagan. But now it raged in one person instead of in two, as the girl sat under the soft darkness of the trees, listening to the eager voice of her boy husband, who was beginning at last to cast the skin of his reserve. The voice went on and on, interrupted only by the doves. But sometimes Catherine felt as if she leaned upon the painted railing of the Pavilion, and heard the distant cries of the golden City. At last Mark said,

"Kitty, that is what I mean to do."

"It is terrible," she said.

And she pursed her lips like her mother.

"Yes," Mark answered, with enthusiasm. "It is terrible. It is ghastly."

Catherine looked at him with an intense and growing surprise. She was wondering how the conception of such horrors could take place in a man so gay as Mark.

At last she said,

"Mark, you feel your own power, do you not?"

"Kitty," he replied quietly, almost modestly, yet with a firm gravity that was strong, "I do feel that I have something to say and that I shall be able to say it in my book. I have waited a long while. Now I believe that I am ready, that it is time for me to begin."

"Then, Mark, if you feel that you have this power, don't you feel a desire to conquer the greatest difficulties in your art, to show that you can succeed where others have failed?"

He looked at her curiously, realising that she had something to say to him, and that she was trying to prepare the way before it.

"Come, Kitty," he said. "Say what you wish to say. You have the right. What is it?"

Catherine told him of her conversation with Jenny.

"That little thin girl," he said. "So she thinks wickedness more interesting, more many-sided than virtue, more dramatic in its possibilities. Well, she and I are agreed. But what was it you wanted?"

"Mark, I want you to prove to her—to everyone—that it is not so."

"How?"

"By writing a different kind of book—a noble book. You can do it. Where others have failed, you can succeed."

He laughed at her, gaily.

"Perhaps, some day, I'll try," he said. "But I can only write at present what I have conceived. Till this book is done, I can think of nothing else. I see you are interested, Kitty. I must tell you all I am intending to do."

He continued, until it was quite evening, expatiating on the force with which he intended to realise in literature the terrors that trooped in his imagination. And by the time he had finished and darkness stood under the trees, Catherine was carried away by the pagan spirit. She thought no more of the possible harm the projected book might work in sensitive natures. She thought only of its power, which she acclaimed.

Mark kissed her with a solemnity of passion he had never shown before, and they went back to the house.

It was an immense relief to Mark to open his book of revelation and to allow Catherine to read these pages in it. But he could not be continuously unreserved to any human being. And that evening he subsided into his former light-hearted gaiety, and shrouded the stranger man in an impenetrable veil. Catherine sat with him in wonderment, while the moon came up behind the trees and shone over the clearing before the house. She did not yet understand the inflexible secrecies of genius. A nightingale sang. Its voice was so sweet that Catherine felt as if the whole world were full of tenderness and of sympathy. She said so to Mark, just as she was turning from him to go to bed.

"Ah, Kitty," he said, "there are other things in the world besides tenderness and sympathy, thank Heaven. There are terrors, there are crimes, there are strange and fearful things both within us and outside of us."

"How sad that is, Mark!" said Catherine.

He smiled at her gaily—cruelly, she thought a moment afterwards when she was alone in her bedroom.

"Sad?" he said. "I don't think so, for I love drama. Life is dramatic. If it were not it would be intolerable."

And still the nightingale sang. But he did not hear it. Catherine heard it till she fell asleep.

Now Mark began to write with assiduity. Catherine busied herself with her household duties, with the garden and with charities in the neighbouring Parish. Her mother's rather hysterical beliefs lost their hysteria in her, at this period, and were softened and rendered large hearted. Catherine's sympathy with the world was indeed a living thing, not simply a fine idea. While Mark was shut up every morning with his writing she visited the poor, sat by the sick, and played with the village children. The Parish—this came out forcibly at her trial,—grew to love her. She was the prettiest Lady Bountiful. The impress made upon her by her mother was visible in all this. For Mrs. Ardagh, rigid, melancholy as she was sometimes, was genuinely charitable, genuinely dutiful. If she adored the forms of religion she loved also its essence,—the doing of good. In these many mornings Catherine was like her mother—improved. But in the evenings she no longer resembled Mrs. Ardagh, but rather, in a degree, echoed her father, and responded to his vehement, if furtive, teachings. For in the evenings Mark read to her what he had written during the day and discussed it with her in all its bearings. He recognised the clear quickness of Catherine's intellect. Yet she very soon noticed that he was exceedingly inflexible with regard to his work. He liked to discuss, he did not like to alter, it.

One night, when he had finished the last completed chapter, he laid down the manuscript and said,

"Well, Kitty?"

Catherine was lying on a couch near the open French window. She did not speak until Mark repeated,

"Well?"

Then she said,

"I think that far the finest chapter of your book— —"

Mark smiled triumphantly.

"But it seems to me terribly immoral," she finished.

"Oh, that's all right, dear. So long as it is properly worked out, inevitable."

"It teaches— —"

"Nothing, Kitty—nothing. It merely describes what is."

"But surely it may do harm."

"Not if it is truly artistic. And you think— —"

"It that? Yes, I do. But, Mark, art is not all."

"Your father would say so."

"My father—yes."

"And he is right. I neither inculcate nor do I condemn. I only produce, or try to produce, a work of art. You admire the chapter? You think it truly dramatic?"

"Indeed I do—that's just why I am afraid of it."

"Little timorous bird."

He came over to the sofa and kissed her tenderly. She shivered. She thought his lips had never been dry and cold like that before.

The book was finished by the end of the summer. It was published in November and created a considerable sensation. Mark issued it under the name of "William Foster." Only Catherine and his friend Frederic Berrand knew who William Foster really was. The newspapers praised the workmanship of the book almost universally. But many of them severely condemned it as dangerous, morbidly imaginative, horrible in subject, and likely to do great mischief because of its undoubted power and charm. It was forbidden at some libraries.

Mark was delighted with its reception. Now, that he had brought forth his child, he seemed more light-hearted, gay and boyish than ever. His too vivid imagination had been toiling. It rested now. Catherine and he came up to town for the winter. They meant to spend only their summers in Surrey. They took a house in Chester Street, and often dined with the Ardaghs in Eaton Square. At one of these dinners Jenny Levita was present. Mark, remembering what Catherine had told him about her in Surrey, looked at her with some interest, and talked to her a little in his most light-hearted way. She replied briefly and without much apparent animation, seeming indeed rather absent-minded and distraite. Presently Mr. Ardagh said,

"This new man, William Foster, is that very rare thing in England—a pitiless artist. He has the audacity of genius and the fine impersonality."

Catherine started and flushed violently. As she did so she saw Jenny's long dark eyes fixed earnestly upon her. Mark smiled slightly. Mrs. Ardagh looked pained.

"His book is doing frightful harm, I am sure," she said.

"Nonsense, my dear," said her husband. "Nothing so absolutely right, so absolutely artistic, can do harm."

An obstinate expression came into Mrs. Ardagh's face, but she said nothing. Catherine looked down at her plate. She felt as if small needles were pricking her all over.

"Have you read the book?" said Mr. Ardagh to his wife.

"Yes," she replied. "It was recommended to me, I began it not knowing what sort of book it was."

"And did you finish it?" asked her husband, with rather a satirical smile.

"Yes. I confess I could not leave off reading it. That is why it is so dangerous. It is both powerful and evil."

Then the subject dropped. Mark was still smiling quietly, but Catherine's face was grave. When she and her mother and Jenny went up into the drawing-room, leaving the men to their cigarettes, Catherine recurred to the subject of "William Foster's" book.

"Do you really think that a novel can do serious harm, mother?" she began. "After all, it is only a work of the imagination. Surely people read it and forget it, as they would not forget an actual fact."

Mrs. Ardagh sighed wearily. She was a pale woman with feverish eyes. The expression in them grew almost fierce as she answered,

"It is the black imagination of this William Foster that will come like a suffocating cloud upon the imaginations of others, especially of——" She suddenly broke off. Catherine, wondering why, glanced up at her mother and saw that she was looking towards the far end of the big drawing-room. Jenny was sitting there, under a shaded lamp. She had some work in her hands but her hands were still. Her head was turned away, but her attitude, the curve of her soft, long, white throat, the absolute immobility of her thin body betrayed the fact that she was listening attentively.

"I would not let that child read William Foster's book for the world," Mrs. Ardagh whispered to Catherine.

Then she changed the subject, and spoke of some charity that she was interested in at the East End of London. Jenny's hands instantly began to move about her embroidery.

That night Catherine spoke to Mark of what her mother had said.

He only laughed.

"I cannot write for any one person, Kitty," he said, "or if I do it must be — —"

"For whom?" she asked quickly.

"Myself," he replied.

Catherine slept very badly that night. She was thinking of William Foster and of Mark. They seemed to her two different men. And she had married — which?

Mark did no work in London. He knew too many people, he said, and besides, he wanted to rest. Catherine and he went out a great deal into society. At Christmas they ran over to Paris and spent three weeks there. During this holiday William Foster, it almost seemed, had ceased to exist. Mark Sirrett was light-hearted, gay, and the kindest, most thoughtful husband in the world. When they came back to London, Catherine went at once to see her mother. Mr. Ardagh had gone to the Riviera and Catherine found Mrs. Ardagh quite alone in the big house in Eaton Square.

"Why, where is Jenny Levita?" she asked.

Mrs. Ardagh made no reply for a moment. Her face, which was rather straw-colour than white, worked grotesquely as if under the influence of some strong emotion that she was trying to suppress. At length she said, in a chill, husky voice,

"Jenny has left me."

"Left you — why?"

"She was taken away from me. She was taken back to the sin from which I hoped I had rescued her."

"Oh, mother! By whom?"

Mrs. Ardagh put her handkerchief to her eyes.

"William Foster," she answered.

Catherine felt cold and numb.

"William Foster—I don't understand," she said slowly.

Mrs. Ardagh rolled and unrolled her handkerchief with trembling fingers.

"She got hold of that book—that black, wicked book," she said, and there was a sort of fury in her voice. "It upset her faith. It tarnished her moral sense. It reminded her of the—the man from whose influence I had drawn her. All her imagination was set in a flame by that hateful chapter."

"Which one?" Catherine asked.

Mrs. Ardagh mentioned the chapter which Catherine had most hated, most admired, and most feared.

"I fought with William Foster for Jenny's soul," she said, passionately. "But I am not clever. I have no power. I am getting old and tired. She cried. She said she loved me, but that goodness was not for her, that she must go, that life was calling her, that she must live—live! William Foster had shown her death and she thought it life. I always knew that in Jenny good and evil were fighting, that her fate was trembling in the balance. That book turned the scale."

She sobbed heavily, then with a catch of her breath, she added,

"William Foster is a very wicked man."

Catherine flushed all over her face. But she said nothing. That night she told Mark of Jenny's fate. She expected him to be grieved. But he was not.

"An author who respects his art cannot consider every hysterical girl while he is writing," he said. "And, besides, it is only your mother's idea that she was influenced by my book. Long ago she showed you the bent of her mind."

"But, Mark, don't you remember how that chapter struck me when you first read it to me?"

"I remember that you thought it the finest chapter in the book, and you were right, Kitty. You've got artistic discernment, like your father. Berrand and you would get on together. Directly he comes back I'll introduce you to each other."

Catherine said no more. From that time she devoted herself more than ever to her mother, who now, under the influence of sorrow, allowed her nature to come to its full flower. Abandoning the pleasures of society, which had long wearied her, she gave herself up to services, charities and good works in the poor parts of London. She carried Catherine with her on many of her expeditions, and there can be no doubt that her fervour and curious exaltation had a marked effect upon the girl. Catherine had always been highly susceptible to influence, but she had been during most of her life attacked perpetually by two absolutely opposite influences. Now one of these, her father's, was removed from her. She came more than ever before under her mother's domination. For Mark, when he was not "William Foster," was simply a high-spirited and happy youth, full of energy and of apparently normal desires and intentions. He had that sort of genius which can be long asleep in the dark, while its possessor dances, like a mote, in sunshine.

In the spring the Sirretts made ready to leave London. As the day drew near for their departure Mark's manner changed, and he displayed symptoms of restlessness and of impatience. Catherine noticed them and asked their reason.

"I am longing to return to 'William Foster,' Kitty," he said.

She felt a sharp pain at her heart, but she only smiled and replied,

"I almost thought you had forgotten him."

"On the contrary, I have been preparing to meet him again all these months."

His dark eyes shone as he spoke. And once again that stranger stood before Catherine. She turned and went upstairs, saying that she must see to her packing. But when she was alone in her bedroom she shed some tears. That afternoon she went to Eaton Square to bid her mother good-bye. Mrs. Ardagh was looking unhappy.

"Your father returns from Italy on Wednesday," she said. "You'll just miss him."

"I am so sorry, mother," Catherine said.

Mrs. Ardagh looked at her in silence for a moment. Then she said in a low voice,

"I am not."

"Mother—but why?"

"I think you are better away from him. My heart tells me so. Oh, Kitty, I thank God every day of my life that Mark is—is such a good fellow, without those terrible ideas and theories of your poor father. You cannot think what I suffer."

It was the first time she had ever spoken so plainly on the subject, and even now she quickly changed to another topic. Mark had never introduced poor Mrs. Ardagh to "William Foster." And Catherine would not add another burden to those she already had to bear.

Surrey was looking very lovely in the spring weather. The trees were just beginning to let out the tips of their green secrets. The ground was dashed with blue and with yellow, where bloomed those flowers that are the sweetest of the year because they come the first, and whisper wonderful promises in the ears of all who love them. There had been some rain and the grass of lawns and hillsides was exquisite in the startling freshness of its vivid colour. Nature seemed uneasy with delight, like a child on a birthday morning. The tender beauty of everything around her reassured Catherine, who had come from town in a mood of strange apprehension. As she looked at the expectant woods awaiting their lovely costume in fragile nudity, at the violets that seemed to sing in odours, at that pale and shallow sky which is a herald of the deeper skies to come, it seemed to her impossible that Mark, who could be so blithe, so radiant, could turn to dark imaginings in such an atmosphere of exquisite enterprise. She was filled with hope and with a species of religious optimism. Some days passed, Catherine and Mark spent them in a renewal of friendship with their domain. They were like two children and were gayer than the spring. Then one evening Mark said,

"And now, Kitty, I am going to start work again. Berrand has written that he will be in England next week and will come on here at once. But he won't disturb me. And my scheme is ready."

Catherine felt the breath fluttering in her throat as she murmured,

"Your scheme is ready?"

"Yes. It's a great one. Berrand thinks so. I have written something of it to him. I am going to trace the downfall of a nature from nobility to utter degradation."

His eyes sparkled with enthusiasm, as he repeated in thrilling tones,

"Utter degradation."

Catherine thought of the spring night, in which such holy preparations for joy were silently being carried on, of all the youthful things just coming into life. An inspiration came to her. She caught her husband's hand and drew him to the window.

"Pull up the blind, Mark," she said.

He obeyed, smiling at her as if in wonder at this freak.

"Now open the window."

"Yes, dear. There! What next?"

In front of the window there was a riband of pavement protected by an overhanging section of roof. Catherine stepped out on this pavement. Mark followed her. They stood together facing the spring night. There was no moon, but the sky was clear and starlit. Nature seemed breathing quietly, like a thing alive but asleep. The surrounding woods were a dusky wall. The clearing was a vague sea of dew. And the air was full of that wonderful scent that all things seem to have in spring. It is like the perfume of life, of life that God has consecrated, of life that might have been in Eden. It is odorous with hope. It stings and embraces. It stirs the imagination to magic. It stirs the heart to tears. For it is ineffably beautiful and expectant.

"How delicious!" Mark said.

Catherine's hand tightened on his arm.

"The trees are talking," he said. "That damp scent comes from their roots, and the flowers and grasses round them."

He drew in his breath with a gasp of pleasure.

"Yes?" Catherine said.

He bent down and touched the lawn with his hand.

"What a dew! Look, Kitty, there goes a rabbit!"

A hunched shadow suddenly flattened and vanished.

"Little beggar! He's gone into the wood. What a jolly time he and his relations must have."

"Yes, Mark. Isn't the night happy, and the spring?"

He drew in his breath again.

"Yes."

"Mark!"

"Well, dear?"

"Mark—don't write this book."

Mark started slightly with surprise.

"Kitty! what are you saying?"

"Write a happy book."

"My dear babe—how uninteresting!"

"Write a good book, a book to make people better and happier."

"A book with a purpose! No, Kitty."

"Well then, a spring book. This night isn't a night with a purpose, because it's lovely."

He laughed quite gaily.

"Humorist! Why did you bring me out into it?"

"To influence you against that book."

He was silent.

"Are you angry, Mark?"

"No, dear."

"Will you do what I ask?"

"No, Kitty."

He spoke very quietly and gently, then changed the subject, talked of the coming summer, the garden, prospective pleasures. But he talked no more of his work. Next day he shut himself up in his study, and thenceforward his life became a repetition of his life during the previous summer. A fortnight later Frederic Berrand arrived.

Catherine had long felt an eager desire to see this one intimate friend of Mark's. She expected him to be no ordinary man, and she was not mistaken. Berrand was much older than Mark. He looked about forty. He was thin, sallow, eager in manner, with shining eyes—almost toad-like—a yellowish-white complexion, and coal-black hair. His vivacity was un-English, yet at the back of his nature there lay surely a stagnant reservoir of melancholy. He was a pessimist, full of ardour. He revelled, intellectually, in the sorrows and in the evils that afflict the world.

It was easy to see that he had a great influence over Mark. And it was easy to see also that the dismal genius of "William Foster" appealed to all the peculiarities of his nature with intense force. He was at once on friendly terms with Catherine, to whom he spoke openly of his admiration of her husband.

"Mrs. Sirrett," he said one evening, when Mark was working—he had taken to working at night now as well as in the morning—"your husband will do great things. He will found a school. The young men will be captivated by his sombre genius, and we shall have less of the thoughtless rubbish that the journalist loves and calls sane, healthy, and all the rest of it."

"But surely sanity and health——"

"My dear Mrs. Sirrett, we want originality and imagination."

"Yes, indeed. But can't they be sane and healthy?"

"Was Gautier healthy when he wrote of the Priest and of the Vampire? This book Mark is writing will be awful in its intensity. It will make the world turn cold. It is terrible. People will shudder at it."

He walked about the room enthusiastically.

"And its terror is the true terror—mental. How the papers will hate it, and how every one will read it!"

"May it—may it not do a great deal of harm?" said Catherine, slowly.

"What if it does? Nothing can prevent it from being a great book."

And he broke out into a dissertation on art that would have delighted Mr. Ardagh.

Catherine listened to him in silence, but when he had finished she said,

"But you are one-sided, Mr. Berrand."

"I!" he cried. "How so?"

"You see only the horrible in life, even in love. You care only for the horrible in art."

"The truth is more often horrible than not," he answered. "We dress it in pink paper as we dress a burning lamp. We fear its light will hurt our weak eyes. Almost all the pretty theories of future states, happy hunting grounds, and so forth, almost all the fallacies of life to which we are inclined to cling, are only pink paper shades which we make to save ourselves from blinking at the light."

"You call it light?" she said.

And she felt a profound pity for him. There was no need of that. Berrand was one of those strange men who are happy in the contemplation of misery.

While Berrand was staying with the Sirretts, Mrs. Ardagh came to them on a visit. She was now in very poor health, and her mind was greatly set, in consequence, on that other world of which the healthy scarcely think, unless they wake at night or lose a near relation unexpectedly. Mr. Berrand immediately horrified her. Of course he did not speak of "William Foster." "William Foster's" existence in the house was a secret. But he freely aired his sentiments on all other subjects, and each sentiment went like a sword through Mrs. Ardagh's soul.

"How can Mark make a friend of such a man," she said to Catherine. "Like your father, he has no religious belief. He worships art instead of God. He loves, he positively loves, the evil of the world. Such men are a curse. They go to people hell."

Her feverish eyes glowed with fanaticism.

"Oh, mother!" said Catherine, thinking of "William Foster."

"They do not care to do good, they do not fear to do harm," continued Mrs. Ardagh. "Why are they not cut off?"

She made her daughter kneel down with her and pray against such men.

Then they went down to dinner, and dined with "William Foster."

Catherine felt like one in a fever. She knew that her mother had an exaggerated mind. Nevertheless, she was deeply moved by it, recognising that it exaggerated truth, not a lie.

At dinner Mrs. Ardagh, by some ill-chance, was led to mention "William Foster's" book. Mark raised gay eyebrows at Berrand and Catherine grew hot. For Mrs. Ardagh denounced the author as she had denounced him in London, but with more excitement.

"I trust," she said, "that he will never live to write another."

Catherine felt as if a knife were thrust into her breast, and even Mark started slightly and looked almost uneasy, as if he fancied that the force of Mrs. Ardagh's desire might accomplish its fulfilment. Only Berrand was undismayed. There was a devil of mischief in him. His eyes of a toad gleamed as he said, turning to Mrs. Ardagh,

"I happen to know that 'William Foster' is writing another book at this very time."

Catherine bent her eyes on her plate. She was tingling with nervous excitement.

"Do you know him, then?" said Mrs. Ardagh, in her fervid, and yet dreary, voice.

"Slightly."

"Then tell him of the dreadful harm he has done."

"What harm?"

Mrs. Ardagh spoke of Jenny Levita. It seemed that she had now fallen into an evil way of life.

"But why should you attribute the folly of a weak girl to William Foster's influence?" said Berrand.

"Her soul was trembling in the balance," said Mrs. Ardagh, striking her thin hand excitedly on the table. "That book turned the scale. She went down. Tell him of her, Mr. Berrand, tell him of the ruin of that poor child. It may influence him."

"I'm afraid not," said Berrand, with a glance at Mark. "William Foster is an artist."

"It is terrible that he should be permitted to work such evil," said Mrs. Ardagh.

During that summer a vague and hollow darkness seemed to brood round the life of Catherine. It stood behind the glory of the golden days. She felt night even at noontide, and a damp mist floated mysteriously to her out of the very heart of the sun. Yet she had some happy, or at least some feverishly excited, moments, for Berrand was generally staying with them, and Catherine — abnormally sensitive as she always was to her undoing, — came under his curious influence and caught some of his enthusiasm for the talent of "William Foster."

Once again Mark began to speak to her of his work, to read parts of it aloud to both his companions. And there were evenings when Catherine, carried away by the intellectual joy of the two men, exulted with them in the horrible fascination of the book and in the intensity of its dramatic force. But, when these moments were over, and she was gone, she brooded darkly over her mother's words. For she knew that the book was evil. Like a snake it carried poison with it, and, presently, it was going to carry that poison out from this house in the woods, out into the world. Ah! the poor world, on which a thousand things preyed, in which a thousand snakes set their poisoned fangs!

And then she wept. Mark and Berrand were eagerly talking of the snake, praising its lustrous skin, marvelling at its jewelled eyes, foretelling its lithe progress through Society. She heard the murmur of their voices until far into the night. And sometimes she thought that distant murmur sounded like the hum of evil, or like the furtive whisper of conspirators.

Berrand did not leave them until the new book was nearly finished. As he pressed Catherine's hand in farewell he said,

"You will have a sensational autumn, Mrs. Sirrett."

"Sensational. Why?" she asked.

"London will ring with William Foster's name. My word how the Journalists will curse! They protect the morality of the nation you know — on paper."

He was gone. As the carriage drove away Catherine saw his beautiful, and yet rather dreadful, eyes gleaming with mischievous excitement.

Suddenly she felt heavy-hearted. Those last words of his cleared away any mist of doubt that lingered about her own terror. She recognised fully for the first time the essential difference between Mark and Berrand. Mark was really possessed by the spirit of the artist, was driven by something strange and dominating within him to do what he did. Berrand was possessed by a spirit of mischievous devilry, by the poor and degrading desire to shock and startle the world at whatever cost. For the moment Catherine mentally saw Mark in a light of nobility; Berrand in a darkness of degradation.

Yet—this thought followed in a moment,—Berrand was harmless to the world, while Mark—

"Kitty, come in here," called her husband's voice from the study. "I want to consult you about this last chapter."

In the Autumn "William Foster's" new book was issued by an "advanced" publisher, who loved to hear his wares called dangerous, and who walked on air when the reviewers said that such men as he were a curse to Society—as they occasionally did when there was nothing special to write about.

In the autumn also Mrs. Ardagh's illness grew worse and it appeared that she could not live much longer. Catherine was terribly grieved, and was for a time so much engaged with her mother that she scarcely heeded what was going on in the world around. Incessantly immured in the sick-room she did not trace the progress of the snake through Society until—as Berrand had foretold—the cries of the Journalists rose to Heaven like cries from a burning city. "William Foster" was held up to execration so universal that his book could hardly be printed in sufficient quantities to satisfy the demands of a public frantically eager to be harmed. In her sick-room Mrs. Ardagh, now not far from death, yet still religiously interested in the well-being of the world she was leaving, heard the echoes of the journalistic cries. Some friend, perhaps, conveyed them. For Catherine was silent on the matter, keeping a silence of fear and of shame. And these echoes stayed with the dying woman, as stay the voices in the hills.

One night, when Catherine came into her mother's room, Mrs. Ardagh was crying feebly. On the sheet of the bed lay a letter which she had crumpled in her pale hands and then tried, vainly, to fling away from her. Catherine leaned over the bed.

"What is it, mother?" she said. "You are not in pain?"

Mrs. Ardagh shifted in the bed. There was a suggestion of almost intolerable uneasiness in the movement.

"I am in pain, horrible pain," she answered. "No—no," as Catherine was about to ring for the nurse, "not in the body—not that."

Catherine sat down by the bed and clasped her mother's hot hand.

"What is it?" she whispered.

Mrs. Ardagh was silent for a moment. She blinked her heavy eyelids to stop the tears from falling on her wasted cheeks. At length she said,

"William Foster has done more evil."

Catherine did not speak. Her heart beat irregularly, and then seemed to stop, and then beat with unnatural force again.

"Catherine," her mother continued, "Jenny is utterly lost."

"No, mother, no!" Catherine said. "I will go to her. Let me go. I will rescue her. I will make her see——"

"Hush—you can't. She is dead and she died in shame."

She paused. Catherine did not speak.

"And now," Mrs. Ardagh continued feebly, "that man is spreading the net for others. Do you know, Catherine, I often pray for him?"

"Do you, mother?"

"Yes. He has great powers. I never let your father know it, but that first book of his made an impression upon me that has never faded. That's why I think of him even now—that and the fate of poor Jenny."

She lifted herself up a little in the bed.

"His last book, I am told, is much more terrible, much more deadly than the first."

"Is it?"

"You haven't read it?"

Catherine hesitated a moment, then she said,

"I know something about it."

Mrs. Ardagh lay still for a while, as if thinking. Presently she said,

"Catherine, such an odd, foolish idea keeps coming to me."

"What is it, mother?"

"That I should like to see 'William Foster' and—and try to make him understand what he is doing. Perhaps he doesn't know, doesn't realise. God often lets the devil blind us, you know. If I told him about Jenny, told him all about her, he might see—he might understand. Don't you think so?"

Catherine was holding her mother's hand. She pressed it vehemently.

"Oh, mother, perhaps he might!"

Mrs. Ardagh sat up still more among her pillows.

"You don't think it's a silly fancy?"

"I don't know. I wonder."

Catherine was crying quietly.

"It keeps coming," said Mrs. Ardagh, "as if God sent it to me. What can I do? How can I send to William Foster? I don't know where he is. Could that Mr. Berrand——?"

"Mother," Catherine said. "Leave it to me, I will bring William Foster to you."

She was trembling. But the invalid, exhausted with the excitement of the conversation, was growing drowsy. She sank down again in her pillows.

"Yes," she murmured. "I—might—tell—him—William Foster."

She slept heavily.

"Mark," Catherine said to her husband the next day. "Mother is dying. She can only live a very few days."

"Oh, Kitty! How grieved I am!"

His face was full of the most tender sympathy. He took her hand gently and kissed her.

"My Kitty, how will you bear this great sorrow?"

"Mark," Catherine said, and her voice sounded curiously strained. "Mother wants very much to see you, before she dies. She has something to say to you. I think she cares more about seeing you than about anything else in the world."

Mark looked surprised.

"I will go to her at once," he said. "What can it be? Ah, it must be something about you."

"No, I don't think so."

"What then?"

"She will tell you, Mark. It is better she should tell you herself."

"I will go to her then. I will go now."

"Wait a moment"—Catherine was very pale—"Promise me, Mark, that you won't—you won't be angry if—if mother—you will——"

She stopped. Her emotion was painful. Mark was more and more puzzled.

"Angry with your mother? At such a time!" he said.

"No—you wouldn't. I am upset. I am foolish. Let me go first to tell her you are coming. Follow me in a few minutes."

She went out leaving her husband amazed. When she arrived in Eaton Square Mr. Ardagh met her in the hall.

"She is worse," he said. "Much worse. The end cannot be far off."

"The beginning," Catherine said, looking him straight in the eyes.

He understood then which parental spirit had conquered the spirit of the child, and he smiled—sadly or gladly? He hardly knew. So strangely does death play with us all. Catherine went upstairs into her mother's room, which was dim and very hot. She shut the door, sent away the nurse, and went up to the bedside.

"Mother," she said, "William Foster is coming. Do you feel that you can see him?"

Mrs. Ardagh was perfectly conscious, although so near death.

"Yes," she said. "God means me to give him a message—God means me."

She lay silent; Catherine sat by her. Presently she spoke again.

"I shall convince him," she said quietly. "That is meant. If I did not God would strike him down. He would be cut off. But I shall make him know himself."

And then she repeated, with a sort of feeble but intense conviction,

"If I did not God would strike him down—yes—yes."

Something—perhaps the fact that her mother was so near death, so close to that great secret,—made her words, faltering though they were, go home to Catherine with the most extraordinary poignancy, as words had never gone before. She felt that it was true, that there was no alternative. Either Mark must be convinced now, by this bedside, in this hot, dark room from which a soul was passing, or he would, by some accident, by some sudden means, be swept away from the world that he was injuring, that he was poisoning.

Mrs. Ardagh seemed to grow more feeble with every moment that passed. And suddenly a great fear overtook Catherine, the dread that Mark would come too late, and then—God's other means! She trembled, and strained her ears to catch the sound of wheels. Mrs. Ardagh now seemed to be sinking into sleep—Catherine strove to rouse her. She stirred and said, "What is it?" in a voice that sounded peevish.

Just then there was a gentle tap on the door. Catherine sprang up, and hastened to it with a fast beating heart. Mr. Ardagh stood there.

"How is she?" he whispered.

"I think she is not in pain. She is just resting. Has Mark come?"

"No."

"Please send him up directly he comes."

She spoke with a hushed, but with an intense, excitement.

"I want him to—to say good-bye to her," she added.

Mr. Ardagh nodded, and went softly downstairs.

"Is that he—is that William Foster?" said Mrs. Ardagh feebly from the bed.

"No, mother. But he will be here directly."

"I'm very tired," said the sick woman in reply. And again her thin voice sounded irritable.

Catherine sat down by her and held her hand tightly, as if that grasp could keep her in this life. A few minutes passed. Then there was the sound of a cab in the Square. It ceased in front of the house. Catherine could scarcely breathe. She bent down to the dying woman.

"Mother!"

"Well?"

"Mother, he has come—but I want to tell you something—are you listening?"

"Move the pillow."

Catherine did so.

"Mother, I want to tell you. William Foster is——"

The bedroom door opened and Mark entered softly. Catherine stood up, still holding her mother's hand, which was now very cold. Mark came to the bed on tiptoe.

"Mother," Catherine said, "William Foster"—Mark started—"is here. Tell him—tell him."

There was no reply from the bed.

"Kitty," Mark whispered, "what is this?"

"Hush!" she said. "Mother—mother, don't you hear me?"

Again there was no reply. Then Catherine bent down and cast a hard, staring glance of enquiry on her mother.

Mrs. Ardagh was dead.

Catherine looked up at Mark.

"God's other means," she thought.

The death of her mother left a strong and terrible impression upon Catherine. She brooded over it continually and over Mrs. Ardagh's last words. The last words of the dying often dwell in the memories of the living. Faltering, feeble, sometimes apparently inconsequent, they appear nevertheless prophetic, touched with the dignity of Eternal truths. Lives have been moulded by such last words. Natures have been diverted into new and curious paths. So it was now. For the future Mr. Ardagh's influence had no force over his daughter. An influence from the grave dominated her. Mr. Ardagh recognised the fact, shrugged his shoulders and travelled. His philosophy taught him to accept the inevitable with the fortitude of the Stoic. From henceforward the Sirretts saw little of him. As to Mark, with his habitual tenderness he set about consoling his wife for her loss. He was kindness itself. Catherine seemed grateful, was indeed grateful to him. Nevertheless, after the death of Mrs. Ardagh, something seemed to stand between her and her husband, dividing them. Mark did not know what this was. For some time he was unconscious of this thin veil dropped between them. Even when he became aware of it he could not tell why it was there. He strove to put it aside, but in vain. Then he strove not to see it, not to think of it. He forgot it in his work. But Catherine always knew what set her apart from her husband. It was that influence from the grave. It was the memory of her mother's last words. She recognised them from the first, blindly, as words of prophecy. Yet the days went by. "William Foster" sat in his study in the Surrey home once more, while the spring grew, imitative of last year's spring. And there was no sign from God. Catherine never doubted that the dying woman had been inspired. She never doubted that "William Foster" would be stayed, however tragically, from working fresh evil in the world. Indeed she waited, as one assured of some particular future, breathless in expectation of its approach. Sometimes she strove to picture precisely what it might be, and, fancifully, she set two men before her—Mark and "William Foster." Even in real life they seemed two different men. Why not in the life of the imagination? And that was sweeter, for then she could look forward to the one standing fast, to the other being stricken. Might not his genius die in a man while the man lived on? There had been instances of men who had written one or two brilliant books and had seemed to exhaust themselves in that effort. And she dreamed of her husband's gift being stolen from him—divinely—of the stranger being slain. Yet this dreaming was idle and fantastic, the image which greets closed eyes. For Mark's energy and enthusiasm were growing. The fury of the papers fed him. The cries of pious fear emboldened his dogged and dreary talent. His genius grew darker as its darkness became recognised.

This third book of his promised to be more powerful, more deadly, than either of its forerunners. He did not speak much of it to Catherine. But now and then, carried away by excitement and by the need of sympathy, he dropped a hint of what he was doing. She listened attentively but said little. Mark noticed her lack of responsiveness, and one night he said rather bitterly,

"You no longer care for your husband's achievements, Catherine."

He did not call her Kitty.

"I fear them, Mark," Catherine replied.

"Fear them! Why?"

"They are doing great harm in the world."

Mark uttered an impatient exclamation. As a man he was kind and gentle, but as an artist he was wilful and intolerant. Soon after this he wrote to Berrand and invited him to stay. Berrand came. This time Catherine shuddered at his coming. She began to look upon him as her husband's evil genius. Berrand did not apparently notice any change in her, for he treated her as usual, and spoke much to her of Mark. And Catherine was too reserved to express the feelings which tortured her to a comparative stranger. For this reason Berrand did not understand the terrible conflict that was raging within her as "William Foster's" new work grew, and he often spoke to her about the book, and described, with mischievous intellectual delight, its terror, its immorality and its pain. Catherine listened with apparent calm. She was waiting for that interruption from heaven. She was wondering why it did not come.

One night in summer it chanced that she and Berrand spoke of Fate. Catherine, dominated by her fixed idea that God would intervene in some strange and abrupt way to interrupt the activities of Mark, spoke of Fate as something inevitably ordained, certain as the rising of the sun or the dropping down of the darkness. Berrand laughed.

"There is no Fate," he said. "There is man, there is woman. Man and woman make circumstance. We fashion our own lives and the lives of others."

"And our deaths?" said Catherine.

"We die when we've done enough, when we've done our best or worst, when we've pushed our energy as far as it will go—that is, if we die what is called a natural death. But of course now and then some other human being chooses to think for us, and to think we have lived long enough or too long. And then——"

He paused with a smile.

"Then——?" said Catherine, leaning slightly forward.

"Then that human being may cut our thread prematurely, and down we go to death."

Catherine drew in her breath sharply.

"But that again," continued Berrand. "Is man—or woman—not the fantasy you call Fate?"

"Perhaps Fate can take possession of a man or a woman," Catherine said slowly and thoughtfully, "govern them, act through them."

"That's a dangerous doctrine. You believe that criminals are irresponsible then?"

"I don't know," she said. "I suppose there must be an agent. Yes, I suppose there must."

She spoke as one who is thinking out a problem.

"God," she continued, after a moment of silence, "may choose to use a man or woman as an agent instead of a disease."

"Oh, well," said Berrand, with his odd, high laugh, "I cannot go with you on that road of thought, Mrs. Sirrett. I am not afflicted with a religion. Oh, here's Mark. How have you been getting on, Mr. William Foster?"

"Grandly," he replied.

His dark eyes were blazing with excitement. Catherine suddenly turned very cold. She got up and left the room. The two men scarcely noticed her departure. They plunged into an eager discussion on the book. They debated it till the night waned and the melancholy breath of dawn stole in at the open window.

Meanwhile, Catherine, who had gone to bed, lay awake. This summer was so like last summer. Now, as then, she was sleepless, and heard the distant, excited voices rising and falling, murmuring on and on hour after hour. Now, as then, they accompanied activity. Now, as then, the activity was deadly, harmful to an invisible multitude, hidden out in the great world. But there was a difference between last year and this, so like in many ways. Mark's power had grown in the interval. He had become more dangerous. And Catherine had developed also. Circumstance—spoken of by Berrand—had changed, twisted into a different shape by dying hands, twisted again by the hands—all unconscious—of that man who talked downstairs, of Berrand. Was he, too, an agent of Fate, at which he scornfully laughed? Why not?

Oh, those everlasting voices! they rang hatefully in the sleepless woman's ears. Their eagerness, their enthusiasm, were terrible to her. For now their joy seemed to summon her to a great darkness. Their sound seemed to call her to the making of a great silence. She put her hands over her ears, but she still heard them till it was dawn. She still heard them when they were no more speaking.

From this time Catherine waited indeed, but with a patience quite different from that which possessed her formerly. Then she was expectant, almost superstitiously expectant, of an abrupt interposition of Fate. Now she waited, but with less expectancy, and with a strange and growing sense of personal obligation which had been totally absent from her before the issue lay between the thing invisible and herself. And each day that passed brought the issue a step nearer to her. How pathetical seemed to her the ignorance of the two men who were her companions in the cloistered house at this time. Tears rose in her eyes at the thought of her secret and their impotence to know it. But then she thought of her mother's death-bed and the tears ran dry. For the spirit of her mother surely was with her in the dark, the spirit that knew all now and that could inspire and direct her.

The book grew and Catherine waited. Would Mark be allowed to complete it? that was the great question. If he was, then the burden of action was laid upon her by the will of God. She had quite made up her mind on that. She had even prayed, and believed that an answer had been given to her prayer, and that the answer was—"In the event you anticipate it is God's will that you should act." She was fully resolved to do God's will. And so she waited, with a strong, but how anxious, patience. The growth of the book was now become ironical to her as the growth of a plant which must die when it attains a certain height; the labour spent upon it, the discussion that raged around it, the decisions that were arrived at as to its course—all these things were now most pitifully pathetic to Catherine. As she watched Mark and Berrand, as she listened to them, she seemed to watch and listen to children, playing idly, chattering idly, on the edge of events that must stop their play, their chatter—perhaps for ever.

For this book would never see the light. No one would ever read it. No one would ever speak of it but these two men, whose lives seemed bound up in it. And Catherine alone knew this.

Sometimes she had a longing to tell them of this knowledge, to say to Mark, "Do not waste yourself in this useless energy!" to say to Berrand, "Do not rejoice over the future of that which has no future." But she refrained, knowing that to speak would be to give the lie to what she spoke. For such revelation must frustrate her contemplated action. So nobody knew what she knew, except the spirit that stood by her in the night. She waited, and the book drew slowly towards its climax and its close. As Berrand grew more excited about it he spoke more of it to Catherine. But Mark—conscious of that veil dropped between him and his wife—scarcely mentioned it to her, and declined to read any passages from it aloud. Catherine understood that he distrusted her and knew her utterly unsympathetic and adverse to his labours. The sign for which she had hoped, which she had once most confidently expected, did not come. And at length she almost ceased to think of it, and was inclined to put the idea from her as a foolish dream.

The burden of action was, it seemed, to be laid upon her. She would accept it calmly, dutifully. So the summer waned, drawing towards autumn. The atmosphere grew heavy and mellow. The garden was languid with its weight of bearing plants and with its fruits. Mists rose at evening in the woods, clouding the trunks of the trees, and spreading melancholy as a sad tale that floats, like a mist, over those who hear it. And, one day, the book was finished.

Berrand came to tell Catherine. He was radiant. While he spoke he never noticed that she closed her hands tightly as one who prepares to face an enemy.

"We are going to London this afternoon," he added. "Mark must see his publisher."

"He is taking up the manuscript?" said Catherine hastily.

"No, no. There are one or two finishing touches to be put. But he must arrange about the date of publishing. He will return by the midnight train, but I shall stay in town for the night."

Mark locked up the manuscript in a drawer of his writing table, the key of which he carried about him on a chain. And the two men took their departure, leaving Catherine alone.

So the time of her duty was fully come. She had waited till now, because, till now, she had not been absolutely sure that she was to be the agent through whom Fate was to work. But she could no longer dare to doubt. The book was finished. Mark had been allowed to finish it. But its deadly work was not accomplished till it was given to the world. It must never be given to the world.

The day was not cold. Yet Catherine ordered the footman to light a fire in Mark's study. When he had done so she told him not to allow her to be disturbed. Then she went into the room and shut the door behind her. She walked up to the writing table, at which Mark had spent so many hours, labouring, thinking, imagining, working out, fashioning that shell which was to burst and maim a world. The silence in the room seemed curiously intense. The fire gleamed, and the sun gleamed too; though already it was slanting to the West. Catherine stood for some time by the table. Then she tried the drawer in which Mark kept his manuscript and found it locked. The resistance of the drawer to her hand roused her.

Two or three minutes later one of the maids in the servant's hall said,

"Whatever's that?"

"What?" said the footman who had lit the study fire.

"Listen!" said the maid.

They listened and heard a sound like a blow struck on some hard substance.

"There it is again," said the maid. "What ever can it be?"

The footman didn't know, but they both agreed that the noise seemed to come from the study. While they were still gossiping about it Catherine stood at Mark's writing table, and drew out from an open drawer the manuscript of the book. She lifted it in her hands slowly and her face was hard and set. Then she turned and carried it to the hearth, where the fire was blazing. By the hearth she paused. She meant to destroy the book in the fire. But now that she saw the book, now that she held it in her hands, the deed seemed so horribly merciless that she hesitated. Then she knelt down on the hearth and leaned towards the flames. Their light played upon her face, their heat scorched her skin. She held the book towards them, over them. The flames flew up towards it eagerly, seeming to desire it. Catherine tantalised them by withholding from them their prey. For now, in this crisis of action, doubts assailed her. She remembered that she had never read the book, though she had heard much of it from Berrand. He was imaginative and essentially mischievous. Perhaps he had exaggerated its tendency, drawn too lurid a picture of its horrible power. Catherine turned a page or two and glanced at the clear, even writing. It fascinated her eyes.

At eight the footman opened the door, announcing dinner.

Catherine started as if from a dream. Her face was white and her eyes were ablaze with excitement. She put the manuscript back in the drawer, went into the dining-room and made a pretence of dining. But very soon she was back again in the study. She sat down under a lamp by the fire and went on reading the book. She knew that Mark would not be home till midnight; there was plenty of time. She turned the leaves one by one, and presently she forgot the passing of time, she forgot everything in the evil fascination of the book. She was enthralled. She was horror-stricken. But she could not cease from reading. Only when she had finished she meant to burn the book. No one else should ever come under its spell. She never heard the clock striking the hours. She never heard the sound of carriage wheels on the gravel of the drive. She never heard a step in the hall, the opening of the study door. Only when Mark stood before her with an exclamation of keen surprise did she start up. The manuscript dropped from her hands on to the hearth. The drawer in the writing table, broken open, gaped wide.

"Catherine," Mark said, and he bent hastily and picked up the book. "Catherine, what is the meaning of this? You have—you have— —"

He stopped, struck dumb by flooding astonishment. She stared up at him without a word and with a dazed expression in her eyes. He looked towards the drawer.

"You have dared to break open my writing table!"

"Yes," she said, finding a voice. "I have dared."

"And to read—to read— —"

She nodded. Mark seemed utterly confused by surprise. He looked almost sheepish, as men do in blank amazement. She got up and stood before him and laid her hands on his, which held the book.

"You see that fire?" she said in a low voice.

He looked at it, as if he had not noticed it before.

"What's it for?" he said, also in a low voice.

"Don't you know?"

They looked into each other's eyes for a moment.

"To—to—you intended to burn— —"

She nodded again, and closed her hands tightly on the book.

"Mark," she said solemnly. "It's an evil thing. Let it go."

His face changed. Astonishment died in fierce excitement.

"You're mad!" he said brutally.

And he struck her hands away from the book with his clenched fist. She did not cry out, but her face became utterly dogged. He saw that.

"D'you hear me?" he said.

"Yes."

His passion rose, as he began fully to grasp the enormity of the deed that his coming had prevented.

"You would destroy my labour, my very soul," he said hoarsely. "You who pretended to love me!"

"Because I love you," she said.

He laughed aloud.

"You hate me," he cried.

"I hate to see you do evil," she said.

"This is fanaticism," he muttered, looking at her obstinate white face, and steady eyes. "Sheer fanaticism."

It began almost to frighten him.

"You shall not do this evil," she said. "You shall not."

Mark stared at her for a moment. Then he turned away.

"I'll not argue with you," he said. "But, if you had done what you meant to do, if you had destroyed my labour, I would have recreated it, every sentence, every word."

"No, Mark!"

"I would, I would," he said. "The world shall have it, the world should have had it even then. Go to your room."

She left him. But her face had not changed or lost its expression.

She went upstairs slowly. And the spirit of her mother went with her. She felt sure of that.

When two days afterwards, late in the evening, Mark Sirrett suddenly died,—from poison, as was proved at Catherine's trial—she had no feeling that Mark was dead. That only came to her afterwards, as she sat by the body, awaiting the useless arrival of the doctor. She only knew that the stranger was gone, the stranger into whose wild eyes she had gazed for the first time in the Pavilion of Granada, when the world was golden beneath them and the roses touched his hair. She looked at the body, and she seemed to hear again the bell of the cathedral, filling the drowsy valley with terrible vibrations of romance. It was a passing bell. For God had stricken down "William Foster."

THE CRY OF THE CHILD

PART I
THE DEAD CHILD

The peasants going homeward at evening, when the last sunbeams slanted over the mountains and struck the ruffled surface of the river, did not hear the cry. The children, picking violets and primroses in the hedgerow by the small white house, did not hear it. The occasional tourists who trudged sturdily onward to the rugged pass at the head of the valley did not hear it.

Only Maurice Dale heard it, and grew white and shivered.

Even to him it had been at first as faint as an echo pulsing through a dream. He had said to himself that it was a fancy of his brain. And then he had pulled himself together and listened. And again, as if from very far off, the little cry had stolen to his ear and faded away. Then he had said to himself that it was the night wind caught in some cranny of the house, and striving to get free. He had thrown open his window and leaned out, and trembled, when he found that the hot night was breathless, airless, that no leaf danced in the elm that shaded his study, that the ivy climbing beneath the sill did not stir as he gazed down at it with straining eyes.

It was not the cry of the wind then. Yet it must be. Or if not that it must be some voice of nature. But the river had no such thrill of pain, of reproach in its song. Then he thought it was some night bird, haunting the eaves of his cottage, or the tangle of wood the country people called his garden. And he put on his clothes eagerly, descended the narrow staircase, and let himself out on to the path that curved to the white gate. But, in the garden there was no sound of birds.

This was a year ago. Maurice remembered very well his long vigil in the garden, and how he had prayed that he might hear one note, one only, of a night-jar, or the hoot of an owl in the forest, so that the black thought just born in his mind might be strangled, and the shadow driven out of his heart. But his prayer had not been granted. And he knew he had not deserved that it should be. Towards dawn he went back into his house again, and on the threshold, just as a pallor glimmered up as if out of the grass at his feet, he heard the cry again. And he knew that it came from within the house.

Then the sweat stood on his forehead, and he said to himself, with pale lips, "It is the cry of the child!"

All the people of Brayfield by the sea were agreed on one point. The new doctor, Maurice Dale, young as he looked, was clever. He had done wonders for Mrs. Bird, the rich old lady at Ocean View. He had performed a quite brilliant amputation on Tommy Lyne, the poor little boy who had been run down by a demon bicyclist. And then he was well born. It got about that his father was an Honourable, and all the young ladies of Brayfield trembled at the thought that he was a bachelor. His looks were also in his favour. Maurice was pale and tall, with black, smooth hair parted in the middle, regular features, and large black eyes. The expression he assumed suited him. It was curiously sad. But, at first, this apparent pathos was a great success in Brayfield. It was only at a later period that it was the cause of unkind tittle-tattle. In the beginning of Maurice's residence at Brayfield eulogy attended it and applause was never far off. People said that Maurice was impressionable, and that the vision of pain upon which the medical student's eyes must look so closely had robbed him of the natural buoyancy of youth. Poor young man, they thought enthusiastically, he suffers with those who suffer. And this was considered—and rightly considered—a very touching trait in Maurice.

Brayfield was well satisfied with its new doctor, and set itself to be ill for his benefit with a fine perseverance. But, as time went on, the satisfaction of Brayfield became mingled with curiosity. The new doctor was almost too melancholy. It would not be true to say that he never smiled, but his smile was even sadder than his gravity. There was a chill in it, as there is a chill in the first light of dawn. One or two particularly impressionable people declared that it frightened them, that it was uncanny. This idea, once started, developed. It went from house to house. And so, gradually, a spirit of whispering awe arose in the little town, and the vision of human pain ceased to be altogether accountable for the pale sorrow of the young doctor. It was decided that his habitual depression must take its rise from some more personal cause, and, upon this decision, gossip naturally ran a wild course. Since nobody knew anything about Maurice Dale except that his father was an Honourable, rumour had plenty of elbow-room. It took advantage of the situation, and Maurice was more talked about than anybody in Brayfield. And Lily Alston, the daughter of Canon Alston, Rector of Brayfield, launched out into surmises which, however, she kept to herself.

Lily, at this time, was a curious mixture of romance and religion, of flightiness and faith. She read French novels all night and went to early service in the morning. She studied Swinburne and taught in the Sunday-school with almost equal ardour, and did her duty and pursued a thousand things outside of her duty with such enthusiasm that she was continually knocked up. On these continual occasions Maurice Dale was invariably sent for, and so an intimacy grew up between him and the Rectory, which contained the Canon, his daughter, and the servants. For Mrs. Alston was dead, and Lily was an only child. Real intimacy with a Rectory means, above all things, Sunday suppers after evening church, and, in time, it became an unalterable custom for Maurice Dale to spend the twilight of his Sabbaths with the Canon and his daughter. The Canon, who was intellectual and desolate, despite his daughter, since his wife's death, liked a talk with Maurice; and Lily, without having fallen in love with the young doctor, thought him, as she said to herself, "a wonderfully interesting study."

Lily's wild surmises, already alluded to, were born on one of these Sabbath evenings in winter, when she, the Canon, and Maurice, were gathered round the fire after supper.

The sea could be heard rolling upon the pebbly beach at a distance, and the wind played about the skirts of the darkness. The Canon, happily at ease after his hard day's work, rested in his red armchair puffing at his well-seasoned pipe. Lily was lying on a big old-fashioned sofa drawn before the flames, a Persian cat, grave in its cloud of fur, nestling against her and singing its song of comfort. Maurice Dale sat upright, pulling at a cigar. It chanced that Lily had been away the week before, paying a visit in London, and naturally the conversation turned idly upon her doings.

"I used to love London," the Canon said, with a half sigh. "In the old days, when I shocked one or two good people here, Lily, by taking your mother to the playhouses. Somehow I don't care for these modern plays. I don't think she would have liked them."

"I love London, too," Lily said, in her enthusiastic voice, "but I think modern plays are intensely interesting, especially Ibsen's."

"They're cruel," the Canon said.

"Yes, father, but not more cruel than some of the older pieces."

"Such as—?"

"I was thinking of 'The Bells.' I saw Irving in it on Friday for the first time. You've seen it, of course, Mr. Dale?"

Maurice, who had been gazing into the fire, looked up. His lips tightened for a moment, then he said:

"No, never!"

"What! Though you lived in London all those years when you were a medical student?"

"I had opportunities of seeing it, of course, but somehow I never took them—and I dislike the subject of the play greatly now."

There was a certain vehemence in his voice.

"Why?" the Canon asked. "I remember my wife was very fond of it."

"I think it morbid and dangerous. There are troubles enough in life without adding to them such a hateful notion as a—a haunting; a horrible thing that—" he looked round with a sort of questioning gaze in his dark eyes—"that must be an impossibility."

"I don't know," the Canon said, without observing the glance. "I don't know. A sin may well haunt a man."

"Perhaps. But only as a memory, not as a jingle of bells, not as a definite noise, like a noise a man may hear in the street any day. That must be impossible. Now—don't you say so?"

Lily, on her sofa, had noticed the very peculiar excitement of the young doctor's manner, and that his denial was really delivered in the form of an ardent interrogation. But the Canon's mind was not so alert after the strain of pulpit oratory. He was calmly unaware of any personal thrill in the discussion.

"I would not be sure," he said. "God may have what men would call supernatural ways of punishment as well as natural ones."

"I decline to believe in the supernatural," Maurice said, rather harshly.

"Granted that these bells might ring in a man's mind, so that he believed that his ears actually heard them. That would be just as bad for him."

"Then, I suppose, he is a madman," Lily said.

Maurice started round on his chair.

"That's a—a rather shocking presumption, isn't it?" he exclaimed.

"Well," the Canon said, knocking the ashes slowly out of his pipe, "if you exclude the supernatural in such a case, and come upon the natural, I must say I think Lily is not far wrong. The man who hears perpetually a non-existent sound connected with some incident of his past will at any rate soon be on the highway to insanity, I fancy."

Maurice said nothing for a moment, but Lily noticed that he looked deeply disturbed. His lips were pressed together. His eyes shone with excitement, and his pale forehead frowned. In the short silence that followed on the Canon's remark, he seemed to be thinking steadfastly. At last he lifted up his head with a jerk and said:

"A man may have a strong imagination, without being a madman, Canon. He may choose to translate a mere memory into a sound-companion, just as men often choose to play with their fancies in various ways. He may elect to say to himself, I remember vividly the cry of—" He stopped abruptly, then went on hastily, "the sound of bells. My mind hears them. Let me—for my amusement—push on my imagination a step further and see what will happen. Hark! It's done. My ears can hear now what a moment ago only my mind could hear. Yes, my ears hear it now."

He spoke with such conviction, and the gesture which he linked with his words, was so dramatic, that Lily pushed herself up on the pillows of the sofa, and even the Canon involuntarily assumed an attitude of keen attention.

"Why, Dale," the latter said after a moment, "you should have been an actor, not a doctor. Really you led me to anticipate bells, and I only hear the wind. Lily, didn't you feel as I did, eh?"

Lily had gone a little pale. She looked across at Maurice.

"I don't know that I expected to hear bells, father," she said slowly.

As she said those words, Maurice Dale, for the first time, felt as if a human being drew very near to his secret. Lily's glance at him asked him a question. "What was it that pierced through the wind so faintly?" it seemed to say.

"What then?" the Canon asked.

"I don't know," she replied.

Maurice got up.

"I must go now," he said.

The Canon protested. It was early. They must have one more smoke. But Maurice could not be induced to stay. As he walked rapidly homeward in the darkness he told himself again and again that he was a fool. How could it be? How could she hear the cry? The cry of the child?

That night Lily did not read a French novel. She lay awake. Her fancy was set on fire by the evening's talk. Her girlish imagination was kindled. In those dark and silent hours she first began to weave a web of romance round Maurice, to see him set in a cloud of looming tragedy. He looked more beautiful to her in this cloud than he had looked before. Lily thought it might be wicked, but somehow she could not help loving mental suffering — in others. And the face of Maurice gazed at her in the blackness beneath a shadowy crown of thorns.

Next day, at the early service, she was inattentive to the ministrations of religion. Her father seemed a puppet at its prayers, the choir a row of surpliced dolls, the organ an empty voice. Only at the end, when silence fell on the kneeling worshippers, did she wake with a start of contrition to the knowledge of her impiety, and blush between her little hands at her concentration upon the suspected sorrow of the young doctor. But in that night and that morning Lily ran forward towards Maurice, set her feet upon the line that divides men from women. She knew that she had done so only when she next encountered him. Then, as their eyes met she was seized with a painful idea of guilt, bred by an absurd feeling that he could see into her mind, and know how all her thoughts had been crowding about him. It is a dangerous symptom that sensation of one's mind being visible to another as a thing observed through glass. Lily did not understand her danger, but she was full of a turmoil of uneasiness. Maurice noticed it and felt conscious also, as if some secret understanding existed between him and Lily, yet there was none, there could be none.

In conclave the individually stupid can sometimes almost touch cleverness. Brayfield only began to talk steadily about Lily and the young doctor from the day of this meeting of self-consciousnesses which had, as it chanced, taken place on the pavement of the curved parade by the sea. Till that day the little town had attributed to Maurice hopelessness, to Lily simply friendship for a sad young man. Now its members talked the usual gossip that attends the flirtations of the sincere, but added to it a considerable divergence of opinions as to the likelihood of Maurice's conversion from despair. Lily, they were all decided, began to love Maurice. But some believed and some denied, that Maurice began to love Lily. This would have been hard for Lily had she noticed it, but her fanciful and enthusiastic mind was concentrated on one thing only and her range of vision was consequently narrowed. She was incessantly engaged in trying to trace the footsteps of the doctor's misery, of which she was now fully convinced. And indeed, since that Sabbath evening already described,

Maurice had scarcely endeavoured to play any part of ordinary happiness to her. Her partial penetration of his secret quickly brought a sense of relief to him. There was something consoling in the idea that this little girl divined his loneliness of soul, if not its reason.

By degrees they grew quietly so accustomed to the silent familiarity existing between their ebbing and flowing thoughts; they were—without a word spoken—so thoroughly certain of the language their minds were uttering to each other, that when their lips did speak at length, the words that came were like a continuance of an already long conversation.

Lily was, once more, knocked up, and the Canon called in Maurice to prescribe. He arrived in the late afternoon and was taken by the Canon into Lily's little sitting-room, where she lay on a couch by the fire. A small, shaded, reading lamp defined the shadows craftily.

"Now, Dale," the Canon said, "for goodness' sake tell her to be more orderly and to do less—mind and body. She behaves as if life was a whirlpool. She swims stupendously, tell her to float—and give her a tonic."

And he went out of the room shaking his head at the culprit on the couch.

When the door had shut upon him, Maurice came up to the fire in silence and looked at Lily. She smiled at him rather hopelessly, and then suddenly she said:

"Poor dear father! To ask you to make me take life so easily!"

That remark was the first onward gliding of their minds in speech, the uttered continuance of the hitherto silent colloquy between them. Maurice sat down. He accepted the irony of the situation suggested by the Canon without attempt at a protest.

"Life can never be easy, if one thinks," he said. Then, trying to adopt the medical tone, he added:

"But you think too much. I have often felt that lately."

"Yes," she said.

Her eyes were bent on him with a scrutiny that was nearly ungirlish. Maurice tried not to see it as he put his fingers on her wrist. She added:

"I have felt that about you too."

Maurice had taken out his watch. Without speaking he timed the fluttering pulsation of her life, then, dropping her hand and returning the watch to his pocket:

"Your too eager thoughts were of me?" he asked.

"Yes, but yours were not of me."

"Not always," he said, with an honesty that pleased her.

And again Lily saw above his face the shadowy crown of thorns. She was really unwell and ready to be unstrung. Perhaps this made her say hastily, as she shifted lower on her cushions:

"I'm partly ill to-day because you let me see how horribly you are suffering."

"Yes," Maurice said heavily. "I let you see it. Why's that?"

There was nothing like a shock to either of them in the directness of their words. They seemed spoken rightly at the inevitable time. No thought of question, of denial, was entertained by them. Maurice sat there by her and dropped his mask utterly.

"Miss Alston, I am a haunted man," he said.

And, in a moment, as he spoke, he seemed to be old. Lily said nothing. She twisted between her little fingers the thin rug that covered her, and was angry with herself because, all of a sudden, she wanted to cry.

"And I am beginning to wonder," Maurice went on, "how much longer I can bear it, just how long."

Lily cleared her throat. It struck her as odd that she did not feel strange with this man who looked so old in the thin light from the lamp. Indeed, now that the mask had entirely fallen from him, he seemed more familiar to her than ever before.

"I suppose we must bear everything so long as God chooses," she said.

"No, so long as we choose."

"But how?"

"To live to bear it. I cannot be haunted after I am dead. That can't be."

He lifted his head and looked at her with a sort of pale defiance, as if he would dare her to contradict him. Lily confronted the horror of his eyes, and a shudder ran over her. The thorns had pierced more deeply even than she had believed as she lay awake in the night. Just then a door banged and a footstep approached on the landing.

"Hush, it's father," Lily whispered.

And the Canon entered to ask the condition of the patient. Maurice prescribed and went away. In the windy evening as he walked, he was conscious of a large change dawning over his life. Either the spirit of prophecy—which comes to many men even in modern days—was upon him, or hope, which he believed quite dead in him, stirred faintly in his dream. In either event he saw that on the black walk of his life there was the irregular, and as yet paltry, line of some writing, some inscription. He could not read the words. He only knew that there were some words to be read. And one of them was surely Lily's name.

He did not meet her until the evening of the following Sunday when, as usual, he went to supper at the Rectory. Lily was better and had been to church. The Canon was delighted and thanked Maurice for his skill in diagnosis and in treatment.

"You cure every one," he said.

Lily and Maurice exchanged a glance. He saw how well she understood that he felt the words to be an irony though they were uttered so innocently. After supper, just as the Canon, with his habitual Sunday sigh of satisfaction, was beginning to light his pipe, Sarah, the parlour maid, came in with a note. The Canon read it and his sigh moved onwards to something not unlike a groan. He put his filled pipe down on the mantelpiece.

"What is it, father?" asked Lily.

"Miss Bigelow," he replied laconically.

"On a Sunday. Oh, it's too bad!"

"It can't be helped," the Canon said. "Excuse me, Dale, I have to go out. But—stay—I shall be back in half an hour."

And he went out into the hall, took his coat and hat and left the house. Miss Bigelow was his cross. She was a rich invalid, portentously delicate, full of benefactions to the parish and fears for the welfare of her soul. She kept the Canon's charities going royally, but, in return, she claimed the Canon's ghostly ministrations at odd times to an extent that sometimes caused the good man's saintly equanimity to totter. Hating doctors and loving clergymen, Miss Bigelow was forever summoning her distracted father confessor to speed that parting guest—her soul, which however, never departed. She remarked in confidence to those about her, that she had endured "a dozen deathbeds." The Canon had sat beside them all. He must now take his way to the thirteenth.

As soon as the hall door banged Maurice looked up at Lily.

"Poor, dear father," she murmured.

"I am glad," Maurice said abruptly.

The remark might have been called rude, but it was so simply made that it had the dignity belonging to any statement of plain truth. Neither rude nor polite, it was merely a cry of fact from an overburdened human soul. Lily felt that the words were forced from the young doctor by some strange agitation that fought to find expression.

"You wish—you wish—" she began.

Then she stopped. The flood of expression that welled up in her companion's face frightened her. She trembled at the thought of the hidden thing, the force, that could loose such a sea.

"What is it?" she said like a schoolgirl—or so, a moment afterwards, she feared.

"I ought not to tell you," Maurice said, "I ought not, but I must—I must."

He had got up and was standing before her. His back was to the fire, and a shadow was over his face.

"I want to tell you. You have made me want to. Why is that?"

He spoke as if he were questioning his own intellect for the reason, not asking it of her. And she did not try to answer his question.

"I suppose," he continued, "it is because you are the only human being who has partially understood that there is something with me that sets me apart from all my kind, from all the others."

"With you?" Lily said.

She felt horribly frightened and yet strong and earnest.

"Yes, with me," he answered. "I told you that I was a haunted man. Miss Alston, can you, will you bear to hear what it is that is with me, and why it comes. It is a story that, perhaps, your father might forbid you to read. I don't know. And, if it was fiction, perhaps he would be right. But—but—I think—I wonder—you might help me. I can't see how, but—I feel—"

He faltered suddenly, and seemed for the first time to become self-conscious and confused.

"Tell me, please," Lily said.

She felt rather as if she were beginning to read some strange French story by night. Maurice still stood on the hearth.

"It is a sound that is with me," he said. "Only that; never anything else but that."

"A sound," she repeated.

She thought of their conversation about the bells.

"Yes, it is a cry—the cry of a child."

"Yes?"

"That's nothing—you think? Absurd for a man to heed such a trifle?"

"Why do you think it comes?"

Maurice hesitated. His eyes searched the face of the little girl with an almost hard gaze of scrutiny, as if he were trying to sum up the details of her nature.

"Long ago—before I came here, before I was qualified, I was cruel, bitterly cruel to a child," he said at last, speaking now very coldly and distinctly.

His eyes were on Lily. Had she made just then any movement of horror or of disgust, had an expression betokening fear of him come into her eyes, Maurice knew that his lips would be sealed, that he would bid her good-night and leave her. But she only looked more intent, more expectant. He went on.

"I was bitterly cruel to my own child," he said.

Then Lily moved suddenly. Maurice thought she was going to start up. If she had intended to she choked the impulse. Was she shocked? He could not tell. She had turned her face away from him. He wondered why, but he did not know that those last words had given to Lily an abrupt and fiery insight into the depths of her heart.

"At that time," Maurice said, still speaking very distinctly and quietly, "I was desperately ambitious. I was bitten by the viper whose poison, stealing through all a man's veins, is emulation. My only desire, my only aim in life was to beat all the men of my year, to astonish all the authorities of the hospital to which I was attached by the brilliance of my attainments and my achievements, I was ambition incarnate, and such mad ambition is the most cruel thing in the world. And my child interfered with my ambition. It cried, how it cried!"

He was becoming less definitely calm.

"It cried through my dreams, my thoughts, my endeavours, my determinations. Do you know what a weapon a sound can be, Miss Alston? Perhaps not. A sound can be like a sword and pierce you, like a bludgeon and strike you down. A little sound can nestle in your life, and change all the colour and all the meaning of it. The cry of the living child was terrible to me, I thought then. But—then—I had never heard the cry of the dead child. You see I wanted to forget something. And the tiny cry of the child recalled it. There were no words in the cry, and yet there were words,—so it seemed to me—telling over a past history. This history—well, I want to say to you—"

Lily had now put a guard on watch over against her impulsive nature. When Maurice stopped speaking she was able to look towards him again and murmur:

"Say all you want to."

"Thank you," he said, almost eagerly. "If you knew—Miss Alston, before this time, when I was a very young student, I had fallen into one of the most fatal confusions of youth. I had made a mistake as to the greatest need of my own nature. I had, for a flash of time, thought my greatest need was love."

"And it wasn't," the girl said, with a note of wonder in her voice.

"No, it was success, to outstrip my fellows. But I thought it was love, and I followed my thought and I sacrificed another to my thought. My child's mother died almost in giving her to me, and, in dying, made me promise to keep the child always with me. I kept that promise. I was a young student, very poor. My love had been secret. Now I was alone with this helpless child. I left my own lodgings and took others. I brought it there, and its presence obliged me to shut my doors against my own family and against my friends. To keep the door shut I put forward the excuse of my ambition. I said that I was giving myself up to work and I shut myself in with the child. I was its nurse as well as its father. I thought I should be sufficient for it. But it missed—her, whom I scarcely missed."

"You had not loved her?"

Maurice bent his head.

"I had made a mistake, as I said. I had only thought so. Long before she died I had almost hated her for crippling my ambition. She was swept out of my path. But the child was left crying for her."

"Yes. I know."

"Its wail came eternally between me and my great desire. When I sat down to work the sound—which I could not quiet—perplexed my brain. When I lay down to get, in sleep, power for fresh work, it struck through my dreams. I heard it when the stars were out over London, and in the dawn, when from my lodging windows I could see the first light on the Thames. Miss Alston, at last it maddened me."

Lily was pale. She scarcely knew of what she was expectant.

"I had tried to comfort the child. I had failed. Now I determined to forget it, to shut it out from my working life. At last, by force of will, I almost succeeded. I read, I wrote, I analysed the causes of disease, the results of certain treatments as opposed to the results of others. And sometimes I no longer heard my child, no longer knew whether it wailed and wept or whether it was silent. But one evening—"

Maurice stopped. His face was very white and his eyes burned with excitement.

"One evening," he repeated, speaking almost with difficulty, and with the obstinate note in his voice of one telling a secret half against his will and better judgement, "I could not work. The wail of the child was so loud, so alarmed, so full of a fear that seemed to my imagination intelligent, and based on a knowledge of something I did not know, that my professional instinct was aroused. At first I listened, sitting at my writing table. Then I got up and softly approached the folding doors. Beyond them, in the dark, the child lamented like one to whom a nameless horror draws near. Never had I known it to weep like this; for this was no cry after a mother, no cry of desire, no cry even of sorrow. It was a half-strangled scream of terror, I did not go into the room, but as I listened, I knew—"

He faltered.

"Yes," Lily said.

"As I listened I knew what the cry meant. Miss Alston, is it not strange that even a baby who scarcely knows life knows so well—death?"

"Death!"

"Yes, recognises its coming, shrinks from it, fears it with the terror of a clear intelligence. Is it not very strange?"

"Death!" Lily repeated.

She too was pale. Maurice continued in a low voice.

"I understood the meaning of the cry, and I did not enter the inner room. No, I walked back to my writing table, put my hands over my ears— to deaden the cry—and gave myself again to work. How long I worked I don't know, but presently I heard a loud knocking at the door of my room. I sprang up and opened it. My landlady stood outside.

"'What do you want?' I asked.

"The good woman's face was grave.

"'Sir, I know that child must be ill,' she said.

"'Ill—why? What do you mean?'

"'Oh, sir, its crying is awful. It goes right through me.'

"I pushed the woman out almost roughly.

"'It is not ill,' I said. 'It is only restless. Leave me. Don't you see I am working?'

"And I shut the door sharply. I sat down again at my table and toiled till dawn. I remember that dawn so well. At last my brain had utterly tired. I could work no longer. I pushed away my papers and got up. The room was misty—so I thought—with a flickering grey light. The dirty white blind was drawn half up. I looked out over the river, and from it I heard the dull shout of a man on a black barge. This shout recalled to me my child and the noise of its lament. I listened. All was silent. There was no murmur from the inner room. And then I remember that suddenly the silence, for which I had so often longed and prayed, frightened me. It seemed full of a dreadful meaning. I waited a moment. Then I walked softly across the room to the folding doors. They were closed, I opened them furtively and looked into the bedroom. It was nearly dark. Approaching the bed I could scarcely discern the tiny white heap which marked where the child lay among the tumbled bedclothes. I bent down to listen to the sound of its breathing. I could not hear the sound. Then I caught the child in my arms and carried it over to the sitting-room window so that the dawn might strike upon its little face. The face was discoloured. The heart was not beating. Miss Alston, while I worked, my child had died in a convulsion. It had striven against death, poor feeble baby, and had had no help from its father. My medical skill might have eased its sufferings. Might have saved it. But I had deliberately closed my ears to its appeal for love, for assistance. I had let it go. I should never hear it again."

Maurice had spoken the last words with excitement. Now he paused. With an obvious effort he controlled himself and added calmly:

"I buried my child and gave myself again to work. My examination was close at hand. I passed it brilliantly. But I shuddered at my success. Those lodgings by the river had become horrible to me. I left them, took a practice in a remote Cumberland valley, and withdrew myself from the world, from all who had known me. In this retirement, however, I had a companion of whose presence at first I was unaware. The dead child followed me, the child of whom now I feel myself to have been the murderer."

"No—no—not that!" Lily whispered. But he did not seem to hear her.

"One night," he continued, "in my lonely house in the valley I was awakened by some sound. I sat up in bed and listened. All was black around me, and at first all was quiet too. I lay down again to sleep. But as I touched the pillow I heard a faint murmur that seemed to come from far away. I said to myself that it was a fancy of my mind but again it came. Then I thought it was the wind caught in some cranny of my house. I opened my window and leaned out. But there was no wind in the trees. What was the noise then? The cry of a bird perhaps. Yes, it must be that. Yet did any note of a bird have a thrill of pain in it? I hurried on some clothes and let myself out into the garden. I would hear that bird again. I would convince myself of its presence. But in the garden I could hear nothing save the thin murmur of the stream that threaded the valley. So I returned to the house, and at the door I was greeted by a little cry from within. Miss Alston, it was the cry of my dead child, full of pain and of eternal reproach. I shut the door, closing myself in with my fate, and since that night I have been a haunted man. Scarcely a day has passed since then, scarcely a night has gone by without my hearing that appeal for help which once I disregarded, which now I can never reply to. I fled from the valley, in a vain hope of leaving that voice behind me. I came here. But the child's spirit is here too. It is forever with me."

He stopped abruptly, then he added, "I can even hear it now, while I look at you, while I touch your hand."

His burning eyes were fixed on Lily's face. His burning hand closed on hers as if seeking assistance.

"What am I to do?" he said, and for the first time his voice broke and failed.

"Pray!" she whispered.

"I have prayed. But God forgives only those who reverse their evil acts. Mine can never be reversed. I can never be kind to my child to whom I have been bitterly cruel. There is no help for me, none. Yet I had a feeling that— that you might help me."

"If I could!" the girl cried with a blaze of sudden eagerness. Her heart leaped up at the words, leaped up from its depth of pity for Maurice to a height of almost fiery enthusiasm.

"But how?" he said.

Then his face hardened and grew stern.

"No," he said, "there can be no help for me, none in this world."

The drawing-room door opened and the Canon appeared.

"Miss Bigelow has not died for the thirteenth time," he said, coming up to the fire.

When the Canon kissed his daughter that night, after Maurice Dale had gone home, he seemed struck by a new expression in her face.

"Why, how excited you look, child!" he said, "what is it?"

But Lily returned his kiss hastily and ran away without a word. Once in her room she locked the door—for no reason except that she must mark the night by some unwonted action—put on her dressing-gown and threw herself down on her bed. Her mind was alive with thoughts. Her imagination was in flames. For so much had come upon her that evening. In the first place she understood that she loved Maurice. She knew that, when he spoke the words, "My child," and jealousy of an unknown woman struck like some sharp weapon to her heart. She realised that he did not love her, yet so great was her simple unselfishness, that she did not dwell on the knowledge, or blame for an instant the selfishness which concentrated Maurice's mind so entirely upon himself and his own sorrow. Her only anxiety was how to help him. Her only feeling was one of tender pity for his agony. And yet, for Lily was a girl of many fancies and full of the wilful side-thoughts of women, she found room in her nature for a highflown sense of personal romance which now wrapped her round in a certain luxury of complacency. She moved in a strange story that was true, a story that she might have read with a quickening of the pulses. She and Maurice, whom she loved, moved in it together heroine and hero of it. And none knew the story but themselves. And then she burst into silent tears, calling herself cruel for having this moment of half joy in the tragedy of another. She pushed down into the depths of Maurice's misery. And then, with a clearer mind, she sat up on the bed. It was dead of night now. Was he listening in the silence to that haunting cry that was destroying him? She wondered breathlessly. And she recalled the conversation about "The Bells." Was Mathias truly haunted? or was he mad? She asked herself that, putting Maurice eventually behind footlights in his place. Was there really a veritable cry, allowed to come out of the other world to Maurice? or did his diseased brain work out his retribution? She could not tell. Indeed she scarcely cared just then. In either event, the result upon him was the same and was terrible. In either event, the outcome might be what she dared not name even to herself. And, though he did not love her, he turned to her for help. Lily flushed in the thought of this. Almost more than if she had his heart it seemed to have his cry for assistance. She must answer it effectually. She must. But how? And then she sprang up and began to pace the room. How to help him. Slowly, and with a minute examination, she went in memory through his story, with its egoism, its cruelty, its ambition, its punishment, its childlike helplessness of to-night, and of many nights. She recalled each word that he had spoken until she came to almost the last, "I have prayed. But God forgives only those who reverse their evil acts. Mine can never be reversed. I can never be kind to my child—" Just there she stopped. Maurice's words flew against what Lily's religion taught her of the Great Being who can pardon simply and fully so long only as the sinner entirely and deeply repents. But she accepted them as true for Maurice. There was the point to be faced. She felt that his nature, haunted indeed or betrayed by its own weakness, but still loved by her, could only be restored to peace if he could fulfil the impossible, reverse—as he expressed it—that act of his past. Ah, that cry of the little dying, helpless child, of his little child. Lily could almost hear it too, the tears came into her eyes. How could she still it? How could she lay the little spirit to rest forever? Peace for child, peace for father, sinned against and sinner—she felt she would gladly sacrifice her own life, her own peace, to work the miracle of comfort on dead and living. Yes, she could give up her love,—if—. Suddenly Lily threw herself down on her bed and buried her burning face deep in the pillows. A thought had come to her, so strange that she wondered whether it were not wicked. The hot red colour surged over her with this thought, and all the woman in her quivered as she asked herself whether, in this life of sorrows and of abnegations, it could ever be that the grief and the terror of another could be swept away by one who, in the endeavour to bring solace, must obtain intense personal happiness. In books it is ever self-sacrifice that purges and persuades, martyrdom of the senses that renews and relieves. Lily was ready indeed to be a martyr for the man she loved. But the strange way she saw of being his possible saviour lay only in a light of the sun forever on herself.

She wept and saw the light, herself and Maurice walking in it together, till the church bell chimed in the morning, and the tide came up in the sunshine to murmur that it was day.

Maurice Dale was puzzled. He noticed a change in Lily so marked that even his self-centred nature could not fail to observe it. This girl, whom he had thought pretty, fanciful, tenderhearted and gently sympathetic, who had attracted his confession by her quick and feminine receptiveness, now seemed developed into a woman of strength and purpose, full of calm and of dignity. Her shining eyes were more steadfast than of old, her manner was less changeful, less enthusiastic, but more reliant. Brayfield wondered what had come to Miss Alston. Maurice wondered too, dating the transformation accurately from the night when he unburdened his soul in search of the help, which, after all, no human being could give to him. It was strange, he thought, that a man's terror, a man's weakness, should endow a weak girl with confidence and with power. It was too strange, and he laughed at himself for supposing that he had anything to do with the new manifestation of Lily's nature. Nevertheless she began to attract him more than he had believed possible. The nightmare in which his life was encircled grew less real when he was with her. There was virtue in her that went out to him. He came to desire always to be with her and yet he could not say to himself that he loved her with the passion of man for woman. Rather was the desire that he felt for her like that of a criminal towards a place of refuge, of a coward towards an asylum of safety. Sometimes he longed that she might share his trouble, selfishly longed that in her ears might ring the cry of pain that tormented his.

One day, when they were together on a down that overlooked the sea, he told her this.

"I wish it too," she answered softly.

"You are all unselfishness, as I am all selfishness," he said, condemning himself, and nearer to loving her than ever before.

The sails went by along the wintry sea, and the short afternoon faded quickly into a twilight that was cold in its beauty like a pale primrose in frost. They were descending slowly towards the little town that lay beneath them in the shadows.

"I have no voice to trouble my life,—no dead voice, that is," Lily said.

"No dead voice?" Maurice asked. "And the living?"

"Oh, in most lives there is some one voice that means almost too much," Lily answered slowly.

Maurice stopped.

"Whose voice means so much to you?" he said.

"Why do you care to ask?"

"Is it mine?"

The girl had stopped too. Her face was set towards the sea and its great sincerity, which murmurs against the lies and the deceptions of many lives that defile the land, and takes so many more to itself that they may persist no longer in their evil doing. And perhaps it was her vision of the sea that swept from Lily any desire to be a coquette, or to be maidenly,—that is, false. She looked from the sea into Maurice's eyes.

"Yes," she answered. "It is yours."

"You love me then, Lily?"

"Yes, I love you, Maurice."

There was no tremor in her voice. There was no shame in her eyes. Alone in her chamber on the night of Maurice's confession she had flushed and trembled. Now she stood before him and made this great acknowledgement simply and fearlessly. And yet she knew that he did not love her with the desire of man to the woman whom he chooses out of the world to be his companion. She was moved by a resolve that was very great to ignore all that girls think most of at such a moment. Maurice took a step towards her. How true and how strong she looked.

"I dare not ask you to share my life," he said. "It is too shadowed, too sad. I have not the right."

"If you will ask me, I will share it."

She put her hand into his. He felt as if her soul lay in it. They walked on. Already the evening was dark around them.

Canon Alston was a little surprised, merely because he was a father, and fathers are always a little surprised when men love their children. But he liked Maurice heartily and gave his consent to the marriage. Miss Bigelow ordered a valuable wedding-present, and resolved to live until over the marriage day at least. And Brayfield gossiped and gloried in possessing a legitimate cause for excitement.

As for Lily, she was strangely happy with a happiness far different from that of the usual betrothed young girl. She loved Maurice deeply. Nevertheless she did not blind herself to the fact that he was still unhappy, restless, self-engrossed and often terror-stricken, although he tried to appear more confident than of old, and to assume a gaiety suitable to his situation in the eyes of the world. She knew he could never be entirely free to love so long as the cry of the child rang in his ears. And he told her that, strangely enough, since their engagement it had become more importunate. Once he even tried to break their contract.

"I cannot link my life with another's," he said desperately. "Who knows—when you are one with me, you may be haunted as I am. That would be too horrible."

It was a flash of real and heartfelt unselfishness. Lily felt herself thrill with gratitude. But she only said:

"I am not afraid."

On another occasion—this was about a month after they became engaged—Maurice said:

"Lily, when shall we be married?"

She glanced up at him, and saw that he was paler even than usual, and that his face looked drawn with fatigue.

"Whenever you wish," she answered.

"Let it be soon," he said. And then he broke out almost despairingly:

"I cannot bear this much longer. Lily, what can it mean? There is something too strange. Ever since you and I have been betrothed the curse that is laid upon me has been heavier, the cry of the child has been more incessantly with me. I hear it more plainly. It is nearer to me. It is close to me. In the night sometimes I start up thinking the child is even beside me on the pillow, complaining to me in the darkness. I stretch out my hand. I feel for its little body. But there is nothing—nothing but that cry of fear, of pain, of eternal reproach. Why does the spirit persecute me now as it never persecuted me before? Is it because it believes that you will make me happier? Is it because it wishes to deny me all earthly joy? Sometimes I think that, once we are actually husband and wife the cry will die away. Sometimes I think that then it will never leave me even for a moment. If that were so, Lily, I should die, or I should lose my reason."

He covered his face with his hands. He was trembling. Lily put her soft hand against his hands. A great light had come into her eyes as he spoke.

"Let us be married, Maurice," she said. "Perhaps the little child wants me."

He looked up at her and his dark eyes seemed to pierce her, hungry for help.

"Wants you?" he said. "How can that be? No, no. It cries against my thought of happiness, against my desire for peace."

"We must give it peace. We must lay it to rest."

"No one can do that. If I have not the power to redeem my deed of wickedness, how can you, how can any one living redeem it for me?"

Lily looked away from him. Her cheeks were burning with a blush. A tingling fire seemed to run through all her veins and her pulses beat.

"There is some way of redemption for every one," she said.

But he answered gloomily:

"Your religion teaches you to say that, Lily, perhaps to believe it. But there is no way. The dead cannot return to earth that we may give them tenderness instead of our former cruelty. No—no!"

"Maurice—trust me. Let us be married—soon."

That night, before she went to bed, Lily knelt down and prayed until the night was old. She asked what thousands of women have asked since the world was young. But surely never woman before had so strange a reason for her request. And when at length she rose from her knees she felt that time must bring the gift she had prayed for, unselfishly, and with her whole heart.

A month afterwards, on a bright spring morning, Maurice and Lily were married. It was a great occasion for Brayfield. The church was elaborately decorated by the many young ladies who had secretly longed to be the brides of the interesting doctor. Crowds assembled within and without the building. Miss Bigelow rose from her fourteenth death-bed in a purple satin gown and a bonnet prodigious with feathers and testified to the possibility of modern resurrection in a front pew. Flowers, rice, wedding marches filled the air. But people remarked that the bridegroom looked like a man who went in fear. Even when he was on the doorstep of the church in the throng of curious sightseers he moved almost as one whom a dream attends, who sees the pale figures, who hears the faint voices that inhabit and make musical a vision of the night. The bride too, had no radiant air of a young girl fulfilling her girlish destiny and giving herself up to a protector, to one stronger, more able to fight the world than a woman who loves and fears. Her face, too, was pale and grave, even—some thought—a little stern. As she passed up the church she glanced at no one, smiled at no friend. Her eyes were set steadfastly towards the altar where Maurice waited. And when, after the ceremony, she came down the church to the sound of music her eyes were fixed on her husband. She took no heed of any one else, for her hand pressed upon his arm, felt that he was trembling. And her ears seemed to hear through all the jubilant music, through all the murmur of the gazing crowd, a cry, far away, yet more distinct than any sound of earth, thin, piercing, full of appeal to her—the spirit-cry of the child.

PART II
THE LIVING CHILD

The honeymoon of Lily and Maurice was short, and many would have called it sad, could they have known how different it was from the marriage holiday of most young couples. Maurice had looked forward to the wedding as a desperate man looks forward to a new point of departure in his life. He had fixed all his hopes of possible peace upon it. He had dated new days of calm, if not of brightness, from it. He had sometimes vaguely, sometimes desperately, looked to it as to a miracle day, on which—how or why he knew not—the shadow would be lifted from his life. The man who is doomed to death has a moment of acute expectation when some new doctor places him under a fresh mode of treatment. For a few days the increased vitality of his anxious mind sheds a dawn of apparent life through his body. But the mind collapses. The dawn fades. The darkness increases, death steals on. So it was with Maurice. Immediately after the wedding, Lily noticed that he fell into a strangely watchful condition of abstraction. He was full of tenderness to her, full of cares for her comfort, but even in his moments of obvious solicitude he seemed to be on the alert to catch the stir of some remote activity, or to be listening for the sound of some distant voice. His own fate engrossed him even in this first period of novel companionship with another soul. The monomania of the haunted man gripped him and would not release him. He thought of Lily, but he thought more, and with a deeper passion, of himself.

The girl divined this, but she did not for an instant rebel. She had set up a beautiful unselfishness in her heart and had consecrated it. Purpose does much for a woman, helps her sometimes to rise higher than perhaps man can ever rise, to the pale and vacant peaks of an inactive martyrdom. And Lily was full of a passion of purpose known only to herself. She loved Maurice not merely as a girl loves a man, but also as the protective woman loves the being dependent upon her. His secret was hers, but hers was not his. She had her beautiful loneliness of silent hope, and that sustained her.

They went away together. In the train Maurice said to her suddenly, with a sort of blaze of hungry eagerness:

"Lily—Lily—to-day there is a silence for me. Oh, Lily, if you have brought me silence."

He seized her hand and his was hot like fire.

"Will it last—can it last?" he whispered.

And he glanced all round the carriage like one anticipating an answer to his question from some unknown quarter, then he said:

"The noise of the train is so loud, perhaps—"

"Hush!" Lily said. "Don't fight your own peace, Maurice."

"Fight it—no, but I can scarcely believe in it. Lately the—it has been so ceaseless, so poignant. Lily, I have had a fancy that you alone could be my saviour. If it is so! Ah, but how can that be?"

She gave him a strange answer.

"Maurice," she said, "it may be so, but do not despair if the cry comes again."

"What!" he exclaimed almost fiercely, "you—do you hear it then?"

"No, no, but it may come."

"It shall not. The silence is so beautiful."

He put his arms around her. The tears had sprung into his eyes.

"How weak I am," he said, with a fury against his own condition, "you must despise me."

"I love you," she said.

He looked at her with a creeping astonishment.

"I wonder why," he said, slowly. "How can you love a man who has been so miserable that he has almost ceased to be a man?"

"I love even your misery. Don't think me selfish, Maurice. But it was your sorrow, you see, that first taught you to think of me."

He leaned from her suddenly towards the window which was open and pulled it sharply up.

"Why do you do that?" Lily said quickly.

"One hears such noises in the air when one travels at this speed," he answered. "With the window down one might fancy anything. I must shut out fancy. There are voices in the wind that passes, in the rustling woods that we rush through. I won't hear them."

The train sped on.

Their destination was an inland village set in the midst of a rolling purple moor, isolated in a heather-clad gold of the land, distant from the sea, distant from the murmur of modern life; a sleepy, self-contented and serene abode of quiet women and ruminant men, living, loving, and dying with a greater calm than often pervades our modern life. A lazy divinity seemed to preside over the place, in spring-time at least. Men strolled about their work as if Time waited on them, not they on Time. The children—so Maurice thought—played more drowsily than the children of towns. The youths were contemplative. Even the girls often forgot to giggle as they thought of wedding rings and Sunday love-making. Little dogs lay blinking before the low-browed doors of the cottages, and cats reposed upon the garden walls round-eyed in sober dreams. If Maurice sought a home of silence surely he had it here. Lily and he put up at a small inn on the skirt of the village and facing the rippling emptiness of the moor. Before going to bed they stepped out into the night and the wide air. Stars were bright in the sky. Cottage lights twinkled here and there behind them in the village. They heard a stream running away into the heart of the long solitude that lay beyond them. Lily was very quiet. Her heart was full. Thoughts, strange and beautiful, overflowed in her mind. She felt just then how much bigger the human soul is than the human body, how much stronger the prisoner is than the prison in which nevertheless it is dedicated to dwell for a time. Her hand just touched the arm of Maurice as she looked across the soft darkness of the moor. He, too, felt curiously happy and safe. Taking off his cap he passed his hand over his hair.

"Lily," he said, "peace is here for me, in this place with you. My brain has been playing me tricks because I have been so much alone, the devil dwells in a man's loneliness. Listen to the silence of these moors. What a music it is!"

The lights in the cottages were extinguished one by one, as bed claimed their owners. But Maurice and Lily, sitting on the dry fringe of the heather, remained out under the stars. Her hand lay in his and suddenly she felt his quiver.

"What is it, Maurice?" she asked.

He got up and made a step forward.

"Lily," he said, "there is—there must be some one near us, a child lost on the moor, or forgotten by its mother. I hear it crying close to us. Say you hear it too. No, no, it is not the old sound. Don't think that. It can't be. There's a natural explanation of this—I'll swear there is. Come with me."

He pulled her hastily up and pressed forward some steps, stumbling among the bushes. Then he stopped, listening.

"It is somewhere just here, by us," he said. "I must see. Wait a moment. I'll strike a light."

He drew out his match-box and struck a match, protecting the tiny flame between his hands. Then he bent down, searching the uneven ground at their feet. The flame went out.

"I wish I had a lantern," he muttered.

"Maurice," Lily said, "let us go back to the inn."

"What! and leave this child out here in the night. I tell you there is a child crying near us."

He spoke almost angrily.

"Let us go back, Maurice."

He stood for a moment as if uncertain.

"You think—" he began, then he stopped. She took his hand and led him towards the village in silence. As they reached the inn door, the faint light from the coffee-room encircled them. Maurice was white to the lips. He looked at Lily without speaking, and he was trembling.

"Wasn't there anything?" he whispered. "Is it here too? Can't you keep it away?"

Lily said nothing. She opened the inn door. Maurice stepped into the passage, heavily, almost like a drunken man. And this was the first night of their honeymoon.

The incident of the moor threw Maurice back into the old misery from which he had emerged for a brief moment, and, indeed, plunged him into an abyss of despair such as he had never known before. For now he had sincerely hoped for salvation, and his hope had been frustrated. He had clung to a belief that Lily's love, Lily's companionship might avail to rescue him from the phantom, or the reality, that was destroying his power, shattering his manhood. The belief was dashed from him, and he sank deeper in the sea of terror. They stayed on for a while in this Sleepy Hollow, but Maurice no longer felt its peace. Remote as it was, cloistered in the rolling moors, the cry of the child penetrated to it, making it the very centre, the very core of all things hideous and terrible. Even the silence of the village, its aloofness from the world, became hateful to Maurice. For they seemed to emphasise and to concentrate the voice that pierced more keenly in silence, that sounded more horrible in solitude.

"I cannot stay here," he said to Lily. "Let us go back. I will take up my work again. I will try to throw myself into it as I did when I was a student. I shut out the living cry then, I will shut out the dead cry now. For you—you cannot help me."

He looked at her while he spoke almost contemptuously, almost as one looks at some woman whose courage or whose faith one has tried and found wanting.

"You cannot help me," he repeated.

Secretly he felt a cruel desire to sting Lily into passion, to rouse her to some demonstration of anger against his cowardice in thus taunting her love and devotion. But she said nothing, only looked at him with eyes that had become strangely steadfast, and full of the quiet light of a great calm and patience.

"D'you say nothing?" he said.

"If you wish to go, Maurice, let us go."

He had got up and was standing by the low window that looked across the moor.

"Don't you see," he said, "that I am going mad in this place? And you do nothing. Why did I ever think that you could help me?"

"Try to think so still."

She, too, got up, followed him to the window and put her two hands on his shoulders.

"Perhaps the time has not come yet," she said.

Suddenly he took her hands in his and pushed her a little way from him, so that he could look clearly into her face.

"What do you mean? What can you mean?" he said. "Sometimes I think you have some secret that you keep from me, some purpose that I know nothing of. You look as if—as if you were waiting for something; were expectant; I don't know—" he broke off, "After all what does it matter? Only let us go from here. Let us get home. I hate that stretch of moorland. At night it is full of bewailing and misery."

He shuddered although the warm spring sunshine was pouring in at the window. Then he turned and left the room without another word. Lily stood still for a moment, with her eyes turned in the direction of the door. Her cheeks burned with a slight blush and her lips were half opened.

"If he only knew what I am waiting for!" she murmured to herself. "Will it ever come?"

She sank down on the broad, old-fashioned window seat, and leaned her cheek against the leaded panes of glass. The bees were humming outside. She listened to their music. It was dull and dreamy, heavy like a golden noon in summer time. And then the white lids fell over her eyes, and the hum of the bees faded from her ears, and she heard another music that made her woman's heart leap up, she heard the first tiny murmur of a new-born child.

It was sweeter than the hum of bees. It was sweeter than the soul the lute gave up to the ears of Nature when Orpheus touched the strings. It was so sweet that tears came stealing from under Lily's eyelids and dropped down upon her clasped hands. She sat there motionless till the twilight came over the moor, and Maurice entered, white and weary, to ask impatiently of what she was dreaming.

As Maurice wished it, they returned the next day to Brayfield and settled into the house that was to be their home. It stood on a low cliff overlooking the sea; a broad green lawn, on which during the season a band played and people promenaded, lay in front of it. Beyond, the waves danced in the sunshine. The situation of the house was almost absurdly cheerful, and the house itself was new and prettily furnished. But the life into which Lily entered was strangely at variance with the surroundings, strangely antagonistic to the brightness of the sea, the sweetness of the air, the holiday gaiety that pervaded the little town in the summer. For work did not abolish, did not even lull the sound of the voice that pursued Maurice with an inexorable persistence. It was obvious that on his return home after the honeymoon, he made a tremendous effort to get the better of his enemy. He called up all his manhood, all his strength of character. He refused to hear the voice. When it cried in his ears, he went to sit with Lily, and plunged into conversation on subjects that interested them both. He made her play to him, or sing to him in the twilight. He read aloud to her. This was at night. By day he worked unremittingly. When he was not driving to see patients he laboured to increase his knowledge of medicine. He pursued the most subtle investigations into the causes of obscure diseases, and specially directed his enquiries towards the pathology of the brain. He analysed the multitudinous developments of madness and traced them back to their beginnings; and when, as was often the case, he discovered that the mad man or woman whose malady was laid bare to him had inherited this curse of humanity, he smiled with a momentary thrill of joy. His ancestors on both sides of the family had been sane. Yet one of the commonest, most invariable delusions of the insane was the imaginary idea that they were pursued by voices, ordering them to do this or that, suggesting crimes to them or weeping in their ears over some tragedy of the past. Maurice knew that the mind which does not inherit a legacy of insanity may yet be overturned by some terrible incident, by a great shock, or by an unexpected bereavement. But surely such a mind would be aware of its transformation, even as a man who, from an accident, becomes disfigured is aware of the alteration of his face from beauty to desolation. Maurice was not aware that his mind had been transformed. Deliberately, calmly, he asked himself, "Am I insane?" Deliberately, calmly, his soul answered, "No." Yet the cry of the child rang in his ears, pursued his goings out and comings in, filled his days with lamentation, and his nights with horror.

Then, leaving the subject of madness, Maurice began to institute a close investigation into the subject of alleged hauntings of human beings by apparitions and by sounds. He read of the actress, whose lover, who had slain himself in despair at her cruelty, remained for ever with her, manifesting his presence, although invisible, by cries, curses, and clappings of the hands. He read of the clergyman who was haunted by the footsteps of his murdered sweetheart, which even ascended the pulpit stairs behind him, and pattered furtively about him when he knelt to pray for pardon of his sin. He filled his mind with visionary terrors, but they seemed remote or even ridiculous to him, and he said to himself that they were the clever inventions of imaginative people. They were worked up. They were moulded into conventional stories. They pleased the magazines of their time. He alone was really haunted of all men in the world, so far as he knew. And then a great and greedy desire came upon him to meet some other man in a like case, to hear from live lips the true and undecorated history of a despair like his own, one of those bald and terse narratives which pierce the imagination of the hearer like a sword, with no tinselled scabbard of exaggeration and of lies. He wondered whether upon the earth a man walked in a darkness similar to that which fell round him like a veil. He wondered whether he was unique, even as he felt. Sometimes he caught himself looking furtively at a harmless stranger, a bright girl tanned by the sea, or a lad just back from a fishing excursion to Raynor's Bay, and saying to himself low and drearily: "Does any spirit trouble you, I wonder? Does any spirit cry to you in the night?" But neither his work, his excursions of the imagination, nor the presence of Lily in his house, availed to cleanse the life of Maurice from the stain of sound, that ever widened and spread upon it. He fought for freedom for a while, strenuously, with all his heart and soul. But the lost battle left him with his energies exhausted, his courage broken. One night he said to Lily:

"Do you know all I have been doing since we came back here?"

"Yes, Maurice, I know."

"And that it has all been in vain," he said, with a passion of bitterness that he could not try to conceal.

"That too I understand, Maurice—I knew it would be in vain."

He looked at her almost as at an enemy, for his heart was so full of misery, his mind was so worn with weariness, that he began to lose the true appreciation of human relations, and to confuse the beauty near him with the ugliness that companioned him so closely.

"You knew it? What do you mean?" he said. "How could you know it?"

"I felt it, Maurice; do not try any longer to work out alone your own redemption."

"You can say that to me?"

"Yes, for I believe that it is useless—you will fail."

He set his lips together and said nothing. But a frown distorted his face slowly.

"Leave your redemption to God. Oh, Maurice, leave it," Lily said, and there were tears in her eyes. "If this cry of the dead child is his punishment to you it must—it will—endure so long as he pleases. Your efforts cannot still it now. You yourself told me so once."

"I told you?"

"Yes—for the dead are beyond our hands and our lips. We cannot clasp them. We cannot kiss them. We cannot speak to them."

"But they can speak to us and mock us. You are right. I can't still the cry—I can't! Then it's all over with me!"

Suddenly, with a sob, Maurice flung himself down. He felt as if something within him snapped, and as if straightway a dissolution of all the man in him succeeded this rupture of the spirit. Careless of the pride of man, before the world and even in his own home, he gave himself up to a despair that was too weak to be frantic, too complete to be angry; a despair that no longer strove but yielded, that lay down in the dust and wept. Then, presently, raising his head and seeing Lily, in whose eyes were tears of pity, Maurice was seized with an enmity against her, unreasonably wicked, but suddenly so vehement that he did not try to resist it.

"You have broken me," he said. "You have told me that there is no redemption, that I am in the hands of God, who persecutes me. You have told me the truth and made me hate you."

"Maurice!"

The cry came from her lips faintly, but there was the ring of anguish in it.

"It is so," he repeated doggedly. "And, indeed, I believe that you have added to the weight of my burden. Since we have been married the persecution has increased. Once, when I was alone, I could bear it. Now you are here I cannot bear it. The child hates you. When you are near—in the night—its cry is so intense that I wonder you can sleep. Yet I hear your quiet breathing. You say you love me. Then why are you so calm? Why do you tell me to trust? Why do you hint that I may yet find peace, and then tell me to cease from working for my own peace? You don't love me, you laugh at my trouble. You despise me."

He burst out of the room almost like a man demented.

It might be supposed that Lily, who loved him, would have been overwhelmed by this ecstasy of anger against her. But there was something that sheathed her heart from death. She might be wounded, she might suffer; but she looked beyond the present time, over the desert of her fate to roses of a future that Maurice, in his misery, could not see, in his self-engrossment could not divine. There is no living thing that understands how to wait, that can feel the beauty of patience, as a woman understands and feels. The curious depth of calm in Lily which irritated Maurice was created by a faith, half religious, half unreasoning, wholly strong and determined, such as no man ever knows in quite the same fullness as a woman. It is such a perfection of faith which gilds the silences in which the souls of many women wait, surrounded by the clouds of apparently shattered lives, but conscious that there is a great outcome, obscure and remote, but certain as the purpose which beats forever in Creation.

From that day Maurice no longer kept up a pretence of energy, or a simulation of even tolerable happiness in his home. The idea that the spirit of the dead child was stirred to an intense disquietude by his connection with Lily, and that, consequently, his marriage had deepened his punishment, grew in him until at length it became fixed. He brooded over it for hours together, his ears full of that eternal complaining. He began to feel that by linking himself with Lily he had added to his original sin, that his wedding had been a ceremony almost criminal, and that if he had scourged himself by living ascetically, and by putting rigorously away from him all earthly happiness, he might at last have laid the child to rest and found peace and forgiveness himself. And this fixed idea led him to shut Lily entirely out from his heart. He looked upon the fate of her being with him in the house as irrevocable. But he resolved that he ought to disassociate himself from her as far as possible, and, without explaining further to her the thought that now possessed him, he ceased to sit with her, ceased to walk out with her.

After dinner at night he retired to his study leaving her alone in the drawing-room. He let her go up to bed without bidding her good-night. When he was obliged to be with her at meals he maintained for the most part an obstinate silence.

Yet the cry of the child grew louder. The spirit of the child was not mollified. Its persecution continued and seemed to him to grow more persistent with each passing day.

What else could he do? How could he separate himself more completely from Lily?

Canon Alston came one day to solve this problem for him. The Canon had resolved on taking a holiday, and being no lover of solitude in his pleasures, he wished to persuade Maurice to become a grass widower for three weeks.

"Can you let Lily go?" he said. "I know it is a shame to leave you alone, but—"

He stopped, surprised at the sudden brightness that had come into Maurice's usually pale and grave face. Maurice saw his astonishment and hastened to allay it.

"I shall miss Lily of course," he began. "Still, if you want her, and she is anxious to go—"

"I have not mentioned it to her," the Canon said.

And at this moment Lily came into the room. The project was laid before her. She hesitated, looking from her father to her husband. Her perplexity seemed to both the men curiously acute, even to Maurice who was on fire to hear her decision. The prospect of solitude was sweet to his tormented heart now that he was possessed by the fancy that Lily's presence intensified his martyrdom. Yet Lily's obvious disturbance of mind surprised him. The two courses open to her were really so simple that there seemed no possible reason why she should look upon the taking of one of them as a momentous matter.

"Well, Lily, what do you say?" the Canon asked, after a pause. "Will you come with me?"

"But Maurice—"

"Maurice permits it, and I want you."

"I—I had not meant to leave home at present, father, not till after—"

She stopped abruptly.

"Till after what, my dear?" enquired the Canon.

She made no answer.

"Lily," Maurice said, trying to make his voice cool and indifferent, "I think you ought to go. It will do you good. Do not mind me. I shall manage very well for a little while."

"You would rather I went, Maurice?"

"I think we ought not to let your father go on his holiday alone."

"I will go," she said quietly.

So it was arranged. The Canon was jubilant at the prospect of his daughter's company, and asked her where they should travel.

"What do you say to the English Lakes, Lily?" he asked, "they are lovely at this time of year, and the rush of the tourist season has scarcely begun. Shall we go there?"

"Wherever you like, father," she said.

The Canon was feeling too gay to notice the preoccupation of her manner, the ungirlish gravity of her voice. That day, in the evening, when she was at dinner with Maurice, Lily said:

"You lived near the Lakes once, didn't you, Maurice?"

"Yes," he said.

"What was the name of the valley?"

He told her.

"And the house?"

"End Cottage. It was close to the waterfall. I hate it," he added almost fiercely. "It was there that I first heard—but I have told you."

He relapsed into silence and sent away the food on his plate untasted. Lily glanced across at him. But she said nothing more. And Maurice was struck by the consciousness that she took his strangeness strangely, with a lack of curiosity, a lack of protestation unlike a woman; almost for the first time since they were married he was moved to wonder how much she loved him, indeed whether she still loved him at all. He had got up from the dinner table and stood with one hand leaning upon it as he looked steadily, with his heavy and hunted eyes, across at Lily.

"Are you glad to go with the Canon?" he asked.

"I am quite ready to go," she said quietly.

"You don't mind leaving me?"

"I think you wish me to leave you—"

"Perhaps I do," he said, watching her to see if she winced at the words.

But her face was still and calm.

"What then?"

"Then it is better for me to go for a little while than to stay."

"For a little while," he repeated, "yes."

He turned and went slowly out of the room, and suddenly his face was distorted. For, in the darkness of the hall, he heard the child crying and lamenting. He stopped and listened to it like a man who resolutely faces his destruction. And, as so many times, he asked himself; "Is this a freak of my imagination, a trick of my nerves?" No, the sound was surely real, was close to him. It thrilled in his ears keenly. He could not doubt its reality. Yet he acknowledged to himself that he could not actually locate it. Only in that respect did it differ from other sounds of earth. As he stood in the half darkness, listening, a horror, greater than he had ever felt before, came over him. The cry seemed to him menacing, no longer merely a cry for sympathy, for assistance, no longer merely the cry of a helpless creature in pain. He turned white and sick, and clapped his two hands to his ears. And just as he did so the dining-room door opened and Lily came out, a thin stream of light following her and falling upon Maurice. He started at the vision of her and at the revealing illumination. His nerves were quivering. His whole body seemed to vibrate.

"Don't come near me," he cried out to Lily. "It is worse since you are with me. Your presence makes my danger. Ah!"

And with a cry he dashed into his study, banging the door behind him, as if he fled from her.

A few days later Maurice stood at the garden gate and helped Lily into the carriage that was to take her to the station. A summons to a patient prevented him from seeing her and the Canon off on their journey northwards. Just before Lily put her foot on the step she stopped and wavered.

"Wait a moment," she said.

She ran back into the little house which had been her home since she was married. Maurice supposed that she had forgotten something. But she only peeped into her bedroom, into the gay drawing-room, into Maurice's den. And as she looked at this last little chamber, at the books, the ruffled writing-table, the pipes ranged against the wall, her photograph standing in a silver frame upon the mantelpiece, her eyes filled with tears, and there was a stricken feeling at her heart.

"Lily, you will miss the train," Maurice called to her.

She hurried out, got into the carriage and was driven away, wondering why she had gone back to take a last glance at her home, why she had scarcely been able to see it for her tears.

That evening Maurice returned from his round of visits in a curious state of excitement and of anticipation, mingled with nervous dread. He felt as if the eyes of the dead child were upon all his doings, as if the mind of the dead child pondered every act of his, as if the brain of the dead child were busy about his life, as if the soul of the dead child concerned itself for ever with his soul, which it had secretly dedicated to a loneliness assured now by the departure of Lily. By living alone, even for a few weeks, was he not in a measure obeying the desire of the little spirit, which possessed his fate like some inexorable Providence? If so, dare he not hope for an interval of peace, for that stillness after which he longed with an anxiety that was like a physical pain?

He entered his house. Twilight was falling, and the hall, in which on the previous night the child had complained in so grievous a manner, was shadowy. He stood there and listened. He heard the distant wash of the sea, the voices of two servants talking together behind the swing door that led to the kitchen. No sound mingled with the sea, or with the chattering voices. Slowly he ascended the stairs and entered the bedroom, in which Lily had slept quietly, while he, by her side, endured the persecution of the child. The blinds were up. The dying daylight crept slowly from the room, making an exit as furtive and suppressed as that of one who steals from a death chamber. Maurice sat down upon the bed and again listened for a long time.

He was conscious of the sense of relief which comes upon a man who, through some sudden act, has removed from his shoulders a terrible burden. He took this present silence to himself as a reward. But would it last? Opening the window he leaned out to hear the sea more plainly. All living voices, whether of Nature or of man, were beautiful to him, they had come to make his silence.

A servant knocked at the door. Maurice went down to dine. He passed the late evening as usual in his study. He slept calmly. He woke—to silence. Did not this silence confirm his fixed idea that his marriage with Lily had vexed that wakeful spirit, had troubled that unquiet soul of the child? Maurice, wrapped in a beautiful peace, felt that it did. And, as the silent lovely days, the silent lovely nights passed on he came gradually to a fixed resolve.

Lily must not return to him, must not live with him again.

He pondered for a long time how he was to compass their further separation. And, at length, he sat down and wrote a letter to Lily telling her the exact truth.

"Think me cruel, selfish," he wrote at the end of his letter. "I am cruel. I am selfish. Despair has made me so. The fear of madness has made me so. I must have peace. I must and will have it, at whatever cost."

He sent this letter to the *poste restante* at Windermere, as Lily had directed. She and her father were moving about in the Lake district, and did not know from day to day where they might be. He received a reply within a week. It reached him at breakfast time, and, happening to glance at the postmark before he opened it, his face suddenly flushed and his heart beat with violence. For the letter came from that lonely village in that sequestered mountain valley in which he had once lived, in which he had first heard the cry of the child. What chance had led Lily's steps there? Maurice read the letter eagerly. It was very gentle, very submissive. And there was one strange passage in it:

"I understand that you are at peace," Lily wrote. "Yet the child is not at peace. It is crying still. You will ask me how I know that. Do not ask me now. Some day I shall send for you and tell you. When I send for you, if it is by day or night, promise that you will come to me. I claim this promise from you. And now good-bye for a time. My father is very unhappy about us. But he trusts me completely, and I have told him that you and I must be apart, but only for a time. I shall not write to you again till I send for you. Even my letter may disturb your peace and I would give up my life to give you peace."

There was no allusion in the letter to the reason which had led Lily and her father to the out-of-the-way valley which had seen the dawn of Maurice's despair. And Maurice was greatly puzzled. Again there came over him a curious conviction that Lily had some secret from him, some secret connected with his fate, and that she was waiting for the arrival of some day, fixed in her mind, on which to make a revelation of her knowledge to him. This mention of an eventual summons, "by day or night." What could it mean otherwise? Maurice read the letter again and again. Its last words touched him by their perfect unselfishness and also by their feminine romance. He had a moment's thought of the many emotional stories Lily had read. "She lives in one now," he said to himself. And then, as usual, he became self-engrossed, saw only his own life, possibly touched for ever with a light of peace.

The Canon returned alone. He met Maurice gravely, almost sternly.

"I trust my child entirely," he said. "She has told me that for a time you must live apart. She has made me promise not to ask you the reason of this separation. I don't ask it, but if you—"

His voice broke and he turned away for a moment. Then he said:

"Lily remains in the place from which she wrote to you."

"She is going to live there!" Maurice exclaimed.

"For the present, I could not persuade her otherwise. Her old nurse, Mrs. Whitehead, is going up to be with her. I cannot understand all this."

The old man cast his eyes searchingly upon Maurice.

"What—?" he began, then, remembering his promise to his daughter, he stopped short.

"We will talk no more about this," he said slowly. "No more."

He bade Maurice good-bye and returned, sorrowful, to the Rectory.

Lily kept her word. Maurice had no more letters from her. He only heard of her from the Canon, and knew that she remained in that beautiful and terrible valley, which he remembered so vividly and hated so ardently. Meanwhile he dwelt in a peace that was strange to him. The little voice had gone out of his life. The cry of the child was hushed. Often, in the past, Maurice had contemplated the coming of this exquisite silence, but he had always imagined it as a gradual approach. He had fancied that if the lamentation of the child ever died out of his haunted life it would fade away as the sound of the sea fades on a long strand when the whispering tide goes down. Day by day, night by night, her crying would grow less poignant, less distinct in a long diminuendo, as if the restless spirit withdrew slowly farther and farther away, till the cry became a whisper, then a broken murmur, then—nothing. This abrupt cessation of persecution, this violent change from something that had seemed like menace to perfect immunity from trouble, was a fact that Maurice had never thought of as a possibility. He had grown to believe that Lily's presence in his home intensified the terror from which he suffered, certainly. But he had never supposed that her removal from him would lay the spirit entirely to rest. And she said that it was not at rest. How could she know that? And if it were not at rest, in what region was it pursuing its weird activity? Whither had it gone? He wondered long and deeply. And then he resolved to wonder no more. Peace had come to him at last. He would not break it by questioning the reason of it. He would accept it blindly, joyfully. Man blots the sunshine out of life by asking "Why?"

Time passed on. Brayfield had gossiped, marvelled and sunk into a sort of apathy of unrewarded and quiescent curiosity. The Canon pursued his life at the Rectory. Maurice visited his patients and continued unremittingly his medical researches. The immunity he now enjoyed gradually wrought a great change in him. He emerged from prison into the outer air. His health rapidly improved. His heavy eyes grew bright. His mind was active and alert. He was a new man. The darkness faded round him. He saw the light at last. For the silence endured. And at last he even forgot to listen, at dawn or in the silent hours of the night, for the cry of the child. Even the memory of it began to grow faint within his heart. So rapidly does man forget his troubles when he still has youth and the years are not heavy on him.

Yet Maurice often thought of Lily. And now that he was no longer bowed under the tyranny of a shattered nervous system he felt a new tenderness for her. He recalled her devotion and no longer linked her with his persecution. He remembered her unselfishness. He wished her back again. And then—he remembered all his misery, and that, with her, it went. And his selfishness said to him—it is better so. And his mental cowardice whispered to him—your safety is in your solitude. And he put the memory of Lily's love and of the beauty of her nature from him.

So his silent autumn passed by. And his silent winter came. One day, in a December frost, he met the Canon, muffled up to the chin and on his way to see Miss Bigelow, who professed herself once again *in extremis*. They stopped in the snow and spoke a few commonplace words, but Maurice thought he observed a peculiar furtiveness in the old man's manner, a hint of some suppressed excitement in his voice.

"How is Lily?" Maurice asked.

"Fairly well," the Canon said.

"She is still at the inn?"

"No, she lately moved into a little house further up the valley."

"Further up the valley," Maurice said. "But there's only one other house in that direction. I have been there you know," he added hastily.

"Lily told me you had stayed there."

"Well, but—" Maurice persisted, "there is only one house, a private house."

"They have been building up there," the Canon said evasively. "Houses are springing up. It is a pity. Good-night."

And he turned and walked away. Maurice stood looking after him. So they had been building in the valley, and End Cottage no longer possessed the distinction of being the finale of man in that Arcadia of woods and streams, and rugged hills on which the clouds brooded, from which the rain came like a mournful pilgrim, to weep over the gentle shrine of nature.

So they had been building in the valley.

Maurice made his way home. His mind was full of memories.

The close of the year drew on. It was a bad season, a cruel season for the poor. Men went about saying to one another that it was a hard winter. The papers were full of reports of abnormal frosts, of tremendous falls of snow, of ice-bound rivers and trains delayed. There were deaths from cold. The starving died off like flies, under hedges by roadsides, in the fireless attics of towns. Comfortable and well-to-do persons talked vigorously of the delights of an old-fashioned Christmas. The doctors had many patients. Among them Maurice was very busy. His talent had monopolised Brayfield and his time was incessantly occupied. He scarcely noticed Christmas. For even on that day he was full of work. Several people managed to be very ill among the plum puddings. The year died and was buried. The New Year dawned, and still the evil weather continued. In early January Maurice came down one morning to find by his plate a letter written in a hand of old age, straggling and complicated. It proved to be from Mrs. Whitehead, Lily's old nurse; and it contained that summons of which Lily had spoken long ago in her letter to her husband. Lily was ill and wished to see Maurice at once. The letter, though involved, was urgent.

Maurice laid it down. There was a date on it but no name of a house. By the date Maurice saw that the letter had been delayed in transit. Blizzards, snow-storms, had been responsible for many such delays. He got up from the table. At that moment there was no hesitation in his mind. He would go to Lily at once, as fast as rail could carry him. In a few moments his luggage was packed. Within an hour he was on his way to the station. He stopped the carriage at the Rectory and asked to see the Canon for a moment. The servant, looking reproachful, told him her master had started three days before to see "Miss Lily," who was ill.

"Miss Lily," Maurice said. "You mean Mrs. Dale. I am on my way to see her too. What is the matter? They do not tell me."

"I don't know, sir," the servant said, softening a little on learning that Maurice was going north to his wife.

Maurice drove on to the station.

In all his after life he never could forget his white journey. It seemed to him as if nature gathered herself together to delay him, to turn him from his purpose of obeying the summons of Lily. Even the line from Brayfield to London was blocked, and when at length Maurice reached London he found the great city staggering under a burden of snow that rendered its features unrecognisable. All traffic was practically suspended. He missed train after train, and when he drove at last into Euston Station and expressed his intention of going north by the night mail the porter shook his head and drew a terrible picture of that arctic region.

"Most of the lines are blocked, sir," he said, "or will be. It's a-coming on for more snow."

"I can't help that," Maurice said. "I must go. Label my luggage."

The train was due to start at midnight. Maurice had a lonely dinner at the station hotel. While he ate in the gaily lighted coffee-room he thought of Lily and of his coming journey. The influence of the weather had surrounded it with a curious romance such as English travel seldom affords. Maurice was very susceptible to the mental atmosphere engendered by outward circumstances, and yielded more readily than the average man to the wayward promptings of the faithful spirit that nestles somewhere in almost every intellect. He began to regard this white journey to the ice-bound and rugged north with something of a child's wide-eyed, half-delighted, half-alarmed anticipation. He thought of the darkness, of the dangers by the way, of the multitudes of lonely snow-wreathed miles the train would have to cover; of the increasing cold as they went higher and higher up the land, of the early dawn over fells and stone walls, of the grey light on the grey sea. Then he listened to the strangely muffled roar of a London hoarse with cold. And he shivered and had feelings of a man bound on some tremendous and novel quest. As he came out of the hotel the wintry air met him and embraced him. He entered the station, dull and sinister in the night, with its haggard gas-lamps and arches yawning to the snow. There were few passengers, and they looked anxious. The train drew in. Maurice had his carriage to himself. The porter wished him good luck on his journey with the voice and manner of one clearly foreseeing imminent disaster and death. The whistle sounded, and the train glided, a long black and orange snake, into the white wonder of the clouded night. Snow beat upon the windows, incrusted with the filagree work of frost, and as the speed of the train increased the carriage filled with the persistent music of an intense and sustained activity. This music, and the thoughts of Maurice fought against sleep. He leaned back with open eyes and listened to the song of the train. Its monotony was like the monotony of an irritable man, he thought, always angry, always expressing his anger. Beneath bridges, in tunnels, the anger was dashed with ripples of fury, with spurts of brutalising passion. And then the normal current of dull temper flowed on again as before. Maurice wished that the windows were not merely thick white blinds completely shutting out the night. He longed to see the storm in which they fled towards greater storms, the country which they spurned as they sprang northwards! Northwards! And to that valley!

His thoughts went to his old life alone there, to the coming into it of the haunting voice, to his terror, his struggle, his flight southward. He had never thought to return there. Yet now he fled towards that place of memories, calm, sane, cleansed of persecution, with his mind fortified, and his heart steadily and calmly beating, unshaken by the agonies of old. Was he the same man? It seemed almost impossible. And now Maurice said to himself again that perhaps after all the cry of the child had been imagination, a symptom of illness in him from which he had—perhaps even through some obscure physical change—recovered completely. Yet Lily had believed in the cry and believed in the unquiet spirit behind it. But women are romantic, credulous—

The train rocked in a rapture of motion. Maurice drew his rugs more closely round him. With the advance of night the cold grew more deadly.

Towards morning the pace of the train incessantly decreased. Huge masses of snow had drifted upon the line. For a rising wind drove it together under hedgerows and walls until expanding upon the track, it impeded the progress of the engines. Maurice let down a window and peered out. He saw only snow, stationary or floating, at rest in shadowy heaps that fled back in the darkness, or falling in a veil before his eyes. It seemed to him now as if a hand were stretched out to stay his impetuous advance to Lily. The train went slower and slower. At last, towards morning, it stopped. A long and distracted whistling pierced the air. There was a jerk, a movement forward, then another stoppage. They were snowed up in the middle of a desolate stretch of country, with a blizzard raging round them.

How many hours passed before they were released Maurice never knew. He lay wrapped up to the eyes, numbed and passive, of body, but mentally travelling with an extraordinary rapidity. At first he was in the valley. He saw it, as he had seen it in old days, in snow, its river ice-bound, its waterfall arrested in the midst of an army of crystal spears. White mountains rose round it to a low sky, curved, like a bosom, in grey cloud shapes. The air was sharp and silent, clearer than southern air, a thing that seemed to hold itself alert in its narrow prison on the edge of solitude. He heard the bark of a dog on the hills, in search of the starving sheep.

Then he came to one of those new houses of which the Canon had spoken, and in it he found Lily. She was pale, but he scarcely noticed that, engrossed in the strangeness of finding her there. For in the south he had never fully realised Lily at home in the valley, walking on the desolate narrow roads by day, sleeping in the shadow of the hills by night. Now he began to realise her there. Where would the house be? Near End Cottage, perhaps in sight of the garden to which he had stolen on that evil night to listen for the voice of a bird!

After many hours the train was dug out of the snow, and sped forward again in daylight. Maurice slept a little, but uneasily. And now, when he was awake, he began to be filled with an unreasonable apprehension, for which he accounted by taking stock of the low temperature of his body, and of the loss of vitality occasioned by want of food and rest. He was seized with fear as he came up into the north and saw vaguely the moors around him, the snowy waves where the white woods rippled up the flanks of the white hills. He began to realise again his former condition when his life was full of the lamentation of the child. He began to feel as if he drew near to that lamentation once more. Perhaps the little sorrowful spirit had only deserted him to return to the valley in which it first greeted him. Perhaps it would come again to him there. He might hear the cry from the garden of the cottage as he hastened past.

He shuddered and cursed his wild fancies. But they stayed with him through all the rest of the journey, through all the delays and periods of numb patience. And they increased upon him. When at last he reached the dreary station by the flat sandbanks, at which he changed into the valley train, he was pale and careworn, and full of alarm.

Very slowly the tiny train crawled up into the heart of the hills as the darkness of the second night came down. Maurice was the only passenger in it. He felt like one alone in a lonely world, fearing inhabitants unseen, but whose distant presence he was aware of. Could Lily indeed be here, beyond him in this desolation? It seemed impossible. But the child might be here, wandering, a lost spirit, in this unutterable winter. That would not be strange to him. And his soul grew colder than his body. He could see nothing from the window, but occasionally he heard the dry tapping of twigs upon the glass, as the train crept among the leafless woods. And this tapping seemed to him to be the tiny fingers of the child, feebly endeavouring to attract his attention. He shrank away from the window to the centre of the carriage.

At the last station in the valley the train stopped. Maurice got out into the darkness, and asked the guard the name of the house in which Mrs. Dale lived.

"Mrs. Dale," he said, in the broad Cumberland dialect, "Oh, she bides at End Cottage."

Maurice stared at his rugged face peering above the round lamp which he held.

"End Cottage?"

"Yes, sir. The poor lady took it on a six months' lease, but I hear she's—"

But Maurice had turned away with a muttered:

"I'll send up for the luggage."

He stumbled out into the white lane and through the little village. One or two lads, roughly dressed and sprinkled with snowflakes, eyed him from the shelter of the inn porch. As he moved past them, he heard their muttered comments. He left the houses behind and found himself among snow-laden trees. End Cottage was hidden in this narrow wood which was generally full of the sound of the waterfall.

Now the waterfall was silent, motionless, a dead thing in a rocky grave. Maurice saw a faint and misty light among the bare trees. It came from his old home, and now his hand touched the white garden gate, prickly with ice. He pushed it open and stole up the path till he reached the little porch of the cottage. As he stood there his heart beat hard and his breath fluttered in his throat. It seemed to him that there must be some strange and terrible meaning in Lily's presence here. With a shaking hand he pulled at the bell. He waited. No one came. He heard no step. The silence was dense, even appalling. After a long pause he turned the handle of the door, opened it, and stood on the threshold of the cottage. Instead of entering at once he waited, listening for any sound of life within the house, for the voices or footsteps of those inhabiting it.

Just so had he waited on a summer night long ago, with the moon behind him and leaf-laden trees. He listened, and, after a moment of profound stillness, he heard—as he had heard in that very place so long ago—the faint cry of a child. It came from within the house, clear and distinct though frail and feeble.

Involuntarily Maurice moved a step backward into the snow. Horror overwhelmed him. The dead child was here then with Lily, in his old abode. The spirit was not laid to rest. It had only deserted him for a while to greet him again here, to take up again here its eternal persecution; and this resurrection appalled and unmanned him more than all the persistent haunting of the past. He was dashed from confidence to despair. The little cry paralysed him, and he leaned against the wall of the porch almost like a dying man.

And again he heard the cry of the child.

How live and how real it was! Maurice remembered that he had said to himself that the cry was a phantasy of the brain, an imaginary sound vibrating from an afflicted body. And now his intellect denied such a supposition; the cry came from a thing that lived, although it lived in another world. It seemed to summon him with a strange insistence. Against his will, and walking slowly as one in a trance, he moved forward up the narrow stairway till he reached the room that had been his old bedroom.

The cry came surely from within that room. The dead child was shut in there. Yes, never before had Maurice been able to locate the cry precisely. Now he could locate it. With shaking fingers he grasped the handle of the door. He stood in a faint illumination, and the cry of the child came louder to his ears. But there mingled with it another cry, faint yet thrilling with joy:

"Maurice!"

He looked and saw Lily, white as a flower. She was propped on pillows, and, stretching out her thin girl's arms, she held feebly towards Maurice a tiny baby.

"Maurice—it is the child!" she whispered.

"The child!" he repeated hoarsely.

For an instant he believed that his fate was sealed, that the spirit, which for so long had pursued him with its lamenting, now manifested its actual presence to his eyes. Then, in a flash, the truth came upon him. He fell upon his knees by the bedside and put out his arms for the child. He held it. He felt its soft breath against his cheek. A cooing murmur, as if of tiny happiness, came from its parted lips. It turned its little face, flushed like a rose, against the breast of Maurice, and nestled to sleep upon his heart.

And Lily's hand touched him.

"I thought you would not come in time," she said, as the nurse, at a sign from her, stole softly from the room.

"In time?"

"To see me before—they say, you know, that—"

"Lily!" he cried.

"Hush! The child! Listen, dear. If I die, take the child. It is your dead child, I think, come to life through me. Yes, yes, it is the little child that has cried for love so long. Redeem your cruelty, oh, Maurice, redeem it to your child. Give it your love. Give it your life. Give it—"

"Lily!" he said again. And there were tears on his cheeks.

"I gave myself to you for this, Maurice. I was waiting for this. Do you understand me now? You scarcely loved me, Maurice. But I loved you. Let me think—in dying—that I have brought you peace at last."

He could not speak. The mystery of woman, the mystery of child was too near to him. Awe came upon him and the terror of his own unworthiness, rewarded—or punished—which was it?—by such compassion, such self-sacrifice.

"When I left you," Lily murmured, and her voice sounded thin and tired, "it seemed as if the spirit of the child came with me, as if I, too, heard its dead voice in the night, crying for its salvation, for its relief from agony. But, Maurice, you cannot hear it now. You will never hear it again—unless—unless—"

She fixed her eyes on him. They were growing dim.

"God has given the dead to you again through me," she faltered, "that you—may—redeem—redeem—your—sin."

She moved, and leaned against him, as if she would gather him and the sleeping child into her embrace. But she could not. She slipped back softly, almost like a snowflake that falls and is gone.

Maurice Dale is a famous doctor now. He lives with his daughter, who never leaves him and whom he loves passionately. Many patients throng to his consulting-room, but not one of them suspects that the grave physician, deep down in his heart, cherishes a strange belief—not based upon science. This belief is connected with his child. Secretly he thinks of her as of one risen from the grave, come back to him from beyond the gates of death.

The cry of the child is silent. Maurice never hears it now. But he believes that could any demon tempt him, even for one moment, to be cruel to his little daughter, he would hear it again. It would lament once more in the darkness, would once more fill the silence with its despair.

And then a dead woman would stir in her grave.

For there are surely cries of earth that even the dead can hear.

HOW LOVE CAME TO PROFESSOR GUILDEA

Dull people often wondered how it came about that Father Murchison and Professor Frederic Guildea were intimate friends. The one was all faith, the other all scepticism. The nature of the Father was based on love. He viewed the world with an almost childlike tenderness above his long, black cassock; and his mild, yet perfectly fearless, blue eyes seemed always to be watching the goodness that exists in humanity, and rejoicing at what they saw. The Professor, on the other hand, had a hard face like a hatchet, tipped with an aggressive black goatee beard. His eyes were quick, piercing and irreverent. The lines about his small, thin-lipped mouth were almost cruel. His voice was harsh and dry, sometimes, when he grew energetic, almost soprano. It fired off words with a sharp and clipping utterance. His habitual manner was one of distrust and investigation. It was impossible to suppose that, in his busy life, he found any time for love, either of humanity in general or of an individual.

Yet his days were spent in scientific investigations which conferred immense benefits upon the world.

Both men were celibates. Father Murchison was a member of an Anglican order which forbade him to marry. Professor Guildea had a poor opinion of most things, but especially of women. He had formerly held a post as lecturer at Birmingham. But when his fame as a discoverer grew he removed to London. There, at a lecture he gave in the East End, he first met Father Murchison. They spoke a few words. Perhaps the bright intelligence of the priest appealed to the man of science, who was inclined, as a rule, to regard the clergy with some contempt. Perhaps the transparent sincerity of this devotee, full of common sense, attracted him. As he was leaving the hall he abruptly asked the Father to call on him at his house in Hyde Park Place. And the Father, who seldom went into the West End, except to preach, accepted the invitation.

"When will you come?" said Guildea.

He was folding up the blue paper on which his notes were written in a tiny, clear hand. The leaves rustled drily in accompaniment to his sharp, dry voice.

"On Sunday week I am preaching in the evening at St. Saviour's, not far off," said the Father.

"I don't go to church."

"No," said the Father, without any accent of surprise or condemnation.

"Come to supper afterwards?"

"Thank you. I will."

"What time will you come?"

The Father smiled.

"As soon as I have finished my sermon. The service is at six-thirty."

"About eight then, I suppose. Don't make the sermon too long. My number in Hyde Park Place is a hundred. Good-night to you."

He snapped an elastic band round his papers and strode off without shaking hands.

On the appointed Sunday, Father Murchison preached to a densely crowded congregation at St. Saviour's. The subject of his sermon was sympathy, and the comparative uselessness of man in the world unless he can learn to love his neighbour as himself. The sermon was rather long, and when the preacher, in his flowing, black cloak, and his hard, round hat, with a straight brim over which hung the ends of a black cord, made his way towards the Professor's house, the hands of the illuminated clock disc at the Marble Arch pointed to twenty minutes past eight.

The Father hurried on, pushing his way through the crowd of standing soldiers, chattering women and giggling street boys in their Sunday best. It was a warm April night, and, when he reached number 100, Hyde Park Place, he found the Professor bareheaded on his doorstep, gazing out towards the Park railings, and enjoying the soft, moist air, in front of his lighted passage.

"Ha, a long sermon!" he exclaimed. "Come in."

"I fear it was," said the Father, obeying the invitation. "I am that dangerous thing—an extempore preacher."

"More attractive to speak without notes, if you can do it. Hang your hat and coat—oh, cloak—here. We'll have supper at once. This is the dining-room."

He opened a door on the right and they entered a long, narrow room, with a gold paper and a black ceiling, from which hung an electric lamp with a gold-coloured shade. In the room stood a small oval table with covers laid for two. The Professor rang the bell. Then he said,

"People seem to talk better at an oval table than at a square one."

"Really. Is that so?"

"Well, I've had precisely the same party twice, once at a square table, once at an oval table. The first dinner was a dull failure, the second a brilliant success. Sit down, won't you?"

"How d'you account for the difference?" said the Father, sitting down, and pulling the tail of his cassock well under him.

"H'm. I know how you'd account for it."

"Indeed. How then?"

"At an oval table, since there are no corners, the chain of human sympathy—the electric current, is much more complete. Eh! Let me give you some soup."

"Thank you."

The Father took it, and, as he did so, turned his beaming blue eyes on his host. Then he smiled.

"What!" he said, in his pleasant, light tenor voice. "You do go to church sometimes, then?"

"To-night is the first time for ages. And, mind you, I was tremendously bored."

The Father still smiled, and his blue eyes gently twinkled.

"Dear, dear!" he said, "what a pity!"

"But not by the sermon," Guildea added. "I don't pay a compliment. I state a fact. The sermon didn't bore me. If it had, I should have said so, or said nothing."

"And which would you have done?"

The Professor smiled almost genially.

"Don't know," he said. "What wine d'you drink?"

"None, thank you. I'm a teetotaller. In my profession and *milieu* it is necessary to be one. Yes, I will have some soda water. I think you would have done the first."

"Very likely, and very wrongly. You wouldn't have minded much."

"I don't think I should."

They were intimate already. The Father felt most pleasantly at home under the black ceiling. He drank some soda water and seemed to enjoy it more than the Professor enjoyed his claret.

"You smile at the theory of the chain of human sympathy, I see," said the Father. "Then what is your explanation of the failure of your square party with corners, the success of your oval party without them?"

"Probably on the first occasion the wit of the assembly had a chill on his liver, while on the second he was in perfect health. Yet, you see, I stick to the oval table."

"And that means— —"

"Very little. By the way, your omission of any allusion to the notorious part liver plays in love was a serious one to-night."

"Your omission of any desire for close human sympathy in your life is a more serious one."

"How can you be sure I have no such desire?"

"I divine it. Your look, your manner, tell me it is so. You were disagreeing with my sermon all the time I was preaching. Weren't you?"

"Part of the time."

The servant changed the plates. He was a middle-aged, blond, thin man, with a stony white face, pale, prominent eyes, and an accomplished manner of service. When he had left the room the Professor continued,

"Your remarks interested me, but I thought them exaggerated."

"For instance?"

"Let me play the egoist for a moment. I spend most of my time in hard work, very hard work. The results of this work, you will allow, benefit humanity."

"Enormously," assented the Father, thinking of more than one of Guildea's discoveries.

"And the benefit conferred by this work, undertaken merely for its own sake, is just as great as if it were undertaken because I loved my fellow man and sentimentally desired to see him more comfortable than he is at present. I'm as useful precisely in my present condition of—in my present non-affectional condition—as I should be if I were as full of gush as the sentimentalists who want to get murderers out of prison, or to put a premium on tyranny—like Tolstoi—by preventing the punishment of tyrants."

"One may do great harm with affection; great good without it. Yes, that is true. Even *le bon motif* is not everything, I know. Still I contend that, given your powers, you would be far more useful in the world with sympathy, affection for your kind, added to them than as you are. I believe even that you would do still more splendid work."

The Professor poured himself out another glass of claret.

"You noticed my butler?" he said.

"I did."

"He's a perfect servant. He makes me perfectly comfortable. Yet he has no feeling of liking for me. I treat him civilly. I pay him well. But I never think about him, or concern myself with him as a human being. I know nothing of his character except what I read of it in his last master's letter. There are, you may say, no truly human relations between us. You would affirm that his work would be better done if I had made him personally like me as man — of any class — can like man — of any other class?"

"I should, decidedly."

"I contend that he couldn't do his work better than he does it at present."

"But if any crisis occurred?"

"What?"

"Any crisis, change in your condition. If you needed his help, not only as a man and a butler, but as a man and a brother? He'd fail you then, probably. You would never get from your servant that finest service which can only be prompted by an honest affection."

"You have finished?"

"Quite."

"Let us go upstairs then. Yes, those are good prints. I picked them up in Birmingham when I was living there. This is my workroom."

They came into a double room lined entirely with books, and brilliantly, rather hardly, lit by electricity. The windows at one end looked on to the Park, at the other on to the garden of a neighbouring house. The door by which they entered was concealed from the inner and smaller room by the jutting wall of the outer room, in which stood a huge writing-table loaded with letters, pamphlets and manuscripts. Between the two windows of the inner room was a cage in which a large, grey parrot was clambering, using both beak and claws to assist him in his slow and meditative peregrinations.

"You have a pet," said the Father, surprised.

"I possess a parrot," the Professor answered, drily, "I got him for a purpose when I was making a study of the imitative powers of birds, and I have never got rid of him. A cigar?"

"Thank you."

They sat down. Father Murchison glanced at the parrot. It had paused in its journey, and, clinging to the bars of its cage, was regarding them with attentive round eyes that looked deliberately intelligent, but by no means sympathetic. He looked away from it to Guildea, who was smoking, with his head thrown back, his sharp, pointed chin, on which the small black beard bristled, upturned. He was moving his under lip up and down rapidly. This action caused the beard to stir and look peculiarly aggressive. The Father suddenly chuckled softly.

"Why's that?" cried Guildea, letting his chin drop down on his breast and looking at his guest sharply.

"I was thinking it would have to be a crisis indeed that could make you cling to your butler's affection for assistance."

Guildea smiled too.

"You're right. It would. Here he comes."

The man entered with coffee. He offered it gently, and retired like a shadow retreating on a wall.

"Splendid, inhuman fellow," remarked Guildea.

"I prefer the East End lad who does my errands in Bird Street," said the Father. "I know all his worries. He knows some of mine. We are friends. He's more noisy than your man. He even breathes hard when he is specially solicitous, but he would do more for me than put the coals on my fire, or black my square-toed boots."

"Men are differently made. To me the watchful eye of affection would be abominable."

"What about that bird?"

The Father pointed to the parrot. It had got up on its perch and, with one foot uplifted in an impressive, almost benedictory, manner, was gazing steadily at the Professor.

"That's the watchful eye of imitation, with a mind at the back of it, desirous of reproducing the peculiarities of others. No, I thought your sermon to-night very fresh, very clever. But I have no wish for affection. Reasonable liking, of course, one desires," he tugged sharply at his beard, as if to warn himself against sentimentality, — "but anything more would be most irksome, and would push me, I feel sure, towards cruelty. It would also hamper one's work."

"I don't think so."

"The sort of work I do. I shall continue to benefit the world without loving it, and it will continue to accept the benefits without loving me. That's all as it should be."

He drank his coffee. Then he added, rather aggressively:

"I have neither time nor inclination for sentimentality."

When Guildea let Father Murchison out, he followed the Father on to the doorstep and stood there for a moment. The Father glanced across the damp road into the Park.

"I see you've got a gate just opposite you," he said idly.

"Yes. I often slip across for a stroll to clear my brain. Good-night to you. Come again some day."

"With pleasure. Good-night."

The Priest strode away, leaving Guildea standing on the step.

Father Murchison came many times again to number one hundred Hyde Park Place. He had a feeling of liking for most men and women whom he knew, and of tenderness for all, whether he knew them or not, but he grew to have a special sentiment towards Guildea. Strangely enough, it was a sentiment of pity. He pitied this hard-working, eminently successful man of big brain and bold heart, who never seemed depressed, who never wanted assistance, who never complained of the twisted skein of life or faltered in his progress along its way. The Father pitied Guildea, in fact, because Guildea wanted so little. He had told him so, for the intercourse of the two men, from the beginning, had been singularly frank.

One evening, when they were talking together, the Father happened to speak of one of the oddities of life, the fact that those who do not want things often get them, while those who seek them vehemently are disappointed in their search.

"Then I ought to have affection poured upon me," said Guildea, smiling rather grimly. "For I hate it."

"Perhaps some day you will."

"I hope not, most sincerely."

Father Murchison said nothing for a moment. He was drawing together the ends of the broad band round his cassock. When he spoke he seemed to be answering someone.

"Yes," he said slowly, "yes, that *is* my feeling—pity."

"For whom?" said the Professor.

Then, suddenly, he understood. He did not say that he understood, but Father Murchison felt, and saw, that it was quite unnecessary to answer his friend's question. So Guildea, strangely enough, found himself closely acquainted with a man—his opposite in all ways,—who pitied him.

The fact that he did not mind this, and scarcely ever thought about it, shows perhaps as clearly as anything could the peculiar indifference of his nature.

II

One Autumn evening, a year and a half after Father Murchison and the Professor had first met, the Father called in Hyde Park Place and enquired of the blond and stony butler—his name was Pitting—whether his master was at home.

"Yes, sir," replied Pitting. "Will you please come this way?"

He moved noiselessly up the rather narrow stairs, followed by the Father, tenderly opened the library door, and in his soft, cold voice, announced:

"Father Murchison."

Guildea was sitting in an armchair, before a small fire. His thin, long-fingered hands lay outstretched upon his knees, his head was sunk down on his chest. He appeared to be pondering deeply. Pitting very slightly raised his voice.

"Father Murchison to see you, sir," he repeated.

The Professor jumped up rather suddenly and turned sharply round as the Father came in.

"Oh," he said. "It's you, is it? Glad to see you. Come to the fire."

The Father glanced at him and thought him looking unusually fatigued.

"You don't look well to-night," the Father said.

"No?"

"You must be working too hard. That lecture you are going to give in Paris is bothering you?"

"Not a bit. It's all arranged. I could deliver it to you at this moment verbatim. Well, sit down."

The Father did so, and Guildea sank once more into his chair and stared hard into the fire without another word. He seemed to be thinking profoundly. His friend did not interrupt him, but quietly lit a pipe and began to smoke reflectively. The eyes of Guildea were fixed upon the fire. The Father glanced about the room, at the walls of soberly bound books, at the crowded writing-table, at the windows, before which hung heavy, dark-blue curtains of old brocade, at the cage, which stood between them. A green baize covering was thrown over it. The Father wondered why. He had never seen Napoleon—so the parrot was named—covered up at night before. While he was looking at the baize, Guildea suddenly jerked up his head, and, taking his hands from his knees and clasping them, said abruptly:

"D'you think I'm an attractive man?"

Father Murchison jumped. Such a question coming from such a man astounded him.

"Bless me!" he ejaculated. "What makes you ask? Do you mean attractive to the opposite sex?"

"That's what I don't know," said the Professor gloomily, and staring again into the fire. "That's what I don't know."

The Father grew more astonished.

"Don't know!" he exclaimed.

And he laid down his pipe.

"Let's say—d'you think I'm attractive, that there's anything about me which might draw a—a human being, or an animal, irresistibly to me?"

"Whether you desired it or not?"

"Exactly—or—no, let us say definitely—if I did not desire it."

Father Murchison pursed up his rather full, cherubic lips, and little wrinkles appeared about the corners of his blue eyes.

"There might be, of course," he said, after a pause. "Human nature is weak, engagingly weak, Guildea. And you're inclined to flout it. I could understand a certain class of lady—the lion-hunting, the intellectual lady, seeking you. Your reputation, your great name— —"

"Yes, yes," Guildea interrupted, rather irritably—"I know all that, I know."

He twisted his long hands together, bending the palms outwards till his thin, pointed fingers cracked. His forehead was wrinkled in a frown.

"I imagine," he said,—he stopped and coughed drily, almost shrilly—"I imagine it would be very disagreeable to be liked, to be run after—that is the usual expression, isn't it—by anything one objected to."

And now he half turned in his chair, crossed his legs one over the other, and looked at his guest with an unusual, almost piercing interrogation.

"Anything?" said the Father.

"Well—well, anyone. I imagine nothing could be more unpleasant."

"To you—no," answered the Father. "But—forgive me, Guildea, I cannot conceive you permitting such intrusion. You don't encourage adoration."

Guildea nodded his head gloomily.

"I don't," he said, "I don't. That's just it. That's the curious part of it, that I——"

He broke off deliberately, got up and stretched.

"I'll have a pipe, too," he said.

He went over to the mantelpiece, got his pipe, filled it and lighted it. As he held the match to the tobacco, bending forward with an enquiring expression, his eyes fell upon the green baize that covered Napoleon's cage. He threw the match into the grate, and puffed at the pipe as he walked forward to the cage. When he reached it he put out his hand, took hold of the baize and began to pull it away. Then suddenly he pushed it back over the cage.

"No," he said, as if to himself, "no."

He returned rather hastily to the fire and threw himself once more into his armchair.

"You're wondering," he said to Father Murchison. "So am I. I don't know at all what to make of it. I'll just tell you the facts and you must tell me what you think of them. The night before last, after a day of hard work—but no harder than usual—I went to the front door to get a breath of air. You know I often do that."

"Yes, I found you on the doorstep when I first came here."

"Just so. I didn't put on hat or coat. I just stood on the step as I was. My mind, I remember, was still full of my work. It was rather a dark night, not very dark. The hour was about eleven, or a quarter past. I was staring at the Park, and presently I found that my eyes were directed towards somebody who was sitting, back to me, on one of the benches. I saw the person—if it was a person,—through the railings."

"If it was a person!" said the Father. "What do you mean by that?"

"Wait a minute. I say that because it was too dark for me to know. I merely saw some blackish object on the bench, rising into view above the level of the back of the seat. I couldn't say it was man, woman or child. But something there was, and I found that I was looking at it."

"I understand."

"Gradually, I also found that my thoughts were becoming fixed upon this thing or person. I began to wonder, first, what it was doing there; next, what it was thinking; lastly, what it was like."

"Some poor creature without a home, I suppose," said the Father.

"I said that to myself. Still, I was taken with an extraordinary interest about this object, so great an interest that I got my hat and crossed the road to go into the Park. As you know, there's an entrance almost opposite to my house. Well, Murchison, I crossed the road, passed through the gate in the railings, went up to the seat, and found that there was—nothing on it."

"Were you looking at it as you walked?"

"Part of the time. But I removed my eyes from it just as I passed through the gate, because there was a row going on a little way off, and I turned for an instant in that direction. When I saw that the seat was vacant I was seized by a most absurd sensation of disappointment, almost of anger. I stopped and looked about me to see if anything was moving away, but I could see nothing. It was a cold night and misty, and there were few people about. Feeling, as I say, foolishly and unnaturally disappointed, I retraced my steps to this house. When I got here I discovered that during my short absence I had left the hall door open—half open."

"Rather imprudent in London."

"Yes. I had no idea, of course, that I had done so, till I got back. However, I was only away three minutes or so."

"Yes."

"It was not likely that anybody had gone in."

"I suppose not."

"Was it?"

"Why do you ask me that, Guildea?"

"Well, well!"

"Besides, if anybody had gone in on your return you'd have caught him, surely."

Guildea coughed again. The Father, surprised, could not fail to recognise that he was nervous and that his nervousness was affecting him physically.

"I must have caught cold that night," he said, as if he had read his friend's thought and hastened to contradict it. Then he went on:

"I entered the hall, or passage, rather."

He paused again. His uneasiness was becoming very apparent.

"And you did catch somebody?" said the Father.

Guildea cleared his throat.

"That's just it," he said, "now we come to it. I'm not imaginative, as you know."

"You certainly are not."

"No, but hardly had I stepped into the passage before I felt certain that somebody had got into the house during my absence. I felt convinced of it, and not only that, I also felt convinced that the intruder was the very person I had dimly seen sitting upon the seat in the Park. What d'you say to that?"

"I begin to think you are imaginative."

"H'm! It seemed to me that the person—the occupant of the seat—and I, had simultaneously formed the project of interviewing each other, had simultaneously set out to put that project into execution. I became so certain of this that I walked hastily upstairs into this room, expecting to find the visitor awaiting me. But there was no one. I then came down again and went into the dining-room. No one. I was actually astonished. Isn't that odd?"

"Very," said the Father, quite gravely.

The Professor's chill and gloomy manner, and uncomfortable, constrained appearance kept away the humour that might well have lurked round the steps of such a discourse.

"I went upstairs again," he continued, "sat down and thought the matter over. I resolved to forget it, and took up a book. I might perhaps have been able to read, but suddenly I thought I noticed ——"

He stopped abruptly. Father Murchison observed that he was staring towards the green baize that covered the parrot's cage.

"But that's nothing," he said. "Enough that I couldn't read. I resolved to explore the house. You know how small it is, how easily one can go all over it. I went all over it. I went into every room without exception. To the servants, who were having supper, I made some excuse. They were surprised at my advent, no doubt."

"And Pitting?"

"Oh, he got up politely when I came in, stood while I was there, but never said a word. I muttered 'don't disturb yourselves,' or something of the sort, and came out. Murchison, I found nobody new in the house—yet I returned to this room entirely convinced that somebody had entered while I was in the Park."

"And gone out again before you came back?"

"No, had stayed, and was still in the house."

"But, my dear Guildea," began the Father, now in great astonishment. "Surely——"

"I know what you want to say—what I should want to say in your place. Now, do wait. I am also convinced that this visitor has not left the house and is at this moment in it."

He spoke with evident sincerity, with extreme gravity. Father Murchison looked him full in the face, and met his quick, keen eyes.

"No," he said, as if in reply to an uttered question: "I'm perfectly sane, I assure you. The whole matter seems almost as incredible to me as it must to you. But, as you know, I never quarrel with facts, however strange. I merely try to examine into them thoroughly. I have already consulted a doctor and been pronounced in perfect bodily health."

He paused, as if expecting the Father to say something.

"Go on, Guildea," he said, "you haven't finished."

"No. I felt that night positive that somebody had entered the house, and remained in it, and my conviction grew. I went to bed as usual, and, contrary to my expectation, slept as well as I generally do. Yet directly I woke up yesterday morning I knew that my household had been increased by one."

"May I interrupt you for one moment? How did you know it?"

"By my mental sensation. I can only say that I was perfectly conscious of a new presence within my house, close to me."

"How very strange," said the Father. "And you feel absolutely certain that you are not over-worked? Your brain does not feel tired? Your head is quite clear?"

"Quite. I was never better. When I came down to breakfast that morning I looked sharply into Pitting's face. He was as coldly placid and inexpressive as usual. It was evident to me that his mind was in no way distressed. After breakfast I sat down to work, all the time ceaselessly conscious of the fact of this intruder upon my privacy. Nevertheless, I laboured for several hours, waiting for any development that might occur to clear away the mysterious obscurity of this event. I lunched. About half-past two I was obliged to go out to attend a lecture. I therefore, took my coat and hat, opened my door, and stepped on to the pavement. I was instantly aware that I was no longer intruded upon, and this although I was now in the street, surrounded by people. Consequently, I felt certain that the thing in my house must be thinking of me, perhaps even spying upon me."

"Wait a moment," interrupted the Father. "What was your sensation? Was it one of fear?"

"Oh, dear no. I was entirely puzzled,—as I am now—and keenly interested, but not in any way alarmed. I delivered my lecture with my usual ease and returned home in the evening. On entering the house again I was perfectly conscious that the intruder was still there. Last night I dined alone and spent the hours after dinner in reading a scientific work in which I was deeply interested. While I read, however, I never for one moment lost the knowledge that some mind—very attentive to me—was within hail of mine. I will say more than this—the sensation constantly increased, and, by the time I got up to go to bed, I had come to a very strange conclusion."

"What? What was it?"

"That whoever—or whatever—had entered my house during my short absence in the Park was more than interested in me."

"More than interested in you?"

"Was fond, or was becoming fond, of me."

"Oh!" exclaimed the Father. "Now I understand why you asked me just now whether I thought there was anything about you that might draw a human being or an animal irresistibly to you."

"Precisely. Since I came to this conclusion, Murchison, I will confess that my feeling of strong curiosity has become tinged with another feeling."

"Of fear?"

"No, of dislike, of irritation. No—not fear, not fear."

As Guildea repeated unnecessarily this asseveration he looked again towards the parrot's cage.

"What is there to be afraid of in such a matter?" he added. "I'm not a child to tremble before bogies."

In saying the last words he raised his voice sharply; then he walked quickly to the cage, and, with an abrupt movement, pulled the baize covering from it. Napoleon was disclosed, apparently dozing upon his perch with his head held slightly on one side. As the light reached him, he moved, ruffled the feathers about his neck, blinked his eyes, and began slowly to sidle to and fro, thrusting his head forward and drawing it back with an air of complacent, though rather unmeaning, energy. Guildea stood by the cage, looking at him closely, and indeed with an attention that was so intense as to be remarkable, almost unnatural.

"How absurd these birds are!" he said at length, coming back to the fire.

"You have no more to tell me?" asked the Father.

"No. I am still aware of the presence of something in my house. I am still conscious of its close attention to me. I am still irritated, seriously annoyed—I confess it,—by that attention."

"You say you are aware of the presence of something at this moment?"

"At this moment—yes."

"Do you mean in this room, with us, now?"

"I should say so—at any rate, quite near us."

Again he glanced quickly, almost suspiciously, towards the cage of the parrot. The bird was sitting still on its perch now. Its head was bent down and cocked sideways, and it appeared to be listening attentively to something.

"That bird will have the intonations of my voice more correctly than ever by to-morrow morning," said the Father, watching Guildea closely with his mild blue eyes. "And it has always imitated me very cleverly."

The Professor started slightly.

"Yes," he said. "Yes, no doubt. Well, what do you make of this affair?"

"Nothing at all. It is absolutely inexplicable. I can speak quite frankly to you, I feel sure."

"Of course. That's why I have told you the whole thing."

"I think you must be over-worked, over-strained, without knowing it."

"And that the doctor was mistaken when he said I was all right?"

"Yes."

Guildea knocked his pipe out against the chimney piece.

"It may be so," he said, "I will not be so unreasonable as to deny the possibility, although I feel as well as I ever did in my life. What do you advise then?"

"A week of complete rest away from London, in good air."

"The usual prescription. I'll take it. I'll go to-morrow to Westgate and leave Napoleon to keep house in my absence."

For some reason, which he could not explain to himself, the pleasure which Father Murchison felt in hearing the first part of his friend's final remark was lessened, was almost destroyed, by the last sentence.

He walked towards the City that night, deep in thought, remembering and carefully considering the first interview he had with Guildea in the latter's house a year and a half before.

On the following morning Guildea left London.

III

Father Murchison was so busy a man that he had little time for brooding over the affairs of others. During Guildea's week at the sea, however, the Father thought about him a great deal, with much wonder and some dismay. The dismay was soon banished, for the mild-eyed priest was quick to discern weakness in himself, quicker still to drive it forth as a most undesirable inmate of the soul. But the wonder remained. It was destined to a crescendo. Guildea had left London on a Thursday. On a Thursday he returned, having previously sent a note to Father Murchison to mention that he was leaving Westgate at a certain time. When his train ran in to Victoria Station, at five o'clock in the evening, he was surprised to see the cloaked figure of his friend standing upon the grey platform behind a line of porters.

"What, Murchison!" he said. "You here! Have you seceded from your order that you are taking this holiday?"

They shook hands.

"No," said the Father. "It happened that I had to be in this neighbourhood to-day, visiting a sick person. So I thought I would meet you."

"And see if I were still a sick person, eh?"

The Professor glanced at him kindly, but with a dry little laugh.

"Are you?" replied the Father gently, looking at him with interest. "No, I think not. You appear very well."

The sea air had, in fact, put some brownish red into Guildea's always thin cheeks. His keen eyes were shining with life and energy, and he walked forward in his loose grey suit and fluttering overcoat with a vigour that was noticeable, carrying easily in his left hand his well-filled Gladstone bag.

The Father felt completely reassured.

"I never saw you look better," he said.

"I never was better. Have you an hour to spare?"

"Two."

"Good. I'll send my bag up by cab, and we'll walk across the Park to my house and have a cup of tea there. What d'you say?"

"I shall enjoy it."

They walked out of the station yard, past the flower girls and newspaper sellers towards Grosvenor Place.

"And you have had a pleasant time?" the Father said.

"Pleasant enough, and lonely. I left my companion behind me in the passage at Number 100, you know."

"And you'll not find him there now, I feel sure."

"H'm!" ejaculated Guildea. "What a precious weakling you think me, Murchison."

As he spoke he strode forward more quickly, as if moved to emphasise his sensation of bodily vigour.

"A weakling—no. But anyone who uses his brain as persistently as you do yours must require an occasional holiday."

"And I required one very badly, eh?"

"You required one, I believe."

"Well, I've had it. And now we'll see."

The evening was closing in rapidly. They crossed the road at Hyde Park Corner, and entered the Park, in which were a number of people going home from work; men in corduroy trousers, caked with dried mud, and carrying tin cans slung over their shoulders, and flat panniers, in which lay their tools. Some of the younger ones talked loudly or whistled shrilly as they walked.

"Until the evening," murmured Father Murchison to himself.

"What?" asked Guildea.

"I was only quoting the last words of the text, which seems written upon life, especially upon the life of pleasure: 'Man goeth forth to his work, and to his labour.'"

"Ah, those fellows are not half bad fellows to have in an audience. There were a lot of them at the lecture I gave when I first met you, I remember. One of them tried to heckle me. He had a red beard. Chaps with red beards are always hecklers. I laid him low on that occasion. Well, Murchison, and now we're going to see."

"What?"

"Whether my companion has departed."

"Tell me—do you feel any expectation of—well—of again thinking something is there?"

"How carefully you choose language. No, I merely wonder."

"You have no apprehension?"

"Not a scrap. But I confess to feeling curious."

"Then the sea air hasn't taught you to recognise that the whole thing came from overstrain."

"No," said Guildea, very drily.

He walked on in silence for a minute. Then he added:

"You thought it would?"

"I certainly thought it might."

"Make me realise that I had a sickly, morbid, rotten imagination—heh? Come now, Murchison, why not say frankly that you packed me off to Westgate to get rid of what you considered an acute form of hysteria?"

The Father was quite unmoved by this attack.

"Come now, Guildea," he retorted, "what did you expect me to think? I saw no indication of hysteria in you. I never have. One would suppose you the last man likely to have such a malady. But which is more natural—for me to believe in your hysteria or in the truth of such a story as you told me?"

"You have me there. No, I mustn't complain. Well, there's no hysteria about me now, at any rate."

"And no stranger in your house, I hope."

Father Murchison spoke the last words with earnest gravity, dropping the half-bantering tone—which they had both assumed.

"You take the matter very seriously, I believe," said Guildea, also speaking more gravely.

"How else can I take it? You wouldn't have me laugh at it when you tell it me seriously?"

"No. If we find my visitor still in the house, I may even call upon you to exorcise it. But first I must do one thing."

"And that is?"

"Prove to you, as well as to myself, that it is still there."

"That might be difficult," said the Father, considerably surprised by Guildea's matter-of-fact tone.

"I don't know. If it has remained in my house I think I can find a means. And I shall not be at all surprised if it is still there—despite the Westgate air."

In saying the last words the Professor relapsed into his former tone of dry chaff. The Father could not quite make up his mind whether Guildea was feeling unusually grave or unusually gay. As the two men drew near to Hyde Park Place their conversation died away and they walked forward silently in the gathering darkness.

"Here we are!" said Guildea at last.

He thrust his key into the door, opened it and let Father Murchison into the passage, following him closely and banging the door.

"Here we are!" he repeated in a louder voice.

The electric light was turned on in anticipation of his arrival. He stood still and looked round.

"We'll have some tea at once," he said. "Ah, Pitting!"

The pale butler, who had heard the door bang, moved gently forward from the top of the stairs that led to the kitchen, greeted his master respectfully, took his coat and Father Murchison's cloak, and hung them on two pegs against the wall.

"All's right, Pitting? All's as usual?" said Guildea.

"Quite so, sir."

"Bring us up some tea to the library."

"Yes, sir."

Pitting retreated. Guildea waited till he had disappeared, then opened the dining-room door, put his head into the room and kept it there for a moment, standing perfectly still. Presently he drew back into the passage, shut the door, and said,

"Let's go upstairs."

Father Murchison looked at him enquiringly, but made no remark. They ascended the stairs and came into the library. Guildea glanced rather sharply round. A fire was burning on the hearth. The blue curtains were drawn. The bright gleam of the strong electric light fell on the long rows of books, on the writing table,—very orderly in consequence of Guildea's holiday—and on the uncovered cage of the parrot. Guildea went up to the cage. Napoleon was sitting humped up on his perch with his feathers ruffled. His long toes, which looked as if they were covered with crocodile skin, clung to the bar. His round and blinking eyes were filmy, like old eyes. Guildea stared at the bird very hard, and then clucked with his tongue against his teeth. Napoleon shook himself, lifted one foot, extended his toes, sidled along the perch to the bars nearest to the Professor and thrust his head against them. Guildea scratched it with his forefinger two or three times, still gazing attentively at the parrot; then he returned to the fire just as Pitting entered with the tea-tray.

Father Murchison was already sitting in an armchair on one side of the fire. Guildea took another chair and began to pour out tea, as Pitting left the room closing the door gently behind him. The Father sipped his tea, found it hot and set the cup down on a little table at his side.

"You're fond of that parrot, aren't you?" he asked his friend.

"Not particularly. It's interesting to study sometimes. The parrot mind and nature are peculiar."

"How long have you had him?"

"About four years. I nearly got rid of him just before I made your acquaintance. I'm very glad now I kept him."

"Are you? Why is that?"

"I shall probably tell you in a day or two."

The Father took his cup again. He did not press Guildea for an immediate explanation, but when they had both finished their tea he said:

"Well, has the sea-air had the desired effect?"

"No," said Guildea.

The Father brushed some crumbs from the front of his cassock and sat up higher in his chair.

"Your visitor is still here?" he asked, and his blue eyes became almost ungentle and piercing as he gazed at his friend.

"Yes," answered Guildea, calmly.

"How do you know it, when did you know it—when you looked into the dining-room just now?"

"No. Not until I came into this room. It welcomed me here."

"Welcomed you! In what way?"

"Simply by being here, by making me feel that it is here, as I might feel that a man was if I came into the room when it was dark."

He spoke quietly, with perfect composure in his usual dry manner.

"Very well," the Father said, "I shall not try to contend against your sensation, or to explain it away. Naturally, I am in amazement."

"So am I. Never has anything in my life surprised me so much. Murchison, of course I cannot expect you to believe more than that I honestly suppose—imagine, if you like—that there is some intruder here, of what kind I am totally unaware. I cannot expect you to believe that there really is anything. If you were in my place, I in yours, I should certainly consider you the victim of some nervous delusion. I could not do otherwise. But—wait. Don't condemn me as a hysteria patient, or as a madman, for two or three days. I feel convinced that—unless I am indeed unwell, a mental invalid, which I don't think is possible—I shall be able very shortly to give you some proof that there is a newcomer in my house."

"You don't tell me what kind of proof?"

"Not yet. Things must go a little farther first. But, perhaps even to-morrow I may be able to explain myself more fully. In the meanwhile, I'll say this, that if, eventually, I can't bring any kind of proof that I'm not dreaming I'll let you take me to any doctor you like, and I'll resolutely try to adopt your present view—that I'm suffering from an absurd delusion. That is your view of course?"

Father Murchison was silent for a moment. Then he said, rather doubtfully:

"It ought to be."

"But isn't it?" asked Guildea, surprised.

"Well, you know, your manner is enormously convincing. Still, of course, I doubt. How can I do otherwise? The whole thing must be fancy."

The Father spoke as if he were trying to recoil from a mental position he was being forced to take up.

"It must be fancy," he repeated.

"I'll convince you by more than my manner, or I'll not try to convince you at all," said Guildea.

When they parted that evening, he said,

"I'll write to you in a day or two probably. I think the proof I am going to give you has been accumulating during my absence. But I shall soon know."

Father Murchison was extremely puzzled as he sat on the top of the omnibus going homeward.

IV

In two days' time he received a note from Guildea asking him to call, if possible, the same evening. This he was unable to do as he had an engagement to fulfil at some East End gathering. The following day was Sunday. He wrote saying he would come on the Monday, and got a wire shortly afterwards: "Yes, Monday come to dinner seven-thirty Guildea." At half-past seven he stood on the doorstep of Number 100.

Pitting let him in.

"Is the Professor quite well, Pitting?" the Father enquired as he took off his cloak.

"I believe so, sir. He has not made any complaint," the butler formally replied. "Will you come upstairs, sir?"

Guildea met them at the door of the library. He was very pale and sombre, and shook hands carelessly with his friend.

"Give us dinner," he said to Pitting.

As the butler retired, Guildea shut the door rather cautiously. Father Murchison had never before seen him look so disturbed.

"You're worried, Guildea," the Father said. "Seriously worried."

"Yes, I am. This business is beginning to tell on me a good deal."

"Your belief in the presence of something here continues then?"

"Oh, dear, yes. There's no sort of doubt about the matter. The night I went across the road into the Park something got into the house, though what the devil it is I can't yet find out. But now, before we go down to dinner, I'll just tell you something about that proof I promised you. You remember?"

"Naturally."

"Can't you imagine what it might be."

Father Murchison moved his head to express a negative reply.

"Look about the room," said Guildea. "What do you see?"

The Father glanced round the room, slowly and carefully.

"Nothing unusual. You do not mean to tell me there is any appearance of — —"

"Oh, no, no, there's no conventional, white-robed, cloud-like figure. Bless my soul, no! I haven't fallen so low as that."

He spoke with considerable irritation.

"Look again."

Father Murchison looked at him, turned in the direction of his fixed eyes and saw the grey parrot clambering in its cage, slowly and persistently.

"What?" he said, quickly. "Will the proof come from there?"

The Professor nodded.

"I believe so," he said. "Now let's go down to dinner. I want some food badly."

They descended to the dining-room. While they ate and Pitting waited upon them, the Professor talked about birds, their habits, their curiosities, their fears and their powers of imitation. He had evidently studied this subject with the thoroughness that was characteristic of him in all that he did.

"Parrots," he said presently, "are extraordinarily observant. It is a pity that their means of reproducing what they see are so limited. If it were not so, I have little doubt that their echo of gesture would be as remarkable as their echo of voice often is."

"But hands are missing."

"Yes. They do many things with their heads, however. I once knew an old woman near Goring on the Thames. She was afflicted with the palsy. She held her head perpetually sideways and it trembled, moving from right to left. Her sailor son brought her home a parrot from one of his voyages. It used to reproduce the old woman's palsied movement of the head exactly. Those grey parrots are always on the watch."

Guildea said the last sentence slowly and deliberately, glancing sharply over his wine at Father Murchison, and, when he had spoken it, a sudden light of comprehension dawned in the Priest's mind. He opened his lips to make a swift remark. Guildea turned his bright eyes towards Pitting, who at the moment was tenderly bearing a cheese meringue from the lift that connected the dining-room with the lower regions. The Father closed his lips again. But presently, when the butler had placed some apples on the table, had meticulously arranged the decanters, brushed away the crumbs and evaporated, he said, quickly,

"I begin to understand. You think Napoleon is aware of the intruder?"

"I know it. He has been watching my visitant ever since the night of that visitant's arrival."

Another flash of light came to the Priest.

"That was why you covered him with green baize one evening?"

"Exactly. An act of cowardice. His behaviour was beginning to grate upon my nerves."

Guildea pursed up his thin lips and drew his brows down, giving to his face a look of sudden pain.

"But now I intend to follow his investigations," he added, straightening his features. "The week I wasted at Westgate was not wasted by him in London, I can assure you. Have an apple."

"No, thank you; no, thank you."

The Father repeated the words without knowing that he did so. Guildea pushed away his glass.

"Let us come upstairs, then."

"No, thank you," reiterated the Father.

"Eh?"

"What am I saying?" exclaimed the Father, getting up. "I was thinking over this extraordinary affair."

"Ah, you're beginning to forget the hysteria theory?"

They walked out into the passage.

"Well, you are so very practical about the whole matter."

"Why not? Here's something very strange and abnormal come into my life. What should I do but investigate it closely and calmly?"

"What, indeed?"

The Father began to feel rather bewildered, under a sort of compulsion which seemed laid upon him to give earnest attention to a matter that ought to strike him—so he felt—as entirely absurd. When they came into the library his eyes immediately turned, with profound curiosity, towards the parrot's cage. A slight smile curled the Professor's lips. He recognised the effect he was producing upon his friend. The Father saw the smile.

"Oh, I'm not won over yet," he said in answer to it.

"I know. Perhaps you may be before the evening is over. Here comes the coffee. After we have drunk it we'll proceed to our experiment. Leave the coffee, Pitting, and don't disturb us again."

"No, sir."

"I won't have it black to-night," said the Father, "plenty of milk, please. I don't want my nerves played upon."

"Suppose we don't take coffee at all?" said Guildea. "If we do you may trot out the theory that we are not in a perfectly normal condition. I know you, Murchison, devout Priest and devout sceptic."

The Father laughed and pushed away his cup.

"Very well, then. No coffee."

"One cigarette, and then to business."

The grey blue smoke curled up.

"What are we going to do?" said the Father.

He was sitting bolt upright as if ready for action. Indeed there was no suggestion of repose in the attitudes of either of the men.

"Hide ourselves, and watch Napoleon. By the way—that reminds me."

He got up, went to a corner of the room, picked up a piece of green baize and threw it over the cage.

"I'll pull that off when we are hidden."

"And tell me first if you have had any manifestation of this supposed presence during the last few days?"

"Merely an increasingly intense sensation of something here, perpetually watching me, perpetually attending to all my doings."

"Do you feel that it follows you about?"

"Not always. It was in this room when you arrived. It is here now—I feel. But, in going down to dinner, we seemed to get away from it. The conclusion is that it remained here. Don't let us talk about it just now."

They spoke of other things till their cigarettes were finished. Then, as they threw away the smouldering ends, Guildea said,

"Now, Murchison, for the sake of this experiment, I suggest that we should conceal ourselves behind the curtains on either side of the cage, so that the bird's attention may not be drawn towards us and so distracted from that which we want to know more about. I will pull away the green baize when we are hidden. Keep perfectly still, watch the bird's proceedings, and tell me afterwards how you feel about them, how you explain them. Tread softly."

The Father obeyed, and they stole towards the curtains that fell before the two windows. The Father concealed himself behind those on the left of the cage, the Professor behind those on the right. The latter, as soon as they were hidden, stretched out his arm, drew the baize down from the cage, and let it fall on the floor.

The parrot, which had evidently fallen asleep in the warm darkness, moved on its perch as the light shone upon it, ruffled the feathers round its throat, and lifted first one foot and then the other. It turned its head round on its supple, and apparently elastic, neck, and, diving its beak into the down upon its back, made some searching investigations with, as it seemed, a satisfactory result, for it soon lifted its head again, glanced around its cage, and began to address itself to a nut which had been fixed between the bars for its refreshment. With its curved beak it felt and tapped the nut, at first gently, then with severity. Finally it plucked the nut from the bars, seized it with its rough, grey toes, and, holding it down firmly on the perch, cracked it and pecked out its contents, scattering some on the floor of the cage and letting the fractured shell fall into the china bath that was fixed against the bars. This accomplished, the bird paused meditatively, extended one leg backwards, and went through an elaborate process of wing-stretching that made it look as if it were lopsided and deformed. With its head reversed, it again applied itself to a subtle and exhaustive search among the feathers of its wing. This time its investigation seemed interminable, and Father Murchison had time to realise the absurdity of the whole position, and to wonder why he had lent himself to it. Yet he did not find his sense of humour laughing at it. On the contrary, he was smitten by a sudden gust of horror. When he was talking to his friend and watching him, the Professor's manner, generally so calm, even so prosaic, vouched for the truth of his story and the well-adjusted balance of his mind. But when he was hidden this was not so. And Father Murchison, standing behind his curtain, with his eyes upon the unconcerned Napoleon, began to whisper to himself the word — madness, with a quickening sensation of pity and of dread.

The parrot sharply contracted one wing, ruffled the feathers around its throat again, then extended its other leg backwards, and proceeded to the cleaning of its other wing. In the still room the dry sound of the feathers being spread was distinctly audible. Father Murchison saw the blue curtains behind which Guildea stood tremble slightly, as if a breath of wind had come through the window they shrouded. The clock in the far room chimed, and a coal dropped into the grate, making a noise like dead leaves stirring abruptly on hard ground. And again a gust of pity and of dread swept over the Father. It seemed to him that he had behaved very foolishly, if not wrongly, in encouraging what must surely be the strange dementia of his friend. He ought to have declined to lend himself to a proceeding that, ludicrous, even childish in itself, might well be dangerous in the encouragement it gave to a diseased expectation. Napoleon's protruding leg, extended wing and twisted neck, his busy and unconscious devotion to the arrangement of his person, his evident sensation of complete loneliness, most comfortable solitude, brought home with vehemence to the Father the undignified buffoonery of his conduct; the more piteous buffoonery of his friend. He seized the curtains with his hands and was about to thrust them aside and issue forth when an abrupt movement of the parrot stopped him. The bird, as if sharply attracted by something, paused in its pecking, and, with its head still bent backward and twisted sideways on its neck, seemed to listen intently. Its round eye looked glistening and strained like the eye of a disturbed pigeon. Contracting its wing, it lifted its head and sat for a moment erect on its perch, shifting its feet mechanically up and down, as if a dawning excitement produced in it an uncontrollable desire of movement. Then it thrust its head forward in the direction of the further room and remained perfectly still. Its attitude so strongly suggested the concentration of its attention on something immediately before it that Father Murchison instinctively stared about the room, half expecting to see Pitting advance softly, having entered through the hidden door. He did not come, and there was no sound in the chamber. Nevertheless, the parrot was obviously getting excited and increasingly attentive. It bent its head lower and lower, stretching out its neck until, almost falling from the perch, it half extended its wings, raising them slightly from its back, as if about to take flight, and fluttering them rapidly up and down. It continued this fluttering movement for what seemed to the Father an immense time. At length, raising its wings as far as possible, it dropped them slowly and deliberately down to its back, caught hold of the edge of its bath with its beak, hoisted itself on to the floor of the cage, waddled to the bars, thrust its head against them, and stood quite still in the exact attitude it always assumed when its head was being scratched by the Professor. So complete was the suggestion of this delight conveyed by the bird that Father Murchison felt as if he saw a white finger gently pushed among the soft feathers of its head, and he was seized by a most strong conviction that something, unseen by him but seen and welcomed by Napoleon, stood immediately before the cage.

The parrot presently withdrew its head, as if the coaxing finger had been lifted from it, and its pronounced air of acute physical enjoyment faded into one of marked attention and alert curiosity. Pulling itself up by the bars it climbed again upon its perch, sidled to the left side of the cage, and began apparently to watch something with profound interest. It bowed its head oddly, paused for a moment, then bowed its head again. Father Murchison found himself conceiving—from this elaborate movement of the head—a distinct idea of a personality. The bird's proceedings suggested extreme sentimentality combined with that sort of weak determination which is often the most persistent. Such weak determination is a very common attribute of persons who are partially idiotic. Father Murchison was moved to think of these poor creatures who will often, so strangely and unreasonably, attach themselves with persistence to those who love them least. Like many priests, he had had some experience of them, for the amorous idiot is peculiarly sensitive to the attraction of preachers. This bowing movement of the parrot recalled to his memory a terrible, pale woman who for a time haunted all churches in which he ministered, who was perpetually endeavouring to catch his eye, and who always bent her head with an obsequious and cunningly conscious smile when she did so. The parrot went on bowing, making a short pause between each genuflection, as if it waited for a signal to be given that called into play its imitative faculty.

"Yes, yes, it's imitating an idiot," Father Murchison caught himself saying as he watched.

And he looked again about the room, but saw nothing; except the furniture, the dancing fire, and the serried ranks of the books. Presently the parrot ceased from bowing, and assumed the concentrated and stretched attitude of one listening very keenly. He opened his beak, showing his black tongue, shut it, then opened it again. The Father thought he was going to speak, but he remained silent, although it was obvious that he was trying to bring out something. He bowed again two or three times, paused, and then, again opening his beak, made some remark. The Father could not distinguish any words, but the voice was sickly and disagreeable, a cooing and, at the same time, querulous voice, like a woman's, he thought. And he put his ear nearer to the curtain, listening with almost feverish attention. The bowing was resumed, but this time Napoleon added to it a sidling movement, affectionate and affected, like the movement of a silly and eager thing, nestling up to someone, or giving someone a gentle and furtive nudge. Again the Father thought of that terrible, pale woman who had haunted churches. Several times he had come upon her waiting for him after evening services. Once she had hung her head smiling, had lolled out her tongue and pushed against him sideways in the dark. He remembered how his flesh had shrunk from the poor thing, the sick loathing of her that he could not banish by remembering that her mind was all astray. The parrot paused, listened, opened his beak, and again said something in the same dove-like, amorous voice, full of sickly suggestion and yet hard, even dangerous, in its intonation. A loathsome voice, the Father thought it. But this time, although he heard the voice more distinctly than before, he could not make up his mind whether it was like a woman's voice or a man's—or perhaps a child's. It seemed to be a human voice, and yet oddly sexless. In order to resolve his doubt he withdrew into the darkness of the curtains, ceased to watch Napoleon and simply listened with keen attention, striving to forget that he was listening to a bird, and to imagine that he was overhearing a human being in conversation. After two or three minutes' silence the voice spoke again, and at some length, apparently repeating several times an affectionate series of ejaculations with a cooing emphasis that was unutterably mawkish and offensive. The sickliness of the voice, its falling intonations and its strange indelicacy, combined with a die-away softness and meretricious refinement, made the Father's flesh creep. Yet he could not distinguish any words, nor could he decide on the voice's sex or age. One thing alone he was certain of as he stood still in the darkness,—that such a sound could only proceed from something peculiarly loathsome, could only express a personality unendurably abominable to him, if not to everybody. The voice presently failed, in a sort of husky gasp, and there was a prolonged silence. It was broken by the Professor, who suddenly pulled away the curtains that hid the Father and said to him:

"Come out now, and look."

The Father came into the light, blinking, glanced towards the cage, and saw Napoleon poised motionless on one foot with his head under his wing. He appeared to be asleep. The Professor was pale, and his mobile lips were drawn into an expression of supreme disgust.

"Faugh!" he said.

He walked to the windows of the further room, pulled aside the curtains and pushed the glass up, letting in the air. The bare trees were visible in the grey gloom outside. Guildea leaned out for a minute drawing the night air into his lungs. Presently he turned round to the Father, and exclaimed abruptly,

"Pestilent! Isn't it?"

"Yes—most pestilent."

"Ever hear anything like it?"

"Not exactly."

"Nor I. It gives me nausea, Murchison, absolute physical nausea."

He closed the window and walked uneasily about the room.

"What d'you make of it?" he asked, over his shoulder.

"How d'you mean exactly?"

"Is it man's, woman's, or child's voice?"

"I can't tell, I can't make up my mind."

"Nor I."

"Have you heard it often?"

"Yes, since I returned from Westgate. There are never any words that I can distinguish. What a voice!"

He spat into the fire.

"Forgive me," he said, throwing himself down in a chair. "It turns my stomach—literally."

"And mine," said the Father, truly.

"The worst of it is," continued Guildea, with a high, nervous accent, "that there's no brain with it, none at all—only the cunning of idiotcy."

The Father started at this exact expression of his own conviction by another.

"Why d'you start like that?" asked Guildea, with a quick suspicion which showed the unnatural condition of his nerves.

"Well, the very same idea had occurred to me."

"What?"

"That I was listening to the voice of something idiotic."

"Ah! That's the devil of it, you know, to a man like me. I could fight against brain—but this!"

He sprang up again, poked the fire violently, then stood on the hearthrug with his back to it, and his hands thrust into the high pockets of his trousers.

"That's the voice of the thing that's got into my house," he said. "Pleasant, isn't it?"

And now there was really horror in his eyes, and in his voice.

"I must get it out," he exclaimed. "I must get it out. But how?"

He tugged at his short black beard with a quivering hand.

"How?" he continued. "For what is it? Where is it?"

"You feel it's here—now?"

"Undoubtedly. But I couldn't tell you in what part of the room."

He stared about, glancing rapidly at everything.

"Then you consider yourself haunted?" said Father Murchison.

He, too, was much moved and disturbed, although he was not conscious of the presence of anything near them in the room.

"I have never believed in any nonsense of that kind, as you know," Guildea answered. "I simply state a fact which I cannot understand, and which is beginning to be very painful to me. There is something here. But whereas most so-called hauntings have been described to me as inimical, what I am conscious of is that I am admired, loved, desired. This is distinctly horrible to me, Murchison, distinctly horrible."

Father Murchison suddenly remembered the first evening he had spent with Guildea, and the latter's expression almost of disgust, at the idea of receiving warm affection from anyone. In the light of that long ago conversation the present event seemed supremely strange, and almost like a punishment for an offence committed by the Professor against humanity. But, looking up at his friend's twitching face, the Father resolved not to be caught in the net of his hideous belief.

"There can be nothing here," he said. "It's impossible."

"What does that bird imitate, then?"

"The voice of someone who has been here."

"Within the last week then. For it never spoke like that before, and mind, I noticed that it was watching and striving to imitate something before I went away, since the night that I went into the Park, only since then."

"Somebody with a voice like that must have been here while you were away," Father Murchison repeated, with a gentle obstinacy.

"I'll soon find out."

Guildea pressed the bell. Pitting stole in almost immediately.

"Pitting," said the Professor, speaking in a high, sharp voice, "did anyone come into this room during my absence at the sea?"

"Certainly not, sir, except the maids—and me, sir."

"Not a soul? You are certain?"

"Perfectly certain, sir."

The cold voice of the butler sounded surprised, almost resentful. The Professor flung out his hand towards the cage.

"Has the bird been here the whole time?"

"Yes, sir."

"He was not moved, taken elsewhere, even for a moment?"

Pitting's pale face began to look almost expressive, and his lips were pursed.

"Certainly not, sir."

"Thank you. That will do."

The butler retired, moving with a sort of ostentatious rectitude. When he had reached the door, and was just going out, his master called,

"Wait a minute, Pitting."

The butler paused. Guildea bit his lips, tugged at his beard uneasily two or three times, and then said,

"Have you noticed—er—the parrot talking lately in a—a very peculiar, very disagreeable voice?"

"Yes, sir—a soft voice like, sir."

"Ha! Since when?"

"Since you went away, sir. He's always at it."

"Exactly. Well, and what did you think of it?"

"Beg pardon, sir?"

"What do you think about his talking in this voice?"

"Oh, that it's only his play, sir."

"I see. That's all, Pitting."

The butler disappeared and closed the door noiselessly behind him.

Guildea turned his eyes on his friend.

"There, you see!" he ejaculated.

"It's certainly very odd," said the Father. "Very odd indeed. You are certain you have no maid who talks at all like that?"

"My dear Murchison! Would you keep a servant with such a voice about you for two days?"

"No."

"My housemaid has been with me for five years, my cook for seven. You've heard Pitting speak. The three of them make up my entire household. A parrot never speaks in a voice it has not heard. Where has it heard that voice?"

"But we hear nothing?"

"No. Nor do we see anything. But it does. It feels something too. Didn't you observe it presenting its head to be scratched?"

"Certainly it seemed to be doing so."

"It was doing so."

Father Murchison said nothing. He was full of increasing discomfort that almost amounted to apprehension.

"Are you convinced?" said Guildea, rather irritably.

"No. The whole matter is very strange. But till I hear, see, or feel—as you do—the presence of something, I cannot believe."

"You mean that you will not?"

"Perhaps. Well, it is time I went."

Guildea did not try to detain him, but said, as he let him out,

"Do me a favour, come again to-morrow night."

The Father had an engagement. He hesitated, looked into the Professor's face and said,

"I will. At nine I'll be with you. Good-night."

When he was on the pavement he felt relieved. He turned round, saw Guildea stepping into his passage, and shivered.

V

Father Murchison walked all the way home to Bird Street that night. He required exercise after the strange and disagreeable evening he had spent, an evening upon which he looked back already as a man looks back upon a nightmare. In his ears, as he walked, sounded the gentle and intolerable voice. Even the memory of it caused him physical discomfort. He tried to put it from him, and to consider the whole matter calmly. The Professor had offered his proof that there was some strange presence in his house. Could any reasonable man accept such proof? Father Murchison told himself that no reasonable man could accept it. The parrot's proceedings were, no doubt, extraordinary. The bird had succeeded in producing an extraordinary illusion of an invisible presence in the room. But that there really was such a presence the Father insisted on denying to himself. The devoutly religious, those who believe implicitly in the miracles recorded in the Bible, and who regulate their lives by the messages they suppose themselves to receive directly from the Great Ruler of a hidden World, are seldom inclined to accept any notion of supernatural intrusion into the affairs of daily life. They put it from them with anxious determination. They regard it fixedly as hocus-pocus, childish if not wicked.

Father Murchison inclined to the normal view of the devoted churchman. He was determined to incline to it. He could not—so he now told himself—accept the idea that his friend was being supernaturally punished for his lack of humanity, his deficiency in affection, by being obliged to endure the love of some horrible thing, which could not be seen, heard, or handled. Nevertheless, retribution did certainly seem to wait upon Guildea's condition. That which he had unnaturally dreaded and shrunk from in his thought he seemed to be now forced unnaturally to suffer. The Father prayed for his friend that night before the little, humble altar in the barely-furnished, cell-like chamber where he slept.

On the following evening, when he called in Hyde Park Place, the door was opened by the housemaid, and Father Murchison mounted the stairs, wondering what had become of Pitting. He was met at the library door by Guildea and was painfully struck by the alteration in his appearance. His face was ashen in hue, and there were lines beneath his eyes. The eyes themselves looked excited and horribly forlorn. His hair and dress were disordered and his lips twitched continually, as if he were shaken by some acute nervous apprehension.

"What has become of Pitting?" asked the Father, grasping Guildea's hot and feverish hand.

"He has left my service."

"Left your service!" exclaimed the Father in utter amazement.

"Yes, this afternoon."

"May one ask why?"

"I'm going to tell you. It's all part and parcel of this—this most odious business. You remember once discussing the relations men ought to have with their servants?"

"Ah!" cried the Father, with a flash of inspiration. "The crisis has occurred?"

"Exactly," said the Professor, with a bitter smile. "The crisis has occurred. I called upon Pitting to be a man and a brother. He responded by declining the invitation. I upbraided him. He gave me warning. I paid him his wages and told him he could go at once. And he has gone. What are you looking at me like that for?"

"I didn't know," said Father Murchison, hastily dropping his eyes, and looking away. "Why," he added. "Napoleon is gone too."

"I sold him to-day to one of those shops in Shaftesbury Avenue."

"Why?"

"He sickened me with his abominable imitation of—his intercourse with—well, you know what he was at last night. Besides, I have no further need of his proof to tell me I am not dreaming. And, being convinced as I now am, that all I have thought to have happened has actually happened, I care very little about convincing others. Forgive me for saying so, Murchison, but I am now certain that my anxiety to make you believe in the presence of something here really arose from some faint doubt on that subject—within myself. All doubt has now vanished."

"Tell me why."

"I will."

Both men were standing by the fire. They continued to stand while Guildea went on,

"Last night I felt it."

"What?" cried the Father.

"I say that last night, as I was going upstairs to bed, I felt something accompanying me and nestling up against me."

"How horrible!" exclaimed the Father, involuntarily.

Guildea smiled drearily.

"I will not deny the horror of it. I cannot, since I was compelled to call on Pitting for assistance."

"But—tell me—what was it, at least what did it seem to be?"

"It seemed to be a human being. It seemed, I say; and what I mean exactly is that the effect upon me was rather that of human contact than of anything else. But I could see nothing, hear nothing. Only, three times, I felt this gentle, but determined, push against me, as if to coax me and to attract my attention. The first time it happened I was on the landing outside this room, with my foot on the first stair. I will confess to you, Murchison, that I bounded upstairs like one pursued. That is the shameful truth. Just as I was about to enter my bedroom, however, I felt the thing entering with me, and, as I have said, squeezing, with loathsome, sickening tenderness, against my side. Then— —"

He paused, turned towards the fire and leaned his head on his arm. The Father was greatly moved by the strange helplessness and despair of the attitude. He laid his hand affectionately on Guildea's shoulder.

"Then?"

Guildea lifted his head. He looked painfully abashed.

"Then, Murchison, I am ashamed to say I broke down, suddenly, unaccountably, in a way I should have thought wholly impossible to me. I struck out with my hands to thrust the thing away. It pressed more closely to me. The pressure, the contact became unbearable to me. I shouted out for Pitting. I—I believe I must have cried—'Help.'"

"He came, of course?"

"Yes, with his usual soft, unemotional quiet. His calm—its opposition to my excitement of disgust and horror—must, I suppose, have irritated me. I was not myself, no, no!"

He stopped abruptly. Then—

"But I need hardly tell you that," he added, with most piteous irony.

"And what did you say to Pitting?"

"I said that he should have been quicker. He begged my pardon. His cold voice really maddened me, and I burst out into some foolish, contemptible diatribe, called him a machine, taunted him, then—as I felt that loathsome thing nestling once more to me,—begged him to assist me, to stay with me, not to leave me alone—I meant in the company of my tormentor. Whether he was frightened, or whether he was angry at my unjust and violent manner and speech a moment before, I don't know. In any case he answered that he was engaged as a butler, and not to sit up all night with people. I suspect he thought I had taken too much to drink. No doubt that was it. I believe I swore at him as a coward—I! This morning he said he wished to leave my service. I gave him a month's wages, a good character as a butler, and sent him off at once."

"But the night? How did you pass it?"

"I sat up all night."

"Where? In your bedroom?"

"Yes—with the door open—to let it go."

"You felt that it stayed?"

"It never left me for a moment, but it did not touch me again. When it was light I took a bath, lay down for a little while, but did not close my eyes. After breakfast I had the explanation with Pitting and paid him. Then I came up here. My nerves were in a very shattered condition. Well, I sat down, tried to write, to think. But the silence was broken in the most abominable manner."

"How?"

"By the murmur of that appalling voice, that voice of a love-sick idiot, sickly but determined. Ugh!"

He shuddered in every limb. Then he pulled himself together, assumed, with a self-conscious effort, his most determined, most aggressive, manner, and added:

"I couldn't stand that. I had come to the end of my tether; so I sprang up, ordered a cab to be called, seized the cage and drove with it to a bird shop in Shaftesbury Avenue. There I sold the parrot for a trifle. I think, Murchison, that I must have been nearly mad then, for, as I came out of the wretched shop, and stood for an instant on the pavement among the cages of rabbits, guinea-pigs, and puppy dogs, I laughed aloud. I felt as if a load was lifted from my shoulders, as if in selling that voice I had sold the cursed thing that torments me. But when I got back to the house it was here. It's here now. I suppose it will always be here."

He shuffled his feet on the rug in front of the fire.

"What on earth am I to do?" he said. "I'm ashamed of myself, Murchison, but—but I suppose there are things in the world that certain men simply can't endure. Well, I can't endure this, and there's an end of the matter."

He ceased. The Father was silent. In presence of this extraordinary distress he did not know what to say. He recognised the uselessness of attempting to comfort Guildea, and he sat with his eyes turned, almost moodily, to the ground. And while he sat there he tried to give himself to the influences within the room, to feel all that was within it. He even, half-unconsciously, tried to force his imagination to play tricks with him. But he remained totally unaware of any third person with them. At length he said,

"Guildea, I cannot pretend to doubt the reality of your misery here. You must go away, and at once. When is your Paris lecture?"

"Next week. In nine days from now."

"Go to Paris to-morrow then, you say you have never had any consciousness that this—this thing pursued you beyond your own front door!"

"Never—hitherto."

"Go to-morrow morning. Stay away till after your lecture. And then let us see if the affair is at an end. Hope, my dear friend, hope."

He had stood up. Now he clasped the Professor's hand.

"See all your friends in Paris. Seek distractions. I would ask you also to seek—other help."

He said the last words with a gentle, earnest gravity and simplicity that touched Guildea, who returned his handclasp almost warmly.

"I'll go," he said. "I'll catch the ten o'clock train, and to-night I'll sleep at an hotel, at the Grosvenor—that's close to the station. It will be more convenient for the train."

As Father Murchison went home that night he kept thinking of that sentence: "It will be more convenient for the train." The weakness in Guildea that had prompted its utterance appalled him.

VI

No letter came to Father Murchison from the Professor during the next few days, and this silence reassured him, for it seemed to betoken that all was well. The day of the lecture dawned, and passed. On the following morning, the Father eagerly opened the Times, and scanned its pages to see if there were any report of the great meeting of scientific men which Guildea had addressed. He glanced up and down the columns with anxious eyes, then suddenly his hands stiffened as they held the sheets. He had come upon the following paragraph:

> "We regret to announce that Professor Frederic Guildea was suddenly seized with severe illness yesterday evening while addressing a scientific meeting in Paris. It was observed that he looked very pale and nervous when he rose to his feet. Nevertheless, he spoke in French fluently for about a quarter of an hour. Then he appeared to become uneasy. He faltered and glanced about like a man apprehensive, or in severe distress. He even stopped once or twice, and seemed unable to go on, to remember what he wished to say. But, pulling himself together with an obvious effort, he continued to address the audience. Suddenly, however, he paused again, edged furtively along the platform, as if pursued by something which he feared, struck out with his hands, uttered a loud, harsh cry and fainted. The sensation

in the hall was indescribable. People rose from their seats. Women screamed, and, for a moment, there was a veritable panic. It is feared that the Professor's mind must have temporarily given way owing to overwork. We understand that he will return to England as soon as possible, and we sincerely hope that necessary rest and quiet will soon have the desired effect, and that he will be completely restored to health and enabled to prosecute further the investigations which have already so benefited the world."

The Father dropped the paper, hurried out into Bird Street, sent a wire of enquiry to Paris, and received the same day the following reply: "Returning to-morrow. Please call evening. Guildea." On that evening the Father called in Hyde Park Place, was at once admitted, and found Guildea sitting by the fire in the library, ghastly pale, with a heavy rug over his knees. He looked like a man emaciated by a long and severe illness, and in his wide open eyes there was an expression of fixed horror. The Father started at the sight of him, and could scarcely refrain from crying out. He was beginning to express his sympathy when Guildea stopped him with a trembling gesture.

"I know all that," Guildea said, "I know. This Paris affair——" He faltered and stopped.

"You ought never to have gone," said the Father. "I was wrong. I ought not to have advised your going. You were not fit."

"I was perfectly fit," he answered, with the irritability of sickness. "But I was—I was accompanied by that abominable thing."

He glanced hastily round him, shifted his chair and pulled the rug higher over his knees. The Father wondered why he was thus wrapped up. For the fire was bright and red and the night was not very cold.

"I was accompanied to Paris," he continued, pressing his upper teeth upon his lower lip.

He paused again, obviously striving to control himself. But the effort was vain. There was no resistance in the man. He writhed in his chair and suddenly burst forth in a tone of hopeless lamentation.

"Murchison, this being, thing—whatever it is—no longer leaves me even for a moment. It will not stay here unless I am here, for it loves me, persistently, idiotically. It accompanied me to Paris, stayed with me there, pursued me to the lecture hall, pressed against me, caressed me while I was speaking. It has returned with me here. It is here now," —he uttered a sharp cry,—"now, as I sit here with you. It is nestling up to me, fawning upon me, touching my hands. Man, man, can't you feel that it is here?"

"No," the Father answered truly.

"I try to protect myself from its loathsome contact," Guildea continued, with fierce excitement, clutching the thick rug with both hands. "But nothing is of any avail against it. Nothing. What is it? What can it be? Why should it have come to me that night?"

"Perhaps as a punishment," said the Father, with a quick softness.

"For what?"

"You hated affection. You put human feelings aside with contempt. You had, you desired to have, no love for anyone. Nor did you desire to receive any love from anything. Perhaps this is a punishment."

Guildea stared into his face.

"D'you believe that?" he cried.

"I don't know," said the Father. "But it may be so. Try to endure it, even to welcome it. Possibly then the persecution will cease."

"I know it means me no harm," Guildea exclaimed, "it seeks me out of affection. It was led to me by some amazing attraction which I exercise over it ignorantly. I know that. But to a man of my nature that is the ghastly part of the matter. If it would hate me, I could bear it. If it would attack me, if it would try to do me some dreadful harm, I should become a man again. I should be braced to fight against it. But this gentleness, this abominable solicitude, this brainless worship of an idiot, persistent, sickly, horribly physical, I cannot endure. What does it want of me? What would it demand of me? It nestles to me. It leans against me. I feel its touch, like the touch of a feather, trembling about my heart, as if it sought to number my pulsations, to find out the inmost secrets of my impulses and desires. No privacy is left to me." He sprang up excitedly. "I cannot withdraw," he cried, "I cannot be alone, untouched, unworshipped, unwatched for even one-half second. Murchison, I am dying of this, I am dying."

He sank down again in his chair, staring apprehensively on all sides, with the passion of some blind man, deluded in the belief that by his furious and continued effort he will attain sight. The Father knew well that he sought to pierce the veil of the invisible, and have knowledge of the thing that loved him.

"Guildea," the Father said, with insistent earnestness, "try to endure this—do more—try to give this thing what it seeks."

"But it seeks my love."

"Learn to give it your love and it may go, having received what it came for."

"T'sh! You talk as a priest. Suffer your persecutors. Do good to them that despitefully use you. You talk as a priest."

"As a friend I spoke naturally, indeed, right out of my heart. The idea suddenly came to me that all this,—truth or seeming, it doesn't matter which,—may be some strange form of lesson. I have had lessons—painful ones. I shall have many more. If you could welcome——"

"I can't! I can't!" Guildea cried fiercely. "Hatred! I can give it that,— always that, nothing but that—hatred, hatred."

He raised his voice, glared into the emptiness of the room, and repeated, "Hatred!"

As he spoke the waxen pallor of his cheeks increased, until he looked like a corpse with living eyes. The Father feared that he was going to collapse and faint, but suddenly he raised himself upon his chair and said, in a high and keen voice, full of suppressed excitement:

"Murchison, Murchison!"

"Yes. What is it?"

An amazing ecstasy shone in Guildea's eyes.

"It wants to leave me," he cried. "It wants to go! Don't lose a moment! Let it out! The window—the window!"

The Father, wondering, went to the near window, drew aside the curtains and pushed it open. The branches of the trees in the garden creaked drily in the light wind. Guildea leaned forward on the arms of his chair. There was silence for a moment. Then Guildea, speaking in a rapid whisper, said,

"No, no. Open this door—open the hall door. I feel—I feel that it will return the way it came. Make haste—ah, go!"

The Father obeyed—to soothe him, hurried to the door and opened it wide. Then he glanced back at Guildea. He was standing up, bent forward. His eyes were glaring with eager expectation, and, as the Father turned, he made a furious gesture towards the passage with his thin hands.

The Father hastened out and down the stairs. As he descended in the twilight he fancied he heard a slight cry from the room behind him, but he did not pause. He flung the hall door open, standing back against the wall. After waiting a moment—to satisfy Guildea, he was about to close the door again, and had his hand on it, when he was attracted irresistibly to look forth towards the park. The night was lit by a young moon, and, gazing through the railings, his eyes fell upon a bench beyond them.

Upon this bench something was sitting, huddled together very strangely.

The Father remembered instantly Guildea's description of that former night, that night of Advent, and a sensation of horror-stricken curiosity stole through him.

Was there then really something that had indeed come to the Professor? And had it finished its work, fulfilled its desire and gone back to its former existence?

The Father hesitated a moment in the doorway. Then he stepped out resolutely and crossed the road, keeping his eyes fixed upon this black or dark object that leaned so strangely upon the bench. He could not tell yet what it was like, but he fancied it was unlike anything with which his eyes were acquainted. He reached the opposite path, and was about to pass through the gate in the railings, when his arm was brusquely grasped. He started, turned round, and saw a policeman eyeing him suspiciously.

"What are you up to?" said the policeman.

The Father was suddenly aware that he had no hat upon his head, and that his appearance, as he stole forward in his cassock, with his eyes intently fixed upon the bench in the Park, was probably unusual enough to excite suspicion.

"It's all right, policeman," he answered, quickly, thrusting some money into the constable's hand.

Then, breaking from him, the Father hurried towards the bench, bitterly vexed at the interruption. When he reached it nothing was there. Guildea's experience had been almost exactly repeated and, filled with unreasonable disappointment, the Father returned to the house, entered it, shut the door and hastened up the narrow stairway into the library.

On the hearthrug, close to the fire, he found Guildea lying with his head lolled against the armchair from which he had recently risen. There was a shocking expression of terror on his convulsed face. On examining him the Father found that he was dead.

The doctor, who was called in, said that the cause of death was failure of the heart.

When Father Murchison was told this, he murmured:

"Failure of the heart! It was that then!"

He turned to the doctor and said:

"Could it have been prevented?"

The doctor drew on his gloves and answered:

"Possibly, if it had been taken in time. Weakness of the heart requires a great deal of care. The Professor was too much absorbed in his work. He should have lived very differently."

The Father nodded.

"Yes, yes," he said, sadly.

THE LADY AND THE BEGGAR

Nothing in life is more rare than the conversion of a person who is "close" about money into one generous, open-handed and lavish. The sparrow will sooner become the peacock than the miser the spendthrift. And if this is so, if such a transformation seldom occurs in life, it is even more unusual for a man or woman to leave behind in dying a manifesto which contradicts in set terms the obvious and universally recognised tendency of their whole existence. Naturally, therefore, the provisions of Mrs. Errington's will surprised the world. Old gentlemen in Clubs stared upon the number of the Illustrated London News which announced the disposal of her money as they might have stared upon the head of Medusa. The fidgety seemed turned to stone as they read. The thoughtless gaped. As for the thoughtful, this will drove them to deep meditation, and set them walking in a maze of surmises, from which they found no outlet. One or two, religiously inclined, recalled that saying concerning the rich individual and the passage of a camel through a needle's eye. Possibly it had come home to Mrs. Errington upon her death-bed. Possibly, as her end drew near she had perceived herself tower to camel size, the entrance to Paradise shrink to the circumference which refuses to receive a thread manipulated by an unsteady hand. Yes, yes; they began to expand in unctuous conjecture that merged into deliberate assertion, when some one remarked that Mrs. Errington had died in exactly three minutes of the rupture of a blood-vessel on the brain. So this comfortable theory was exploded. And no other seemed tenable. No other explained the fact that this wealthy woman, notorious during her life for her miserly disposition, her neglect of charity, her curious hatred of the poor and complete emancipation from the tender shackles of philanthropy, bequeathed at death the greater part of her fortune to the destitute of London, and to the honest beggars whom fate persistently castigates, whom even Labour declines to accept as toilers at the meanest wage.

Only Horace Errington, the dead woman's sole child, and Captain Hindford, of the Life Guards, exactly knew the truth of the matter. And this truth was so strange, and must have seemed so definite a lie to the majority of mankind, that it was never given to the world. Not even the rescued poor who found themselves received into the Errington Home as into some heaven with four beautiful walls, knew why there had sprung up such a home and why they were in it. The whole affair was discussed ardently at the time, argued about, contested, and dropped. Mystery veiled it. Like many things that happen, it remained an inexplicable enigma to the world. And finally, the world forgot it. But Horace Errington remembered it, more especially when he heard light-hearted people merrily laughing at certain strange shadows of things unseen which will, at times, intrude into the most frivolous societies, turning the meditative to thoughts deep as dark and silent-flowing rivers, the careless to frisky sneers and the gibes which fly forth in flocks from the dense undergrowths of ignorance.

The Erringtons were magnets, and irresistibly attracted gold instead of steel. Mr. Errington died comparatively young, overwhelmed by the benefits showered upon him by Fortune, which continued to dog persistently the steps of his widow, whom he left with one child, Horace. This boy was destined by his father's will to be a millionaire, and had no need of any money from his mother, so that, eventually, Mrs. Errington did him no wrong by the bequest which so troubled the curious. She was a brilliant and an attractive woman, sparkling as a diamond, and apparently as hard. That she loved Horace there was no doubt, and he had adored her. Yet he could not influence her as most only sons can influence their mothers. She was liberally gifted with powers of resistance, and in all directions opposed impenetrable barriers to the mental or spiritual assaults of those with whom she came in contact. It seemed impossible for Mrs. Errington to receive, like a waxen tablet, a definite impression. She was so completely herself that she walked the world as one clad in armour which turned aside all weapons. This might have been partly the reason why men found her so attractive, partly, also, the reason why Horace considered her, even while he was not yet acquainted with trousers, as so very wonderful among women.

Among many indifferences, Mrs. Errington included a definite indifference to the sufferings of those less fortunate than herself. Legacies came to her as often as mendicants to Victor Hugo's Bishop of D— —. She received them with a quiet greediness so prettily concealed at first that nobody called it vulgar. As time went on this greediness grew to gluttony. Mrs. Errington began to feel that fatal influence which came upon the man who built walls with his gold, and each day longed to see the walls rise higher round him. A passion for mere possession seized her and dominated her. Even, she permitted the world, always curiously nosing, like a dog, in people's gutters, to become aware of this passion. This beautifully dressed, gay and clever woman was known to be an eager miser by her acquaintance first, and last by her own son Horace. It is true that she spent money on the so-called "good things" of life, gave admirable dinners, and would as soon have gone without clothes as without her opera-box. But she practised an intense economy in many secret and some public ways, and, more especially, she was completely deaf to those appeals of suffering, and sometimes of charlatanry, which besiege our ears in London, so full of wily outcasts and of those who are terribly in need. Mrs. Errington's name figured in no charitable lists. She seldom even gave her patronage to a bazaar, and, above all things, she positively abhorred the beggars who make the streets and parks their hunting-grounds, who hover before doorsteps, and grow up from the ground, like mustard-seeds, when a luggage-laden cab stops or a carriage unblessed with a groom pauses before a shop.

Horace knew this hatred very well, so well that, although his nature was as lavish as his mother's was mean, he seldom sought to rouse any pity in her pitiless heart, or to strike the rock from which experience had taught him that no water would gush out. Every habit of conduct, is, however, broken through now and then, when the moment is exceptional and the soul is deeply stirred. And this reticent mood of the boy when with his mother one day received a shock which drove him into a contest with her, and moved him to strive against the obedience which his love for her habitually imposed upon him.

It was spring-time. Horace, now sixteen, and long established at Eton, was at home for the Easter vacation, which he was spending with Mrs. Errington, not at their country place, but in her town house in Park Lane. One morning, when the City was smiling with sunshine, and was so full of the breath of the sweet season that in quiet corners it seemed in some strange and indefinite way almost Countrified, Horace went into Mrs. Errington's boudoir and begged her to come out for a walk in the Park, where he had already been bicycling before breakfast. When there was no question of money she was always ready to accede to any request of the boy's, and she got up at once from her writing-table—she was just sending a short note of refusal to subscribe to some charity pressed upon her attention by a hopeful clergyman—and went to her room to put on her hat. Five minutes later she and Horace set forth.

Weather may have a softening or a hardening influence on the average person. On Mrs. Errington it had neither. She felt much the same essentially in a thunderstorm or in midsummer moonlight, on a black, frost-bound winter's day, or on such a perfect and tender spring morning as that on which she now passed through the park-gate with her son. She never drew weather into her soul, but calmly recognised it as a fact suitable for illustration on the first page of the Daily Graphic. Now she walked gaily into the Row with Horace, looking about her for acquaintances. She found some, and would not have been sorry to linger with them. But Horace wanted her to go further afield, and accordingly they soon moved on towards the

Serpentine. It was when they were just in sight of the water that they met Captain Hindford, already alluded to as a man who had eventually more knowledge than other people of the events which led to the drawing-up of Mrs. Errington's strange will. He was one of the many men who admired Mrs. Errington while wondering at her narrow and excommunicative disposition. And he stopped to speak to her with the eager readiness which is so flattering to a woman. The spring, so much discussed, was lightly discussed again, and, by some inadvertence, no doubt, Captain Hindford, who was almost as genial as if he had lived in the days of Dickens, was led to exclaim—

"By Jove, Mrs. Errington, this first sunshine's as seductive as a pretty child—makes one ready to do anything! Why, I saw an old crossing-sweeper just now sweeping nothing at all—for it's as dry as a bone, you see—and I had to fork out a sixpence; encouraged useless industry just because of the change in the weather, 'pon my word, eh?"

Mrs. Errington's lips tightened ever so little.

"A great mistake, Captain Hindford," she said drily.

Horace looked at his mother with a sort of bright, boyish curiosity. Although he knew so well what her nature was like, it did not cease to surprise him.

"You think so?" said the Captain. "Well, perhaps, you're right; I don't know. Daresay I've been a fool. Still, you know a fool in sunshine is better than a wise man in a fog; 'pon my word, yes, eh?"

Mrs. Errington did not verbally agree, and they parted after the Captain had accepted an invitation to dine quietly in Park Lane that evening.

"Devilish odd woman, devilish odd!" was Hindford's comment. And he watched the mother's and son's retreating figures with a certain astonishment.

"Wonder what the boy thinks of her?" he muttered. "Jove, if there isn't a beggar going after them! She'll soon settle him!"

And he remained standing to watch the encounter. From where he stood he had seen the beggar, who had been half-sitting, half-lying, on a bench facing the water, glance up at Mrs. Errington and her son as they passed, partially raise himself up, gaze after them, and finally rise to his feet and follow their footsteps. Hindford could only see the man's back. It was long, slightly bending, and apparently youngish. A thin but scrupulously neat coat of some poor shiny and black material covered it, and hung from the man's shoulders loosely, forming two folds which were almost like two gently rounded hills with a shallow valley running between them up to the blades of the shoulders. Certainly the coat didn't fit very well. The Captain watched, expecting to see this beggar address an appeal to Mrs. Errington or Horace. But apparently the man was nervous or half-hearted, for he followed them slowly, without catching them up, until the trio vanished from view on the bank of the Serpentine.

When this disappearance took place the Captain was conscious of an absurd feeling of disappointment. He could not understand why he felt any anxiety to see Mrs. Errington refuse a beggar alms. Yet he would gladly have followed, like a spy, to behold a commonplace and dingy event. Despite the apparent reluctance of the beggar to ply his trade, Hindford felt convinced that presently the man would approach Mrs. Errington and be promptly sent about his business. Her negative would, no doubt, be eager enough even upon this exquisite and charitable morning. Wishing devoutly that, being a gentleman, he had not to conform to an unwritten code of manners, Hindford walked away. And, as he walked, he saw continually the back of the beggar with that black coat of the two hills and the valley between the shoulder-blades.

Meanwhile, Mrs. Errington and Horace, quite unaware that they were being followed, pursued their way. There were a few boats out on the water, occupied by inexpert oarsmen whose frantic efforts to seem natural and serene in this to them new and complicated art drew the undivided attention of the boy, a celebrated "wet Bob." Mrs. Errington was thinking about her latest investments and watching the golden walls grow higher about her. Mother and son were engrossed, and did not hear a low voice say, "I beg your pardon!" until it had uttered the words more than once. Then Horace looked round. He saw a tall and very pale young man, neatly though poorly dressed in dark trousers and a thin loose black coat that might have been made of alpaca, and fitted badly. This man's face was gaunt and meagre, the features were pointed, the mouth was piteous. His eyes blazed with some terrible emotion, it seemed, and when Horace looked round a sudden patch of scarlet burned on his white and bony cheeks. Horace's attention was pinned by his appearance, which was at the same time dull and piercing, as the human aspect becomes in the tremendous moment of an existence. This man's soul seemed silently screaming out in his glance, his posture, his chalk-white cheeks starred with scarlet spots, his long-fingered hands drooping down in the shadow of his ill-fitting coat, which fluttered in the breeze. Horace turned, looked, and stood still. The man also stood still. Mrs. Errington looked sharply round.

"What is it, Horace?" she said.

She glanced at the man, and her lips tightened.

"Come along, Horace," she said. "Come!"

But Horace, who seemed fascinated by the spectre that had claimed their attention, still hesitated, and the man, noticing this, half held out one hand and murmured in a husky voice—

"I am starving."

With the words, the scarlet spots in his cheeks deepened to a fiercer hue, and he hung his head like one abruptly overwhelmed with shame.

"For God's sake give me something!" he muttered. "I've—I've never done this before."

Horace's hand went to his waistcoat pocket, but before he could take out a coin Mrs. Errington had decisively intervened.

"Horace, I forbid you," she said.

"Mater!"

"Understand—I forbid you."

She took his arm and they walked on, leaving the man standing by the water-side. He did not follow them or repeat his dismal statement, only let his head drop forward on his bosom, while his fingers twisted themselves convulsively together.

Meanwhile a hot argument was proceeding between Mrs. Errington and Horace. For once it seemed that the boy was inclined to defy his mother.

"Let me give him something—only a few coppers," he said.

"No; beggars ought not to be encouraged."

"That chap isn't a regular beggar. I'll wager anything it's true. He is starving."

"Nonsense! They always say so."

"Mater—stop! I must——"

Horace paused resolutely and looked round. In the distance the man could still be seen standing where they had left him, his head drooped, his narrow shoulders hunched slightly forward.

"Let me run back," the boy went on; "I won't be a minute."

But Mrs. Errington's curious parsimony was roused now to full activity.

"I will not allow it," she said; "the man is probably a thief and a drunkard. Hyde Park swarms with bad characters."

"Bad character or not, he's starving. Anyone can see that."

"Then let him starve. It's his own fault. Let him starve! Nobody need unless they have committed some folly, or, worse, some crime. There's bread enough for all who deserve to live. I have no sympathy with all this preposterous pauperising which goes by the name of charity. It's a fad, a fashion—nothing more."

She forced her son to walk on. As they went he cast a last glance back at the beggar.

"Mater, you're cruel!" he said, moved by a strength of emotion that was unusual in him—"hard and cruel!"

Mrs. Errington made no reply. She had gained her point, and cared for little else.

"You'll repent this some day," Horace continued.

He was in a passion, and scarcely knew what he was saying. Strings seemed drawn tightly round his heart, and angry tears rose to his eyes.

"You'll repent it, I bet!" he added.

Then he relapsed into silence, feeling that if he spoke again he would lose all the self-control that a boy of sixteen thinks so much of.

All that day Horace thought incessantly of the beggar, and felt an increasing sense of anger against his mother. He found himself looking furtively at her, as one looks at a stranger, and thinking her face hard and pitiless. She seemed to him as someone whom he had never really known till now, as some one whom, now that he knew her, he feared. Why his mind dwelt so perpetually upon a casual beggar he couldn't understand. But so it was. He saw perpetually the man's white face, fierce and ashamed eyes, the gesture at once hungry and abashed with which he asked for charity. All day the vision haunted the boy in the sunshine.

Mrs. Errington, on her part, calmly ignored the incident of the morning and appeared not to notice any change in her son's demeanour. In the evening Captain Hindford came to dine. He was struck by Horace's glumness, and in his frank way openly chaffed the boy about it.

"What's up with this young scoundrel?" he said to Mrs. Errington.

Horace grew very red.

"Horace is not very well to-day," said his mother.

"Mater, that's not true—I'm all right."

"I think it more charitable to suppose you seedy," she replied.

"Charitable!" Horace cried. "Well, Mater, what on earth do you know about charity?"

Captain Hindford began to look embarrassed, and endeavoured to change the subject, but Horace suddenly burst out into the story of the beggar.

"It was just after you left us," he said to the Captain.

"I saw the fellow following you," the Captain said. Then he turned to Mrs. Errington. "These chaps are the plague of the Park," he added.

"Exactly. That is what I tell Horace."

"I don't care!" the boy said stoutly. "He *was* starving, and we were brutes not to give him something. The Mater'll be sorry for it some day. I know it. I can feel it."

Captain Hindford began to talk about French plays rather hastily.

When Mrs. Errington went up to the drawing-room, Horace suddenly said to the Captain—

"I say, Hindford, do me a good turn to-night, will you?"

"Well, old chap, what is it, eh?"

"When you say 'good-night,' don't really go."

The Captain looked astonished.

"But——" he began.

"Wait outside a second for me. When the Mater's gone to bed I want you to come into the Park with me."

"The Park? What for?"

"To find that beggar chap. I bet he's there. Lots of his sort sleep there, you know. I want to give him something. And—somehow—I'd like you to come with me. Besides, it doesn't do to go looking for anyone in the Park alone at night."

"That's true," the Captain said. "All right, Errington; I'll come."

And, after bidding Mrs. Errington good-night, he lingered in Park Lane till he was joined by Horace. They turned at once into the Park and began to make their way in the direction of the Serpentine. It was a soft night, full of the fine and minute rain that belongs especially to spring weather. The clocks of the town had struck eleven, and most of the legitimate sweethearts who make the Park their lover's walk had gone home, leaving this realm of lawns and trees and waters to the night-birds, the pickpockets, the soldiers, and the unhealthily curious persons over whom it exercises such a continual and gloomy fascination. Hindford and Horace could have seen many piteous sights had they cared to as they walked down the long path by the Row. The boy peered at each seat as they passed, and once or twice hesitated by some thin and tragic figure, stretched in uneasy slumber or bowed in staring reverie face to face with the rainy night. But from each in turn he drew back, occasionally followed by a muttered oath or a sharp ejaculation.

"I bet he'll be somewhere by the Serpentine," the boy said to Hindford.

And they walked on till at length they reached the black sheet of water closely muffled in the night.

"We met him somewhere just here," Horace said.

"I know," Hindford rejoined. "He got up from this seat. But he may be a dozen miles off by now."

"No," Horace said, with a curious pertinacity; "I'm sure he's about here still. He looked like a man with no home. Ugh! how dreary it is! Come along, Hindford."

The good-natured Captain obeyed, and they went on by the cheerless water, which was only partially revealed in the blackness. Suddenly they both stopped.

"What's that?" Horace exclaimed.

A shrill whistle, followed by shouts, came to them, apparently from the water. Then there was an answering whistle from somewhere in the Park.

"It's the police," said Hindford. "There's something up."

They hurried on, and in a moment saw what looked like a great black shadow, rising out of the water, lifting in his arms another shadow, which drooped and hung down with the little waves curling round it. As they drew close they saw that the first shadow was a policeman, up to his waist in the water, and the second shadow was a man whom he held in his arms, as he waded with difficulty to the shore.

"Lend a hand, mates," he shouted as he saw them.

Just then a light shone out over the black lake from the bull's-eye of a second policeman who had hurried up in answer to his comrade's whistle. Between them they quickly got the man on shore, and laid him down on the path on his back. The bull's-eye lantern, turned full on him, lit up a face that seemed all bony structure, staring eyes, a mouth out of which the water dripped. He had no coat on and his thin arms were like those of a skeleton.

"Dead as a door-nail," said the first policeman. "A case of suicide."

"God! Hindford, it's he! It's the chap who asked me for money this morning!" whispered Horace. "Is he really dead?"

The Captain, who had been examining the body and feeling the heart, nodded. Horace gazed upon the white face with a sort of awful curiosity. He had never before looked at a corpse.

"Look here, Errington," Hindford said to the boy that night as he parted from him in Park Lane, "don't tell your mother anything of this."

"But—but, Hindford——"

"Come, now, you take my advice. Keep a quiet tongue in your head."

"But perhaps it was her fault; it was—if we'd given the poor chap something he'd——"

"Probably. That's just the reason I don't want you to tell Mrs. Errington anything of it. Come, promise me on your honour."

"All right, Hindford, I'll promise. How horrible it's all been!"

"Don't think about it, lad. Good-night."

Horace trembled as he stole up the black staircase to bed. He meant to keep his promise, of course, but he wondered whether the Mater would have owned that she was in the wrong that morning if she had heard his dreary tale of the beggar's death in the night.

The next day it was Mrs. Errington who asked Horace to go out walking. She looked rather pale and fatigued at breakfast, but declared her intention of taking a constitutional.

"Come with me, Horace," she said.

"Very well," he answered, with a curious and almost shy boyish coldness.

"Not into the Park, Mater," he said, as they were starting.

"Why not? We always walk there. Where else should we go?"

"Anywhere—shopping—Regent Street."

"No, Horace, I've got a headache to-day. I want a quiet place."

He didn't say more. They set out, and Mrs. Errington took the precise route they had followed the day before. She glanced rather sharply about her as they walked. Presently they reached the seat on which the beggar had been sitting just before he got up to follow them. Mrs. Errington paused beside it.

"I'm tired. Let us sit down here," she said.

"No, Mater, not here."

"Really, Horace," Mrs. Errington said, "you are in an extraordinary mood to-day. You have no regard for me. What is the matter with you?"

And she sat down on the seat. Horace remained standing.

"I shan't sit here," he said obstinately.

"Very well," Mrs. Errington replied.

She really began to look ill, but Horace was too much preoccupied with his own feelings to notice it. There was something abominable to him in his mother sitting calmly down to rest in the very place occupied a few hours ago by the wretched creature who had, so Horace believed, been driven to death by her refusal of charity. He felt sick with horror in that neighbourhood, and he moved away, and stood staring across the Serpentine. Presently Mrs. Errington called to him in a faint voice — —

"Horace, come and give me your hand."

He turned, noticed her extreme pallor, and ran up.

"What's the row? Are you ill, Mater?"

"No. Help me up." He put out his hand. She got up slowly.

"We'll go home," he said. "You look awfully seedy."

"No; let us walk on."

In spite of his remonstrances she insisted on walking up and down at the edge of the Serpentine for quite an hour. She appeared to be on the look-out for somebody. Over and over again they passed the spot where the beggar had drowned himself. Their feet trod over the ground on which his dead body had been laid. Each time they reached it Horace felt himself grow cold. Death is so terrible to the young. At last Mrs. Errington stopped.

"I can't walk much more," she said.

"Then do let's go home now," Horace said.

She stood looking round her, searching the Park with her eyes.

"I suppose we must," she said slowly. Then she added, "We can come here again to-morrow."

Horace was puzzled.

"What for? Why should we?" he asked.

But his mother made no reply, and they walked home.

Next day she insisted on going again to the same place, and again she was obviously on the look-out. Horace grew more and more puzzled by her demeanour. And when the third day came, and once more Mrs. Errington called him to set forth to the Serpentine, he said to her, with a boy's bluntness— —

"D'you want to meet someone there?"

Mrs. Errington looked at him strangely.

"Yes," she said, after a minute's silence.

"Why, who is it?"

"That beggar I wouldn't let you give money to."

Horace turned scarlet with the shock of surprise and the knowledge— which he absurdly felt as guilty knowledge—that the man was dead, perhaps even buried by now.

"Oh, nonsense, Mater!" he began, stammering. "He won't come there again. Besides, you never give to beggars."

"I mean to give this man something."

Horace was more and more surprised.

"Why?" he exclaimed. "Why now? You wouldn't when I wanted you to, and now—now it's too late. What do you wish to give to him for now?"

But all she would say was, "I feel that I should like to, that—that his perhaps really was a deserving case. Come, Horace, let us go and try to find him."

And the boy, bound by his word to Captain Hindford, was forced to go out in search of a dead man. He felt the horror of this quest. To-day Mrs. Errington carried her purse in her hand, and looked eagerly out for the beggar. Once she fancied she saw him in the distance.

"There he is!" she cried to Horace. "Run and fetch him."

The boy turned pale, and stared.

"Where, Mater?"

"Among those trees."

"It can't be! Nonsense!"

"No," she said; "you are right. I made a mistake. It's only somebody like him. Why, Horace, what's the matter?"

"Nothing," he answered.

But he was shaking. The business was too ghastly. He felt he couldn't stand it much longer, and he resolved to go to Captain Hindford and persuade the Captain to absolve him from his promise. In the afternoon of the same day, accordingly, he went off to Knightsbridge. He rang, and was told that Captain Hindford had gone to Paris and was afterwards going for a tour on the Continent. His heart sank at the news. Was he to go on day after day searching with his mother for this corpse, which was rotting in the grave? He asked for Hindford's address. It was Poste Restante, Monte Carlo. But the servant added that letters sent there might have to wait for two or three days, as his master's immediate plans were unsettled. Horace, however, went to the nearest telegraph-office and wired to Hindford—

"Let me off promise; urgent.—Horace Errington."

Then, having done all he could, he went back to Park Lane. He found his mother in a curiously restless state, and directly he came in she began to talk about the beggar.

"I must and will find that man," she said.

"Mater, why?"

"Because I shall never be well till I do," she said. "I don't know what it is, but I cannot be still by day, and I cannot rest by night, for thinking of him. Why did I not let you give him something?"

"Mater, I wish to God you had!" the boy said solemnly.

Mrs. Errington did not seem to notice his unusual manner. She was self-engrossed.

"However, we shall see him again, no doubt," she went on. "And then I shall give him something handsome. I know he needs it."

Horace went hastily out of the room. He longed for a wire from Captain Hindford. Next day he "shammed ill," as he called it to himself, so as to get out of going into the Park. So Mrs. Errington went off by herself in a condition of almost feverish anticipation.

"I know I shall see him to-day," she said, as she left Horace.

She returned at lunch-time, and came up at once to his room.

"I have seen him," she said.

Horace sat up, staring at her in blank amazement.

"What, Mater? What d'you say?"

"I have seen him."

"No?"

"Yes. I went to the place where he asked you for money, and walked up and down for ages. But he wasn't there. At last I gave it up and crossed the bridge. I took it into my head to come home on the other side of the water. Well, when I was half-way along it, I looked across, and there I saw him."

"Rot, Mater!"

"He was standing alone by the water, staring straight across at me, just as if he saw me and was trying to attract my attention."

"No, no!"

"Horace, don't be silly! Why do you contradict me? He looked just the same as when we saw him first, only he had no coat on."

Horace gave a sort of gasp.

"I suppose his poverty had compelled him to pawn it," Mrs. Errington continued. "Don't you think so, Horace? People can pawn clothes, can't they?"

The boy nodded. His eyes were fixed on her.

"I looked across at him," Mrs. Errington continued, "and made a sign to him to come round to meet me by the other end, near the Row. I held up my purse so that he might understand me."

"What did he do?"

"He turned away and hurried off among the trees."

"Ah!"

"Do you know, Horace," Mrs. Errington continued rather excitedly, "I think if you had beckoned to him he would have come. He's afraid of me, perhaps, because—because I wouldn't let you give to him. To-morrow you must come out with me. Till I've relieved that man's wants I shall have no peace."

She hastened out of the room, apparently in a quiver of unusual agitation. Horace sat petrified. If only Hindford would telegraph! That cursed promise!

On the following day it rained. Nevertheless, Mrs. Errington almost violently insisted upon Horace accompanying her to search for the beggar.

"We shall go to the far side of the water," she said. "I believe when we go to the other side he sees us coming and avoids us. But if we can catch sight of him, as I did yesterday, you can beckon to him, and I am certain when he sees you he will come."

Horace said nothing. He felt cold about the heart, not so much with fear as with awe and wonder. They went to the far bank, and almost directly Mrs. Errington cried out——

"There he is, and without his coat again! How wet he must be getting!"

Horace looked across the dull water, through the driving rain. He saw no one on the opposite bank.

"He sees us," Mrs. Errington added. "Horace, you beckon to him. Here, take my purse. Hold it up, and then point to him to come round and meet us."

Mechanically the boy obeyed.

"Ah, I knew it! This time he is coming," said Mrs. Errington.

"He is coming, Mater?"

"Yes; come along."

She hurried towards the end of the Serpentine. Horace walked by her side, staring in horror through the rain.

"Poor man!" Mrs. Errington said presently. "How ghastly he looks!"

"Mater—I say——"

"Well?"

"Is he near?"

"Near?"

Mrs. Errington stopped in amazement.

"Why, what do you mean, Horace?"

"What I say. Is he near now?"

"Near? He's just coming up."

Suddenly the boy fainted.

When he came to he was lying in the shelter of the Rescue Society.

"Ah, Horace," his mother said, "you ought to have stayed in bed another day."

"Yes, Mater."

"You frightened that poor man. He made off when you fainted."

That evening Horace received a telegram from Monte Carlo——

"Very well but better say nothing.—Hindford."

He read it, laid it down, and told Mrs. Errington the truth.

As already stated, she died very suddenly not long afterwards, leaving behind her the will which so astonished London.